"You need this, S

She stared at him, this ___ ___ ___
business making her fee ___ ___ ___

Right then, they weren't rivals. They were ___ ___
and a man who needed each other. The entir ___ ___
to exist in that moment, could be held at b ___
she'd allow it.

Here, in this place, she didn't have to be stronger, colder,
hungrier than anyone else in the room. She could fall asleep
in Beckett's strong arms. With him holding her, she could
believe, if only for the night, that no matter how bad things
got, it would all be okay in the end.

It's only a single night.

"What do you say, Samara?"

Really, there was only one answer. "Okay."

"Good. Then we can begin." He gave her a downright
wolfish grin.

Acclaim for Katee Robert's Novels

Undercover Attraction

"Pick it up as soon as possible. The story is packed with all the action, scandal, sexual tension, and family drama you could ask for, and I, for one, loved it."

—All About Romance

"Robert combines strong chemistry, snappy plotting, and imperfect yet appealing characters...This installment is easily readable as a standalone, and it's a worthy addition to a sexy series."

—*Publishers Weekly*

Forbidden Promises

"A tension-filled plot full of deceit, betrayal, and sizzling love scenes will make it impossible for readers to set the book down. This installment stands alone, but new readers will certainly want to look up earlier books."

—*Publishers Weekly*

"A great read from the talented Robert!"

—*RT Book Reviews*

"4.5 Stars! My favorite book so far in this series! You will finish it in one sitting...This was one sexy ride!"

—Night Owl Reviews, Top Pick

An Indecent Proposal

"Robert proves she is one of the bright new stars of romance, and readers who love tortured heroes...will snap up the latest in her brilliantly imaginative and blisteringly hot O'Malley series." —*Booklist*

"Top Pick! The chemistry between Cillian and Olivia is amazingly hot and the connection they have is wicked... Another amazing addition to a very addictive series. 5 stars." —Harlequin Junkie

"A romance that takes your breath away and will you have you on the edge of your seat...truly wonderful!!" —Addicted to Romance

"A fast-paced, intriguing story with deceit and betrayal; heartbreak and family; grief and retribution; falling in love and letting go of the past. The premise is imaginative and intoxicating. The characters are passionate and intense; the romance is forbidden but dynamic." —The Reading Cafe

The Wedding Pact

"I really cannot recommend this series enough. It's definitely one of my favorites over the past few months. Katee has this way of getting down to the nitty gritty and making her characters shine, making them real." —Books by Migs

"*The Wedding Pact* is original, and very cleverly plotted...
And what can I say about the ending? Absolutely fantastic."
—Fresh Fiction

"I loved every second. A–"
—All About Romance

The Marriage Contract

"Robert easily pulls off the modern marriage-of-convenience trope...This is a compulsively readable book!
It's more than just sexy times, too, though they are plentiful
and hot!...An excellent start to a new series."
—*RT Book Reviews*

"*Romeo and Juliet* meets *The Godfather*...Unpredictable,
emotionally gripping, sensual and action-packed, *The Marriage Contract* has everything you could possibly need or
want in a story to grab and hold your attention."
—Nose Stuck in a Book (ycervera.blogspot.com)

"A definite roller coaster of intrigue, drama, pain, heartache,
romance, and more. The steamy parts were super steamy,
the dramatic parts delivered with a perfect amount of flair."
—A Love Affair with Books

THE LAST KING

THE
LAST KING

KATEE ROBERT

FOREVER

NEW YORK   BOSTON

Copyright © 2018 by Katee Hird
Excerpt from *The Marriage Contract* copyright © 2015 by Katee Hird
Cover design by Elizabeth Stokes. Cover image © Geber86/GettyImages.
Cover copyright © 2018 by Hachette Book Group, Inc.

Forever
Hachette Book Group
1290 Avenue of the Americas, New York, NY 10104
forever-romance.com
twitter.com/foreverromance

First Edition: April 2018

Forever is an imprint of Grand Central Publishing. The Forever name and logo are trademarks of Hachette Book Group, Inc.

The publisher is not responsible for websites (or their content) that are not owned by the publisher.

The Hachette Speakers Bureau provides a wide range of authors for speaking events. To find out more, go to www.hachettespeakersbureau.com or call (866) 376-6591.

ISBNs: 978-1-4555-9710-9 (mass market), 978-1-4555-9709-3 (ebook)

Printed in the United States of America

OPM

10 9 8 7 6 5 4 3 2 1

To Kristen Nave

ACKNOWLEDGMENTS

This book was definitely a labor of love, and that old saying that it takes a village was never truer than while drafting and editing it. I may have been the one writing, but this book would not have come into being without several key folks.

More thanks than I can ever say to Leah Hultenschmidt for helping me whip this beast into shape. Thank you for having faith in me despite a few false starts, and for helping me get Beckett into true hero shape. I love this story so much, and I wouldn't have pulled it off without your input!

I will be forever grateful to Cherry Adair for picking apart my plot in all of thirty seconds—and then giving me the tools to fix the issues. I'm officially a reformed pantser, and shall be plotting with sticky notes forevermore!

Thank you to the ladies in the IECRWA for sitting down and plotting with me, and then giving me high fives and positive vibes for tackling the story. You're the best!

Big, big, BIG thanks to Lauren Hawkeye and Piper J. Drake for holding my hand through the emotional roller coaster of drafting and editing and rewriting. You ladies were always there to whip out the pom-poms and override the doubt that this would be the book that beat me. You were right! It wasn't! And it ended up being a better book for your support. Thank you!

Huge thanks to Kristen Nave and Terri Wakefield for always being there in a pinch to wrangle the resident honey badger so I could work, and for your words of encouragement. Thanks to Hilary Brady for showing up at opportune times for coffee and snacks.

Last, but never least, thanks to Tim for being my rock in the midst of the insanity of this year. You never doubted that I could do this, and you never hesitated to kick my ass into gear when I needed it and take over dinner duty for weeks on end. I love you like a love song!

THE LAST KING

PROLOGUE

Beckett King had no good reason to be in the hotel bar. If he wanted to celebrate winning the bid for his father's company, he should have gone out to be sure he wouldn't run into the competition. Instead, he stood there in the entrance-way, scanning the dim room for a distinctive head of dark hair.

A low laugh drew him like a magnet to a lodestone. He might not like the woman it was attached to all that much, but she never failed to make an impression. Beckett shifted, zeroing in on the sound.

There.

Samara Mallick leaned against the bar, laughing at something the bartender said. She wore the same black dress she'd had on to give her presentation, and it hugged her mouthwatering curves and left miles of her medium brown skin exposed. She'd taken her hair down since he'd seen her last, and it fell around her shoulders in wild waves of black.

She looked good enough to taste.

Beckett took a step toward her before he caught himself. Samara worked for the competition. There wasn't a woman more off-limits. They'd gone head-to-head over bids for oil territory leases half a dozen times over the last few years, and while Beckett won the contracts more often than he lost them, he couldn't afford to miss a step. If he did, Samara would be there, stealing the next bid out from under him before he had a chance to blink.

He couldn't blink.

She caught sight of him and grimaced, which was enough to propel him toward her. *Just need the reminder of why she's not for me.* They couldn't be in the same room without bickering, and he needed that vicious edge to regain control of himself.

Samara raised dark brows and swept her hair off one shoulder. "The heir decides to make an appearance. Come to gloat, Beckett?" She made a show of looking at the muted beige carpet beneath her heels. "I'd get down on my knees in the presence of royalty, but... Oh wait, no I wouldn't."

The pull he felt didn't dim with her words. If anything, their proximity only made it worse. This close, he could see the tempting curve of her bottom lip, a little fuller than her top, and he caught a whiff of her lavender scent. *Damn it.* Beckett ordered a whiskey and took the spot next to her. "Don't play coy, Samara. You spend plenty of time on your knees for my aunt." Samara's boss. The CEO and owner of Kingdom Corp, the single biggest competitor Beckett came up against time and time again.

He shouldn't have said it. The image of Samara on her knees in front of him was enough to make a man forget himself. Beckett had spent more time than he should have imagining the smirk she'd wear when she took his cock into her mouth...

Fuck.

"Why wouldn't I? She's superior to you in every way."

He smiled in thanks to the bartender as the woman slid a tumbler across to him. "We just spent four days fighting for this account. Let's not talk business."

"Business is the only thing we have to talk about." Three empty shot glasses sat in front of her, lined in a neat little row. As he watched, Samara took a fourth and turned the empty glass over.

"Bitter isn't a good look for you."

As he anticipated, she turned on him, dark eyes flaring in challenge. "You won this round. That doesn't mean a damn thing about the next one." She leaned forward, getting into his space, and lowered her voice. "Besides, we both know Norway's contract is small potatoes. If you need to pat yourself on the back for winning at softball, then go right on ahead."

"Samara, you don't have to pretend that every time I win doesn't needle the hell out of you." He closed what little remained of the space between them. They were alone in the bar, and the music floating from the speakers overhead was so low there was no need to whisper. But he found himself doing it all the same. "I like your hair down. You should wear it like that more often."

Her mouth dropped open for half a second before she recovered. "I don't know what gave you the impression I care what you like." She pressed her full lips together and tilted her head to the side, considering. "Though if we're playing that game, you need a shave, Beckett. You look like you just rolled out of bed. It's embarrassing and sloppy."

He grinned because her body language told a different story. She leaned into him like a flower seeking the sun. They didn't quite touch, but he could feel the heat of her body and it would take nothing more than a single deep breath to press his chest against hers. He had to fight not to take that breath, not to relish the slow drag of her breasts against him. *This* was why he'd taken great pains to ensure they were never alone.

They weren't alone now, but they might as well have been.

She was off-limits.

He didn't give a fuck.

They were in Norway, not Houston. No one here knew them or the roles they played in warring companies. His father didn't have to know. Neither did his aunt.

What's one night?

"You know, there's one way to test that theory out." *Let me take you to bed.*

Her brows shot up and she shook her head. "You're unbelievable. I know you're a King and all, but your arrogance is out of control."

It wasn't arrogance. If there was a sure thing, it wasn't Samara Mallick. She was too prickly, too ambitious, too loyal to someone who hated both Beckett's father and his company.

That didn't stop him from wanting her.

It sure as hell didn't stop him from leaning down and brushing his lips against her ear. "Why don't you put me in my place?" He took her hand and slipped his hotel-room key into it. "Room 311."

Beckett should have turned and walked out right then. It was the smart thing to do. But Samara pressed her hands against his chest, her fingers gripping his shirt in a kneading motion that rooted his feet to the spot. He felt a shudder work its way through her body as if she fought for the same control that flitted through his grip. "That's a terrible idea."

"All the best nights start with terrible ideas."

Samara had all the right words ready. *No. Fuck off, Beckett. Stop trying to add insult to injury. You got the contract—you don't get* this, *too.*

The right words weren't what came out of her mouth when she finally managed to speak. "Yes."

It wasn't her fault.

Beckett King was a force of nature both in and out of the conference room. The charisma she worked so hard to exhibit seemed to come as naturally as breathing to him. Men wanted to be him—or be his best friend—and women just plain wanted him. Samara managed to keep her distance out of sheer spite, but she didn't stand a chance with him leaning so close, his expensive cologne teasing her senses the same way his presence seemed to wrap around her even though *she* was the one touching *him.*

Just blame it on the tequila.

She tightened her grip on his shirt when he started to move back. "Two conditions."

"I'm listening." Damn him to hell for sounding amused.

"No one can know." She had a reputation to protect—they both did.

He splayed his hand across her lower back, guiding her to close the last little bit of distance between them. She sucked in a breath. It was so easy to forget how big Beckett was when they stood a respectable distance apart. His expensive suits toned down his broad shoulders, gave him a more civilized air.

There was nothing civilized in the possessive way the

heat of his hand seared through her thin dress and his hard cock nudged her stomach. *Oh God.*

"No one will know," Beckett growled in her ear. "It'll be our secret."

She had no reason to trust him, but... Neither his father nor her boss would be thrilled if they found out. He might be better positioned to weather the storm of disapproval, but that didn't mean he wanted to borrow trouble.

He exerted the slightest bit of pressure on her back, urging her to arch against him. Her body throbbed everywhere she touched him, but there were too many barriers in place. Samara tilted her head back and looked up into his face, searching his expression.

Chiseled jawline, strong brows, deep brown eyes that seemed to telegraph the ability to fulfill her darkest desires. His sinful mouth curved in a slow smile that drew a shiver from her. "What's your second condition?"

"I'm in charge tonight." It was her only hope of walking away with a little dignity intact. Beckett was everything she was supposed to hate: arrogant, old money, a family line leading back to the first oil struck in Texas. The only way she could look at herself in the mirror tomorrow was if *she* controlled this interaction.

If anything, his smile widened. "You're in charge...for now."

The trip up to his room was a blur. One moment Beckett was paying for their drinks, and the next Samara's back hit his door and his mouth took hers. All her competition and desire was mirrored back at her in that kiss, his tongue sliding against hers as they both fought for dominance. Each move had a corresponding response as if they were dancing—or fighting. She dug her fingers into his dark hair and nipped his bottom lip. He slid her dress up enough to hook the backs of her thighs and hitched her up so she could wrap her legs around his waist. She yanked his shirt out of his slacks so she could run her hands up his chest. He ripped her panties off.

They froze, their harsh breaths the only sound in his dim hotel room. Beckett leaned his forehead against hers. "Are we moving too fast?"

She pressed two fingers to his lips. "I'm fucking you tonight, Beckett."

He didn't move. "You had a lot of tequila."

She smiled before she caught herself. Who would have thought that Beckett King had an honorable streak? He wasn't the biggest dick in their industry, but she'd always found him to be ruthless with a single-minded intensity when it came to pursuing foreign bids. She didn't know what drove him—and she didn't care—but honor didn't come into the equation. Until now.

"I'm buzzed, but not enough that I can't consent." When he didn't move, she kissed his jaw and hooked her fingers into his slacks. "Touch me, Beckett. Kiss me. Fuck me." She punctuated each word with another kiss. "Make me come enough times I forget all the reasons this is a terrible idea." She wrapped her hand around his cock and gave him a squeeze. "Now."

"Bossy."

"Assertive."

He turned and carried her deeper into the room. Beckett laid her on the bed and backed up enough to draw her dress over her head. He was on her in seconds, kissing her neck, her shoulders, her collarbones. He used his mouth to inch down her bra and before closing around her nipple, she thought she heard him mutter, "Fucking perfect."

She was too impatient to let him tease her. Samara fought her way out of her bra. She went after Beckett's shirt next, nearly popping the buttons off as she hauled it over his head. Seconds later, she shoved off his pants and then she was in bed with a naked Beckett King.

Her control tried to reassert itself and clamor that this was the worst idea she'd ever had, but with Beckett's big body laid out for her, there was no going back. She straddled him and traced the muscles lining his chest down to his stomach, stopping to drag her thumbs over the dips below his hips. There were so many things she could say: *You're beautiful, too. Your body makes me crazy. I want to memorize every inch of you so I can replay this when I'm alone.*

Samara kissed him before she could make a fool of herself. She *needed*. "Condoms."

"In a minute." He toppled her and pushed two fingers into her. She moaned before she could stop herself. For all that she'd claimed to want control, with him half on top of her, his mouth against her skin, and his hand working her between her thighs—it was beyond words.

Mistake.

She clasped the back of his neck and dragged him up for another deep kiss. Pleasure sparked as he pressed his thumb to her clit even as he stroked her. *Not yet.* She broke away. "*Condom.* Now, Beckett. I want you inside me."

For a second it looked like he might keep fucking her with his fingers until she came apart on his hand, but he finally cursed. "Next time we go slow."

"Sure." There wasn't going to be a next time and they both knew it, but she wasn't about to ruin tonight by saying as much. Samara propped herself on her elbows and watched as he stalked naked to his suitcase and came back with a string of condoms. She raised her eyebrows. "Ambitious."

Beckett hooked the back of her knees and towed her to the edge of the bed. "If we only have tonight, we're sure as fuck going to make it count."

A sentiment she could appreciate. Samara tore off one condom and sat up to roll it down his cock. She took her time, watching the frustrated desire play across his expression. She stroked him once. Twice. A third time.

"Samara—"

She didn't know what he intended to say, and she didn't care. She pulled him onto the bed and climbed on top. "Not now."

"By not now, you mean never."

That was exactly what she meant, but she wasn't about to say so and risk ruining what they had going. Samara reached between them to stroke him. "Do you really want to talk right now? Or do you want me to ride you until we both forget our own names?"

Beckett's mouth went tight, but he grabbed her hips and ground her against him. "We'll talk another time."

"Thought so." There was no point in talking. Trying to turn this into something more than it was would only end in pain for both of them. Beckett had his future mapped out— heir to Morningstar Enterprise, only son to the CEO and owner. A legacy that had been his from the moment he was born.

Samara's path led in a different direction.

She guided his cock into her and sank onto him until he was sheathed to the hilt. The fullness drew her breath from her lungs and she had to brace her hands on his chest for a few moments to get accustomed to the feeling. "You feel good, Beckett."

His only answer was to run his hands from her thighs up over her hips and waist to cup her breasts. He teased her nipples with his fingers the same way he'd done with his mouth earlier. "You get this orgasm, Samara." He met her gaze, his brown eyes so dark in the shadows they might as well have been as black as hers. "But as soon as you come on my cock, you're mine for the rest of the night. I'm dying for a taste of that pretty pussy."

"I'm in charge," she whispered as she started to move over him.

"You can be in charge while I fuck you with my tongue." He bent up and took her mouth, sliding his tongue against hers even as his cock slid in and out of her. She should argue on principle, but the tension of the last few days left her too tightly wound to do anything but pursue her own pleasure.

Or that was what she told herself as she came on his cock and he ate the sound.

She barely had a chance to relish the orgasm before Beckett flipped them, and then the delicious fullness of his cock was gone and he descended between her thighs. His first lick arched her back and drew a cry from her lips. By all reason, she should be sated and done with the whole experience, but as he thrust his tongue into her, Samara forgot everything but the need for *more*.

Tonight, she'd enjoy everything he had to give her.

Tomorrow, she'd go back to hating Beckett King.

CHAPTER ONE

Six months later

Beckett King was a monumental pain in the ass.

The man was a force of nature, and he never did what Samara expected, which made it impossible to counter his moves.

Probably shouldn't have slept with him, then.

Shut up.

There was no point in stalling further. Samara had a job to do, and the longer she took to do it, the later her night would run. She smoothed down her pencil skirt, bolstered her defenses, and marched through his office door before she could talk herself out of it.

Beckett himself sat on a small couch rather than behind the shiny desk, his head in his hands. His dark hair was longer than she'd seen it last, and he wore a faded gray T-shirt and jeans, looking completely out of place in the sleek, pristine office. His broad shoulders rose and fell in what must have been a deep sigh.

If Samara didn't dislike him so much, she might almost feel sorry for him.

She shifted, her heel clicking against the marble floor,

and Beckett raised his head. He caught sight of her and stood, his expression guarded, his mouth tight.

"Are you here on behalf of my aunt?" he asked. "She really hates my father so much she sends someone else for the reading of his will?"

Samara considered half a dozen responses and discarded all of them. Tonight, at least, she could keep control of her tongue. "I'm sorry about your father."

He snorted. "It was no secret there wasn't a whole lot of love lost between us." And yet the exhausted lines of his face showed that no matter what he said, he cared that his father was dead. It was there in the permanent frown pulling down the edges of his lips, and in the barely banked fury of his chocolate brown eyes.

He sighed again. "If Lydia doesn't want to be here herself, fine. We might as well get this started." He stalked to his desk and pushed a button. "Walter, Lydia's..." He glanced up at her with smoldering eyes. "...*representative* is here."

A few seconds later, a thin man opened the door she'd just walked through and shuffled his way to the desk. He wore an ill-fitting suit and looked about thirty seconds from passing out right where he stood. His pale blue gaze landed on her, his eyes too large in his narrow face. "Ms. Mallick. I'd say it's a pleasure, but the circumstances are hardly that."

"Mr. Trissel. It's nice to see you again." Empty, meaningless words. So much of her job required her to spill white lies and smooth ruffled feathers, and Samara was usually damn good at figuring out what a person needed and leveraging it to get what *she* wanted.

Or what her boss, Lydia King, wanted.

That skill had abandoned her the second she walked

through the doors of Morningstar Enterprise. Her movements lost their normal grace, and words she had no business saying crowded her throat. Beckett always made her feel like an amateur, and they'd been going head-to-head for years, his aunt's company against his father's. But right now, he looked like the walking wounded and she didn't know how to process it. Samara wasn't a nurturer. Even if she was, she wouldn't comfort *him*.

Beckett doesn't matter. The will does.

The reminder kept her steady as Walter separated two folders from the stack and looked at each of them in turn. He passed one folder to Beckett. "It's a lot of legalese, but the bottom line is that Mr. King left you nearly everything. Morningstar and all his shares are yours, which puts you firmly in the role as majority shareholder. As of the moment you sign this, you are acting CEO."

No surprise showed on his face. Why would it? For all his tumultuous relationship with his father, Beckett was the only King suitable to take over once Nathaniel was gone. Of course he'd been named CEO.

Beckett leafed through the file but didn't appear to read any of it. "You said almost everything."

"Yes, well..." The lawyer fidgeted. "There was a change in the most recent version of the will."

He went still. "What change?"

The lawyer passed Samara the second file. "Nathaniel King has left the residence of Thistledown Villa to Lydia King and her children."

"The fuck he did!" Beckett slammed his hands down on the desk, making it clang hollowly. "There's been a mistake. No way in hell my father left the family home to her."

"I'm sorry, Mr. King, but there's been no mistake. As I

mentioned earlier, the paperwork is all in order. Your father was in his right mind when he signed this will, and I stood as his witness. While you're welcome to contest it in court, I have to advise you that it's a losing battle."

Samara read through the paperwork quickly. She'd been told to expect the family home to be willed to Lydia, but she still wanted to make sure everything was in order. As Walter had said, there was a lot of legalese, but it was exactly what he said. *Good.* It meant she could get the hell out of there. "Thank you for your time." She turned on her heel and headed for the door.

She barely made it into the hallway before a large hand closed over her upper arm, halting her forward progress. "Let me go, Beckett."

"Samara, just hold on a damn second." He released her but didn't step back. "That house should have been mine and you know it. My father leaving it to Lydia makes no sense. She hasn't set foot in the place in thirty years."

"It's none of my business what your father did or didn't leave to Lydia. I'm not a King." She forced herself to move away despite the insane urge to touch him. It was second nature to inject her tone with calm and confidence. "Nothing you can say is going to change what that will said. I know it's your childhood home, but your father obviously had a reason for leaving it to his sister. Maybe he was finally trying to fix the hurt *his* father caused by passing her over for CEO and cutting her out of the family. It's not like you were close enough for him to confide in you if he *had* decided to fix things with Lydia."

Hurt flickered through Beckett's dark eyes, and Samara battled a pang of guilt in response. The King family's messed-up past wasn't Beckett's fault any more than it was hers, but that didn't mean she had to throw it in his face.

His jaw set, hurt replaced by fury. "Stop trying to handle me. I'm not some client you're trying to talk into an oil lease."

She took him in, from the top of his hair that looked like he'd been raking his fingers through it for roughly twelve hours straight, over the T-shirt fitted tightly across his broad shoulders and muscled chest, down to the faded jeans that hugged his thighs lovingly, ending on the scuffed boots. "If you were a client, I would already have a contract in hand. You're easy pickings right now, Beckett." *That's it. Remember who you are to each other: enemies.*

He reached out and twisted a lock of her hair around his finger, pulling her a little closer despite her best intentions. "Don't try that snooty attitude with me. It doesn't work."

"You're just full of orders tonight, aren't you?"

"You like it." His thumb brushed her cheek, sending a zing down her spine that curled her damn toes in her expensive red heels. "You like a lot of things I do when you're not thinking so hard."

She had to get the hell out of there right then and there, or she'd do something unforgivable like kiss Beckett King. *Never should have let him get this close. I know what happens when we're within touching distance.* It had only been once, but once was more than enough to imprint itself on her memories. No amount of tequila could blur out how intoxicating it was to have his hands on her body, or the way he'd growled every filthy thing he'd wanted to do to her before following through on it. Things would be a lot easier if she'd just blacked out the entire night and moved on with her life.

He lowered his head and she blurted out the first thing she could think of to make him back off. "Beckett, your father just *died*."

"I'm aware of that."

Nathaniel King was dead.

That reality was almost impossible to wrap her head around. For all her thirty-two years, Nathaniel had loomed large over Houston. The King family was an institution that had been around for generations, all the way back to the founding of Houston itself, and Nathaniel was its favored son. It was that favoritism that caused his father to pass over Lydia for the CEO position. The unfairness of that call had driven her to cash out her shares and start her own company—Kingdom Corp—in direct competition with her family. Thirty years later, it didn't matter what Samara had told Beckett, because that rift was nowhere near closing. Time might heal some wounds, but it only cemented Lydia's ill will for the family that had cut her off when she wouldn't play by their rules.

And now there was nothing left of that side of the family but Beckett.

He released Samara and took a step back, and then another. "Just go. Run back to your handler." He let her get three steps before he said, "But make no mistake—this isn't over."

She wasn't sure if he meant contesting the will or *them*, and she didn't stick around to ask. Samara kept her head held high and the file clutched tightly in her grip as she took the elevator down to the main floor, walked out the doors, and strode two blocks down the humid Houston streets to Kingdom Corp headquarters. The only person lingering at this time in the evening was the security guard near the front door, and he barely looked up as she strode through the doors.

Another quick elevator ride, and she stepped out at the executive floor. Like the rest of the building, it was mostly deserted. Kingdom Corp employees worked long hours, but no one worked harder than Lydia King. She was there before the first person showed up, and she didn't leave until long after they'd gone home. *She* was the reason the company had made unprecedented leaps in the last two decades. Samara admired the hell out of that fact.

"I have it." She shut the door behind her and moved to set the papers on the desk.

"I appreciate you going. It's a difficult time." Lydia leaned forward and glanced over the paperwork. She didn't *look* like she was grieving, for all that her brother had died in a terrible car accident two days ago. Her long golden hair was twisted up into a more sophisticated version of Samara's updo and, despite a long day in the office, her white and gold color-blocked dress didn't have a single wrinkle on it.

Samara glanced at the clock and resigned herself to another long night. "Is there anything I can do?"

Lydia smiled, her berry lipstick still in perfect condition. "How did my nephew look?"

"He's in rough shape." It wasn't just the fact that he'd obviously dropped everything in Beijing and come directly home upon hearing the news of his father's death. Everyone in Houston knew that the King men could barely be in the same building for more than a few days without clashing spectacularly, but that didn't change the fact that Nathaniel was Beckett's father, his last remaining parent, and now he was dead. "I was under the impression that they didn't have much of a relationship."

Lydia shrugged. "Family is complicated, my dear. Especially fathers."

Years of building her defenses ensured that she didn't flinch at the dig. "What's the next move?"

But Lydia wasn't through. She ran her hands over the papers almost reverently. "Was he upset when he found out about the villa?"

She pictured the look in Beckett's dark eyes, something akin to panic. "Yes. He didn't understand why Nathaniel would leave it to you."

"He grew up there. We all did." Lydia's smile took on a softer edge. "Nathaniel and I were born there. So was Beckett. My children would have been if not for how things fell out."

It was just a building, albeit a beautiful one. Samara didn't understand the reverence in Lydia's tone, or the pain Beckett obviously felt to lose it. Who cared about an old mansion on the outskirts of Houston—especially after the King family had essentially cut Lydia off when she wouldn't dance to their tune?

Doesn't matter if I get it. It's important to Lydia, which means I have to plan on dealing with that damn house in the future.

She realized the silence had stretched on a little too long and tried for a smile. "That's nice."

"Oh, Samara." Lydia laughed. "Don't pretend I'm not boring you to death with my nostalgia. At least Nathaniel managed to do one thing right before he did us all the favor of dying."

There she is. This was the Lydia that Samara knew, not the sentimental woman she'd just been talking to. "Nathaniel was handling the upcoming bid personally. With him gone, it will leave Beckett scrambling to catch up." Her fingers tingled, and she clenched her fists. *Excitement. Not guilt. I'm beyond guilt when it comes to men who have had everything handed to them from birth. Losing this contract won't sink Beckett's company, but it* will *damage it.*

"Yes, well, don't get cocky. This is important, Samara."

"I won't drop the ball."

Lydia looked at her for a long, uncomfortable moment. Staring into those hazel eyes was like glimpsing a lion stalking through the tall grass. Samara was reasonably sure the danger wasn't directed at *her*, but her heart still kicked in her chest. Finally, Lydia nodded. "I know you won't let me down. Why don't you get some rest? You need to hit the ground running tomorrow."

Samara paused. "I hope you'll be able to get some rest soon, too." When Lydia just shook her head and chuckled, Samara gave up and left before she could do or say something else ill advised.

She hesitated on the corner. The smart move would be to go back to her little condo, have a glass of wine, and go over her proposal for the government contract yet again. She *knew* she had it locked down, but insidious doubt wormed through her at the thought of facing Beckett King. *I have the advantage this time.* It didn't matter. He had advantages she couldn't even see, ones that had been gifted to him just because he held the King last name.

Samara closed her eyes. She wanted to go *home*. She wanted to call a Lyft and travel across town to the little house her mother had lived in since she was born. She wanted to hug her *amma* until the fear of losing her only parent dissipated.

Get ahold of yourself.

Amma would already be asleep, her alarm set for some ungodly hour so she could get to work on time. If Samara showed up now, it would mean a long conversation while her mother tried to figure out what the problem was. No matter how nice that sounded, Samara was stronger than this. She couldn't lean on her *amma* just because seeing Beckett's grief left her feeling strange.

She was *not* weak. She refused to let a man she barely knew derail her path. Kingdom Corp needed that contract, and *Samara* needed to be the one to get it. It was a shame Beckett's father had died, but ultimately she couldn't let pity for him take root.

He was the enemy.

Samara couldn't afford to forget that.

CHAPTER TWO

Beckett spent a restless few hours in his condo in the city. He'd owned this place since he'd moved out after graduation, but these days he spent as many nights in hotel rooms around the world as he did in his own bed. He listened to the traffic outside his window and wished for the relative silence of Thistledown Villa. Not even the happy memories that haunted his childhood home would be enough to create a shelter in this storm. If anything, the empty, echoing halls would only make him feel worse, more alone than he already was.

The desire to go home just proved all the accusations his father had thrown at him over the years. Too soft. Too weak. Too goddamn stubborn. *That makes two of us, old man.*

But not old enough. Sixty was too young to die. There was no warning or slow decline of health. No chance for reconciliation. Despite what the rest of Houston thought, Beckett didn't hate his father. They were just too different— or too similar, depending on who he asked. All Beckett ever wanted was some semblance of a relationship with the cold bastard, but any hint of softness had died alongside Beckett's mother all those years ago.

He scrubbed a hand over his face, trying to focus past his exhaustion and the first stirrings of something that might be grief. *Or relief.* The battle was over, for better or worse. There would be no more tense dinners that inevitably ended in fights about the future of Morningstar. No more awkward holidays that spotlighted the missing piece of their family and the loss of what could have been. No more trips for Beckett that were barely concealed excuses to get him the hell out of Texas, at least long enough for them to cool off about the argument of the month.

The future stretched before him, a single path forward that he was destined to walk alone.

What the hell were you even doing driving, let alone driving drunk?

He paced around the kitchen island for the fifth time, but his restless energy didn't dissipate now any more than it had in the hours leading up to that moment. There were no answers there, and if answers *did* exist, they were in Thistledown Villa, currently forbidden to him. He could sneak in—he'd been sneaking out of that place since he was fifteen years old—but it would muddy the inevitable legal wars if he got caught and...

Fuck it.

He pulled on a new pair of jeans and a black T-shirt and headed for the parking garage. His old Harley had been to hell and back with him, but he'd kept it out of some perverse need to stick it to his old man. It didn't make a lick of sense as he stood in the darkness, flipping the key from his palm and out and back again. Nathaniel had been a remote and harsh father, but that didn't mean Beckett had been the easiest kid to deal with. He was as responsible for the times they butted heads as his father was.

His phone rang, dragging him from his thoughts. He yanked it from his pocket. "Yeah?"

"You back in town?"

Beckett closed his eyes. All he had to do was make his excuses, get on his motorcycle, and drive the forty minutes out of town to the mansion. Instead, he answered truthfully. "Yeah, I got back a few hours ago."

"Want to go get a beer?" Frank Evans, his longtime friend, offered him a lifeline he hadn't known he needed.

"Yeah." It was even the truth. With one last look at his Harley, he pocketed his keys and headed for the elevator. "Usual place?"

"I'm already here."

That surprised a laugh out of him. It felt good, almost cathartic. "I'll be there in fifteen."

It only took him ten minutes to walk from his condo to the Salty Chihuahua, a tiny bar sandwiched between a Mexican restaurant and a high-end spa that catered specifically to pets. Inside, the theatrically dimmed lights gave hints of the vintage pinup posters plastered on the walls, and all the tables were adorned with fishnet-clad plastic legs instead of normal table legs. He veered around a group of drunk college kids and made his way back to the corner booth tucked near the door to the kitchen.

As expected, Frank lurked there. He'd managed to find a specifically dark shadow to sit in. Beckett never knew if the man did it on purpose, but he seemed to melt into the shadows the way some people always sought the sun. Combined with his fierce scowl and the height and body that would fit right in with any NFL player. No one fucked with Frank. Though, truth be told, that had as much to do with Frank's money and influence in Houston as it had to do with his forbidding looks.

He slid a beer bottle over as Beckett sank into the opposite side of the booth. "Thanks, man."

"How you holding up?"

He didn't know how to answer that. Even though he'd known Frank damn near twenty years, they didn't do the braiding-each-other's-hair-and-whispering-secrets bullshit. That didn't change the fact that, at the end of the day, Beckett trusted the man with his life. Their friendship had lasted despite life hauling them apart for months and sometimes years at a time. It never seemed to matter. When he needed him, Frank was there—and vice versa.

That still didn't mean he wanted to unload all his emotional bullshit. "Fine."

Frank snorted. "More like you're not completely torn up the bastard is dead and *that's* bothering you as much as being an orphan is."

Orphan.

It felt like a dirty word, for all that it was the truth now—had been the truth, if not the reality, since Beckett's mom died. *God, could I get any more morose?* Beckett drained half the beer in a single pull. "I'm fine, Frank. Not okay, but fine." There was no damn reason he should feel like a ship without an anchor, drifting from wave to wave, no land in sight. Nathaniel King had been many things, but a safe harbor didn't enter into the equation.

Beckett eyed his beer. "Tonight might be a whiskey night." Even as he said it, he knew he wouldn't get shitfaced drunk no matter how much he wanted to. Work waited, and it was time sensitive. His conflicting feelings about his old man's death would hold until he had the time and space to work through them. In the meantime, Morningstar needed him.

"You want to talk about it?"

He shook his head. "I don't know. The thing I keep coming back to is that he was drunk behind the wheel. Where the hell was his driver? My old man hasn't driven in decades, but he suddenly decided it was a good idea—and then promptly drove into a telephone pole? It doesn't make any sense."

Frank shrugged. "People do weird shit when they drink."

He couldn't argue that, and yet...Nathaniel King *did* drink, often and far too much, and he'd never made the choice to drive before. Beckett glared at his bottle. "It doesn't make any sense," he repeated.

Frank drank his beer and watched Beckett in the eerie way he did sometimes, as if he could read thoughts. His dark skin seemed to drink up the shadows around him, giving the impression of menace that wasn't quite an illusion. "You want me to look into it?" Frank had his fingers in countless pies in the city. Officially, he was a real estate mogul, but he also dealt in information, though to what endgame Beckett had never quite figured out.

He hesitated. It might be that the very same guilt Frank accused him of feeling was driving this insistence that something was wrong. It was entirely possible—probable, even—that the night of his father's death had played out exactly like everyone said. He could be sending Frank on a wild-goose chase that would only result in Beckett looking bad, no matter how discreet the search for answers was. The last thing he needed was for word to get out that the new CEO of Morningstar Enterprise was paranoid and full of conspiracy theories.

He took another pull from his beer, forcing himself to drink more slowly this time. But what if something fishy *was* going on? If he turned a blind eye and pushed forward without looking into things, he'd always wonder if he could have done more. If he could have found answers. "I'd appreciate it."

"Consider it done." Frank motioned for two more beers and sat back. "I hear you saw Samara."

Beckett slumped down in the booth. "How the hell would you know that?" He glanced at his phone. "It was three hours ago. There were exactly two other people in the room, and I know for a fact that Samara isn't running to you and telling tales." For whatever reason, Frank seemed to enjoy needling Kingdom Corp whenever the opportunity arose. Since Beckett's aunt held grudges like no one's business, it had created a mutual animosity and ensured that none of her employees gladly dealt with Frank.

"Maybe that's exactly what I have set up."

He rolled his eyes and flipped his friend off. "For real, how did you know?"

"A guy I know was getting coffee across the street and saw her leave." Frank grimaced. "It doesn't sound as intimidating when put like that."

"Trust me, you have the market cornered when it comes to intimidation." He finished off his beer as the bartender sauntered up with another pair. She gave Frank a lingering look and put a little more swing into her walk as she headed back the way she'd come.

Frank didn't look over once. "Nice dodge. Samara."

Beckett could tell the man to drop it and Frank would—their unspoken rule—but Beckett found himself wanting to talk about something that wasn't his old man. His feelings regarding Samara weren't any less complicated, but they were still easier to deal with. "She was standing in for my aunt at the reading of my father's will. That's it." That, and for a moment there in the hall, she'd given off definite vibes. She'd locked it down fast, but there was no denying the chemistry between them. Their single night together hadn't even taken the edge off.

"That's it."

"You don't have to sound so put out about it. I don't know what you expected me to say."

Frank crossed his arms over his chest. "Seems the two of you have unfinished business."

"The only unfinished business we have is the upcoming government contract. Once I secure that, I won't have to see her again." Until the next time.

When Frank only raised his brows, Beckett growled. "What do you want me to say? I can barely stand to be in her presence without losing my fucking mind—and not in a pleasant way. We hooked up. It's done. End of story." He glanced at the clock again, and pushed to stand. "I'm out. I need some sleep before I face down the dragon tomorrow."

"Good luck." Now it was Frank's turn to hesitate. "If you change your mind about wanting to talk...I'm here. If anyone knows about complicated relationships with parents, it's me."

"I'll keep that in mind." He wouldn't put them both through the agony of that conversation, though. If Beckett really wanted to purge his demons, he'd find a bottle or a shrink—or both, since he wasn't willing to face down the latter without the former in hand. "Catch up with you later."

He paused by the bar to pay for their drinks and headed out into the night. The sticky air clung to his exposed skin and he inhaled deeply, pulling it into his lungs as if the humidity was solid enough to keep him on his feet. He needed to sleep but his racing thoughts wouldn't still, a hamster on its wheel, frantically spinning, spinning, spinning. He headed for the condo because there was nothing else left to do. He couldn't wander the streets indefinitely, and if he was going to speak to his aunt in the morning, he couldn't walk in there with bloodshot eyes and swaying on his feet. She was a predator, and she wouldn't hesitate to capitalize on perceived weakness.

Beckett strode across the street, the emptiness of his condo looming. *It shouldn't matter that it's empty now. It's always been empty.* He slowed and stopped, looking up at the building.

I've never been completely alone in the world before.

"Fuck," he breathed and shook his head. Now wasn't the time to focus on that bullshit. He *wasn't* alone. He might be the last King in this particular family branch, but there were cousins. They despised him, but they existed. Beyond that, he had Morningstar.

That was the one thing that *hadn't* changed with his father's death. He'd always had Morningstar. He'd have to find someone to replace his role as closer and the main contact for all the business they conducted overseas, but in the end Beckett had been training to take over the business since he was a teenager. If there was nothing else he and his father could agree on, they could agree on *that*.

He pulled his phone out and started walking again. A quick check of the time showed it was well after two in the morning. *It's not a good idea...* He stopped scrolling through his contacts and started at the name his thumb hovered over. *Samara.*

It was possible that he'd call, she'd answer, and she'd come to him and help dispel the hushed silence of his condo. She'd bring life into the cold rooms the same way she brought life and energy into every room she walked into. Even if they spent the next couple hours arguing and verbally sniping at each other, it would be better than walking through that door into the tomblike silence of his place.

With a sigh, Beckett shoved his phone back into his pocket. *Not an option.* If he didn't want to broadcast any weaknesses to his aunt, calling her second-in-command to keep him company because he couldn't bear to be alone was counterintuitive.

He would have to push through this without leaning on anyone.

There wasn't anyone to lean on, anyway.

Beckett woke up disoriented. He reached for the nightstand, only to knock over a lamp that shouldn't have been there. The events of the last few days rolled through him. His father dead. Losing Thistledown Villa. Samara. Frank. A couple hours of sleep hadn't magically solved the problems niggling around in the back of his mind.

He sat up and scrubbed a hand over his face. There was no point in lying around and wondering what the hell his father had been thinking getting behind the wheel, let alone doing it drunk. Frank would ask questions on his side of things, but the thought of just sitting back and waiting left Beckett twitchy. He couldn't drop everything to investigate a death that had already been ruled a drunk driving accident. Even if there was some question of foul play, there was Morningstar to think about. It needed someone at the helm, and with the clock ticking down to when he had to submit the proposal for renewing the government contract they'd held for decades, he didn't have time to dick around just to assuage his own guilt.

But he still had to go see his aunt. She and his father might have loathed each other, but they were siblings. She was still family, even if it was a broken family that had no hopes of healing. It didn't matter. Speaking to her was the right thing to do.

If in the process he managed to get an idea of what her company was offering to secure the lease for the oil in the Gulf, so much the better.

Beckett took a quick shower and chose his suit with care. At Morningstar, he preferred to keep it casual when dealing with in-house things, but outside of the company, perceptions mattered. Lydia King might technically be family, but she was still an inherited enemy. If there was someone capable of fixing those burned bridges, it wasn't Beckett.

Satisfied he was as ready as he was going to be, he dialed Kingdom Corp. A few minutes and several transfers later, the phone connected to Lydia's direct line.

She barely let it ring. "Beckett. What a lovely surprise."

He highly doubted that. "We need to talk." Now that he had some time and distance between the reading of the will and this call, he hoped against hope that he and his aunt could discuss things like reasonable adults. Over the years, she'd been just as ruthless and ambitious as his father was, but if they could put that shit aside for a little bit it would be really nice. He didn't like the odds of that happening—he'd never managed to see eye-to-eye with Nathaniel, after all. It was possible she'd surprise him—unlikely, but possible.

"I'm very busy."

So we're going to play it like this. Normally, he'd go back and forth with a renitent client until they felt they were in control of the situation, but Lydia wasn't a client. It might be seven in the morning, but he was already so fucking done with today. "Make time."

Lydia paused. "I'll create a window if you can be here in twenty."

He didn't have to ask where "here" was—Kingdom Corp offices. When Lydia had split from the family thirty years ago, she hadn't gone far to create her own business—she'd bought a building two blocks away and proceeded to renovate it to be even more ostentatious than Morningstar Enterprise was. "I'll fit you into my schedule."

"You do that." She hung up.

He took his time walking to the offices. He'd be late, but he wasn't too worried about it—showing up out of breath and having run to make the absurd time Lydia set would put her in the power position for their talk. He couldn't afford that. Beckett paused to look around the lobby. It was a classy white that was intimidating and distant—it conveyed the impression of money, but it wasn't beating people over the head with their wealth.

The secretary outside Lydia's office was tiny and dark, her curly hair cut short to her head. Like every other member of the staff he'd caught a glimpse of, she was painfully attractive. She stopped him with a sharp look. "Mrs. King will be with you shortly. Please take a seat."

Another power play—just like his taking his time had been. Beckett sighed, already bored with the game. "Yeah, I don't think so." He marched past her before she had a chance to push back her chair and shoved through the massive dark wood doors into Lydia's office.

His aunt looked up from her computer, her mouth opened

to deliver something cutting, without a doubt, but she stopped when she recognized him. "You're late, Beckett."

"You're busy. I'm busy, too. Let's get this over with."

The sharp clip of the receptionist's heels stopped right behind him. He glanced over his shoulder—she barely came up to his chest, but she looked ready to whoop his ass. "Shall I have him removed from the building, Mrs. King?"

"No, thank you. I have it from here."

The receptionist nodded and shut the doors behind him, but not before sending another searing glare his way. *Not making friends here, am I?* He hadn't expected to be welcomed with open arms, but blatant hostility was unexpected. *Then again, it shouldn't be.*

He dropped into one of the comfortable chairs across from Lydia's desk. It put him low enough that she looked down at him from her current position, and he had no doubt that was intentional. Everything about this place was a power move. Speaking first was a sign of weakness, but he didn't give two fucks. His gaze snagged on the ornate metal forged sign on the wall behind her desk. *Kingdom Corp.* He said the first thing that popped into his head. "How come you never took Elliott's name? How is he, by the way? I haven't seen him in years."

"Some women choose to follow the archaic tradition of taking their husband's name. I didn't. Why be a Bancroft, when I was born a King?" She raised her eyebrows. "As for Elliott, he's currently out of town, probably with one of his mistresses, but I'm sure he'll be back when he needs more money to gamble with."

The casual way she said it bespoke many years' worth of acceptance, which didn't jibe with the Lydia he knew by reputation. Beckett had intended to get right down to business, but now he hesitated. No point in asking why she didn't divorce him. Elliott Bancroft was the second son of a family that rivaled the Kennedys for political pull. They'd generated one president, four senators, a governor, and were almost universally loved within Texas. Their support of Kingdom Corp gave the company certain freedoms that might go away if Lydia's marriage to Elliott ended.

He never expected to feel pity for his aunt. "I'm sorry. I didn't know."

"How could you?" She said it almost gently. "You've spent your entire life in a gilded room as the favored son—the only son. You might be my nephew by blood, but you're nothing more than a rival business associate."

The lack of heat in her words struck him as much as the words themselves. To Lydia, he *wasn't* family. He was just an obstacle in her way. *Can't afford to forget that.* He sat back. "My father gave you Thistledown Villa."

"It certainly appears that way, doesn't it?"

He fully intended to fight her on that ownership, but it would have to wait for the time being. That house was his main link to his past—to the times when the good parts of his family outweighed the bad. Beckett loathed leaving that battle before it started, but he had to think of the people who worked for Morningstar. They were depending on him to ensure that they still had jobs in a year, two, more. Compared to that, his family home didn't measure up, no matter the personal value it held for him. Some things *couldn't* wait, though. "I need access to the house for a few hours."

Lydia picked up an expensive-looking pen. "I don't know that I'm inclined to give it to you."

"Lydia, shelve the act for a few minutes. Most of the furniture in Thistledown Villa might be heirloom and go with

the house, but there are things I'm entitled to. No court in
this state is going to deny me that right and you know it."

Her hazel eyes sharpened on him. She tapped the pen
against her dark red lips. "What is it worth to you?"

Anger flared, hot and potent. He wanted to get in her
face, to yell at her for being so fucking callous in the wake
of his father's death, about the fact that Beckett's loss was
twofold in both the house and his last remaining parent.

Beckett examined the office, partly to make Lydia sweat,
and partly to give himself time. The room was decorated
much the same way as the rest of the building's interiors—
white marble floors and massive windows. The only soft
touches were the chair he currently sat on and its mate next
to him, both a deep purple to match the basic coloring of
the trio of photographs lining each wall on either side of
the desk. He recognized different shots of the fields that
composed most of the property around Thistledown Villa.
During the spring, wildflowers bloomed there, turning it into
something out of a fairy tale.

*She grew up there, too. No matter how many years she's
been banned from the property, it's obviously important to
her.*

He took a careful breath and released his anger. He
wasn't pissed at *her* so much as at the situation, and it would
do well for him to remember that. "My father wants his
ashes scattered at the property."

She set the pen down and steepled her fingers. He
searched her face for the slightest bit of thawing, but there
was only a deep freeze he felt in his bones. "I can arrange for
it. I'll see that your belongings are returned to you as well."

He met her gaze steadily, feeling like he was staring
down the barrel of a gun. One flinch and it would go off.

"With all due respect, Lydia, I can't come up with a single reason to trust you with my father's ashes." *Or with anything else important to me.*

"Excuse me?"

"You heard me." He pushed slowly to his feet. "You hated him, and while I don't think that's unfounded, I'm also going to honor his final wish. I'm asking your permission out of respect, but if you don't give it, I'm going to see this done regardless."

The only sign of her anger was a slight tightening around her eyes. The smile she gave him was as practiced as it was warm. "Of course you can scatter my darling brother's ashes on the property. I'll be sure to have someone waiting to ensure you don't have any problems."

"Generous of you, but that won't be necessary."

Lydia stood. She wore a perfectly tailored white pantsuit that molded to her lean form. "On the contrary, it's entirely necessary." She rounded the desk and leaned against it, the very picture of a successful businesswoman. "I'd like to make you an offer."

This should be good. "I'm listening."

"I'm more than happy to hand over Thistledown Villa and the accompanying land, along with a hefty amount of money—in exchange for Morningstar Enterprise."

He stared, waiting for the punch line. When none came, Beckett shook his head. "I'm not selling you my company."

Lydia sighed. "Beckett, stop reacting and think for a moment. Do you really want to be the CEO of that company? Up until this point you've been living the life of the unfettered, traveling and partying, and, while there was undoubtedly business in the mix, your focus was elsewhere. I don't think you've stayed in Houston for more than a few months since you graduated college and took over the VP position for your father. Running Morningstar isn't going to be fun. It's going to be hard, thankless work."

Beckett gritted his teeth. She *would* see his business travel as evidence that he wasn't prepared. The truth was that Beckett had been helping run the company for years, though up until this point he and his father had divided things right down the center—Nathaniel took everything in Houston, and Beckett handled everything else. It had the dual purpose of letting him expand Morningstar's reach while keeping them mostly apart over the years. Minimizing conflict.

Not that he expected Lydia to understand. By all accounts, she ruled her four children with an iron fist. "It's a moot point what you believe. My father named *me* as CEO and willed me his shares—not you. Morningstar is mine, Lydia. It's not for sale, and neither am I."

"Beckett..." She considered him. "I know for a fact he kept you from the worst of what being a CEO of a company like this means. You'd be much happier finding some nice girl, having a handful of babies, and living off your trust fund."

Guess the gloves are off. He crossed his arms over his chest and stared down at her. "Cute speech. Were you practicing that while my father's body lay cold in the morgue until I made it back from Beijing to identify him? He always said you were a—" He cut himself off before finishing the sentence. There was no damn point. This whole meeting had been a waste of time.

"A what? A harpy. A bitch."

He forced himself not to flinch. Beckett shook his head. "I would never call you any of those things." His dislike of her might be growing by the second, but there had to be lines.

She gave him a viper's smile, as if she could hear his thoughts. "Morals won't get you anywhere in this business, Beckett."

"Yeah, well, I like being able to sleep at night. See you around, Lydia." Beckett walked through the door and shut it softly behind him. He took the elevator down to the main floor and headed out onto the street, his thoughts whirling. She hadn't wasted a single second before trying to pounce on Morningstar. There were plenty of cold people in this business—it was essentially a requirement—but this went above and beyond *cold*.

Lydia King wasn't cold. She was fucking subzero.

CHAPTER THREE

Samara was almost out her door when her phone rang. She cursed and then cursed again when she saw who was calling. After taking a second to make sure she didn't sound out of breath or frazzled, she forced a smile and answered. "Good morning, Lydia."

"I'm afraid I need another favor."

After the long night before, all Samara really wanted to do was meet her friend for their coffee date and then head into the office to work on the presentation part of the proposal. If Lydia needed something at this hour, it didn't mean anything good for Samara's plan for the day. *Doesn't matter. I'm her number two for a reason, and that means no bitching about more work. Not now, when we're so close to edging out Morningstar Enterprise.* "What do you need from me?"

"It's a bit delicate, but you're the one best suited for the job."

This isn't going to be good. "What job?"

"My darling nephew came to see me this morning. He's got it into his head that he needs to scatter his father's ashes at Thistledown Villa. I can't very well have him traipsing out there without supervision, so I need you to accompany him."

She blinked. Of all the things she'd expected, that didn't even make the list. Samara started to point out that she wasn't a babysitter but stopped. Lydia wasn't stupid. In all Samara's years of working for the company—for Lydia—she'd never seen the woman waste a resource, and sending Samara on a babysitting mission was a waste of resources.

Which meant there was something more she wanted to accomplish.

"Beckett is off his stride, and if you put a little effort into it, I'm sure you can convince him to talk with you. The more you speak, the higher the chance that he lets something vital slip."

Convince him.

She closed her eyes and pressed her lips together. She could point out that it wasn't in her job description to *convince* Beckett to do anything, or to comment on the fact that there were other hot buttons Lydia could push instead of sending Samara. Could Lydia know about their indiscretion in Norway? It wouldn't surprise Samara—the woman seemed to know everything. But still, while Samara wasn't above using a little flirtation to get what she wanted, she drew the line at sex.

I already had sex with Beckett.

Not because of who he was, or the company he was connected to.

It didn't matter. At the end of the day, they were both grown-ups and she had her bottom line to worry about. "Will today work for taking him out there?"

"Of course. I haven't had a chance to change the locks,

so there's no reason you can't meet Beckett at the house. I'll call him now." She hung up.

Samara cursed one last time, but there was no heat in it. Her grand plan had been to avoid Beckett until she could look at him without thinking about his body sliding against hers. Sliding *into* hers.

Beckett wasn't stupid. He'd see right through the choice to send *her* rather than some lowly employee with nothing better to do. That wouldn't stop her from doing what it took to keep him distracted and talking. His barriers were already down from grief—it wouldn't take much to nudge him in the right direction.

No matter how unsettled the plan made her.

Her phone buzzed. She pulled up the message from a number she didn't recognize. *I'll meet you out there in an hour.* Just that. Nothing more. No details. Beckett.

She rolled her eyes and typed back a response. *Very cryptic. I'll be there.* After a hesitation, she sent a second one. *Wait in the car. Lydia doesn't want you wandering.*

I'll consider it.

"Damn it, Beckett." She slipped into her heels, grabbed her purse, and practically flew out the door. Samara made the drive in forty-five minutes, breaking more than a few speed limits in the process, and Beckett still beat her there.

She pulled up next to where he straddled his motorcycle, and stared. *God, he looks good.* Today he wore a black T-shirt and a different pair of jeans. He turned to look at her, his dark eyes hidden by a pair of sunglasses, the set of his square jaw giving away nothing of his mood. He nudged the kickstand into place and swung off the bike, giving her an excellent view of just how well his jeans hugged his bite-able ass.

Get it together, Samara.

She was incredibly grateful for her own pair of sunglasses hiding the way her gaze followed him. *Business. This is just business, and you don't even like him.* It didn't matter. She didn't have to like the man to want him, and the glowing ember of desire that had never quite extinguished after that night six months ago chose that moment to make itself known.

There was nothing to do but shut off the car and remove the last obstacle between them. Her heels sank into the gravel, and she wobbled a little as she stepped out of the car. "You made good time."

"Could say the same thing of you."

She turned and surveyed the building in whose driveway they stood. Samara had heard about the legendary King estate more than a few times and she'd even seen pictures, but nothing compared to the reality of standing there, dwarfed by the mansion. It had to be twenty thousand square feet and three stories high, the faintly Victorian style making her feel like a peasant trespassing on royalty's property. *Probably intentional.*

She swallowed. No matter how overwhelming, it was still just a building, and one that Lydia now owned. "Shall we?"

"After you." He bit out the words, tension rising in waves off his body. Beckett obviously didn't want to be there any more than she did. He moved to his saddlebags and pulled out a plain gray metal container, the sight of which stopped her cold.

Nathaniel's ashes.

She moved on autopilot, crunching her way across the gravel and up the imposing front steps to the door. It opened easily in her hand, which might have made her wonder if

Beckett's presence at her back wasn't driving her before him.

Samara stopped in the entranceway—foyer—looking up, up, up to the arching ceiling a good twenty feet above their heads. "Wow."

"Built to impress." He started past her but hesitated, obviously torn. Finally, Beckett pulled the sunglasses off. "There are a few things I want out of my old room, and then I'll scatter the ashes."

He obviously wasn't asking permission, but she nodded. "That's reasonable."

"Reasonable." He snorted. "God, you kill me. I wasn't giving you a choice. I was telling you how it's going to go."

Irritation flared, the familiar feeling welcome after the uncertainty of their last interaction. Samara didn't know how to deal with a grieving Beckett. But the prickly ass currently striding deeper into the house as if he had no doubt she'd trail behind him like a good little dog? *That* she could handle, and gladly.

She followed him at her own pace as he moved up the grand staircase and down the left hall, allowing herself to study the long line of his back muscles that the damn shirt only seemed to accent. Beckett would never be pretty. His features were a little too rough for that, too masculine. He was all man, and his body matched his face—strong.

He'd been strong when he lifted her against the door and ground against her until the need for more had her begging.

Stop it.

But there was no stopping the onslaught of memories. His big hands on her ass, squeezing as he guided her onto his cock. The way he'd made a cage of his arms when he rolled them, effortlessly changing positions without missing a beat. His rough five-o'clock shadow scraping against her inner thighs as he sucked her clit.

"Samara?"

She blinked to find Beckett less than a foot in front of her. "Sorry, I didn't hear what you said."

"What were you thinking about just then?" His gaze fell to her mouth. "Never mind. You don't have to tell me. It's written all over your face."

She licked her lips as he stepped closer, as he backed her against the wall and bracketed her in with his hands on either side of her head. He felt bigger in this position, as if his shoulders could block out the very sun. *You have to get him to back off. You're too close.* She leaned against the wall, the move arching her back just a little. Beckett's gaze dropped to where her breasts pressed against her blouse, and he dragged in an unsteady breath. As if he was using every ounce of willpower not to touch her. He dragged his eyes up to meet hers. "You were thinking about that night."

She could deny it, but it would be pointless. "Yeah."

Slowly, oh so slowly, he moved one hand to sift his fingers through her hair. When she didn't immediately answer, he leaned closer yet. "I think about it, too." He trailed his fingers through her hair until he reached her shoulder and his thumb dipped beneath the fabric of her shirt. "All the fucking time." He dropped his hand farther, the tips of his fingers tracing over her breast in a touch so light she was half sure she imagined it.

Might have convinced herself she imagined it if her entire body wasn't tuned to his in that moment.

Touch me.

As if reading her thoughts, he shifted closer, his leg sliding between hers. The move forced her skirt up as she spread her legs to accommodate his thigh. Higher and higher until he was firmly pressed against her clit. It throbbed in time with her heartbeat, and it was everything she could do not to rub on his thigh like a mindless version of herself.

She *felt* mindless. Samara gave up her determination not to touch him. She couldn't wrap her legs around his waist because of her damn skirt, but she ran her hands up his chest. "We can't."

"I know." But he didn't stop. He slid his hands down to her ass, urging her to grind against his thigh. Slowly, so incredibly slowly, as if he had all the time in the world. He dragged his mouth over her collarbone, the faint rasp of whiskers drawing a whimper from her lips.

Samara dug her fingers into his hair, and he went still. Waiting. She pulled him up and took his mouth the way she'd wanted to since she'd snuck out of that hotel room six months before. She flicked his tongue with hers, teasing him even as he resumed the delicious movement between them again. *Yes, yes, do that, don't stop.*

Beckett let her have control for all of two seconds, and then he deepened the kiss, pressing her more firmly against the wall. He took with his mouth even as he gave with his body, hitching her higher until her toes barely touched the floor and she was completely at his mercy. Pleasure sparked through her, and she kissed him harder. It wasn't enough, might never be enough, but she couldn't stop.

Not when she knew that, as good as this was, what came next was even better.

He tore his mouth from hers. "I don't give a fuck if this is a shitty idea. I want you again, Samara. I need you."

I need you.

She stared into the storm barely contained in his eyes. He

held perfectly still, waiting for her response. As if she had the slightest bit of control in this situation.

She *didn't* have control, though.

If she followed through on the promise Beckett's body was making, it would be good. It would be so far beyond good that there were no words for it.

That wasn't why she'd come out here, though. She'd been tasked with searching out his secrets. If she said yes now, she'd spend the next few hours coming on Beckett's cock, his mouth, his hands, and she'd have compromised herself and her future in the process. No matter how phenomenal the pleasure he could give her, a few hours wasn't worth the rest of her life.

Her mother had learned that the hard way. Samara would be worse than a fool if she made the same mistake.

"Let..." She had to take a shallow breath and try again. "Let me down."

He shifted back just enough for her to slide down his body until her feet were firmly rooted to the floor again. "You want this."

"Yes, I do." Taking that first step away from him felt like tearing her own arm off. It was too *right* to have Beckett's body pressed against hers. As if they fit in a way that defied logic and comprehension.

That was the problem. The second he touched her, she stopped thinking, and being quick on her feet was the only thing that had gotten Samara to where she was today. She couldn't compromise that, even for a man who made her blood sing in her veins and her entire body yearn.

He's the enemy.

She couldn't afford to forget that.

The next step was easier, and she paused to right her

skirt. Her thighs shook with denied pleasure, but she managed to smooth her expression. *Remind him what's at stake. Get your barriers back in place.* "That's not why we're here, Beckett. Get your things and then we'll scatter your father's ashes. After that, you should probably say good-bye to Thistledown Villa."

Beckett couldn't look at Samara. Not with her taste still stinging his tongue and the memory of her heat searing him through his jeans. She was right about stopping, right about not complicating things further, but fuck if he cared about it. They could be in his old bed, losing themselves in each other. The temptation to forget everything for a little while was almost as strong as the temptation for the woman herself.

Liar.

He grabbed an ancient backpack from his closet and looked around the room to distract himself. He'd lived in this space from the time he was a baby to when he moved out at eighteen. He hadn't gone far—just to his brand-new condo in Houston to attend college—but it had still been a new distance that was never there before. Memories crowded the corkboard, trophies lined the shelf running the length of the room, and paperbacks filled the shelf below it. The walls were still the bright blue he'd convinced his mother to paint when he was eight. The weekend they cleared out this room and went to town on the walls was one of the last good ones they'd had before the cancer took first her energy and then her life.

All of it held significance, but the truth was that he'd taken most of the important things when he'd bought his condo in the heart of the city. Nathaniel King could be a bastard and a half, and it would have been in character for him to purge Beckett's room of any hint of his dead wife the same way he'd purged the rest of the house.

He walked to the corkboard and took down the two pictures of his mother he'd left behind. The rest were of friends from high school who he'd barely talked to after graduation, let alone now. They were good memories, but ultimately forgettable.

"Is that your mother?"

He tensed against the urge to shove the photos in his pocket to shield them from Samara. But it wasn't like Beckett's mother was a big secret. She was ancient history, at least according to his father. She'd never *felt* like ancient history to Beckett, though. Everywhere he looked in Thistledown Villa he saw evidence of her despite his old man's best efforts. Nathaniel King could take down her pictures, dig up the flowers she'd planted in front of the house, and even go so far as to change the curtains she'd chosen for the whole house, but he couldn't erase the memories Beckett had with her. No matter how hard he'd tried.

"Yeah. She died when I was nine." The woman in the picture held a baby in a blue blanket—Beckett—and smiled broadly at the camera. Her blond hair looked like it'd been tossed in the wind, and the fields of Thistledown Villa peeked out of the background. They'd played in those fields for days on end during the summers, picking wildflowers while she wove stories about the magical creatures that made their home there. Fantastical adventures his father had always been too busy to come along on.

"She looks happy." There was a strange hushed tone to Samara's words.

"She was." He slid the photo into his pocket. "They both

were." Maybe things would have been different if Nathaniel wasn't so damn determined to smite out every piece of her. It might have been grief pushing him to destroy his own memories with his late wife, but it had only ever seemed a betrayal to Beckett. She was barely gone a week before the purge started. He still vividly remembered walking into the kitchen and finding Nathaniel ripping the photos from the fridge and tossing them into the trash. Even now, twenty-five years later, anger flushed hot and painful in his chest. "My father would have been a different person if she'd lived."

"Maybe." Samara shrugged, her expression guarded. "Or maybe she would have lived long enough for it all to fall apart."

Old wound.

Like recognized like, and they stood in perfect understanding for the space of a heartbeat. Beckett broke the moment, turning away to the desk taking up the corner nearest the window. He found the key taped to the underside of it and unlocked the bottom drawer. The only thing it held was a faded baby book. He'd left it here because it seemed fitting that his childhood home held the first memories that were diligently recorded by the mother whose death neither he nor Nathaniel had ever quite gotten over.

On the dark days in his teenage years, when he and his father would clash violently and then retreat to their respective wings, he'd pull out this book and remember the woman whose neat script detailed adventures she and baby Beckett had together. His first staggering steps in the grand hall that, to his mother's delight, turned into running almost immediately. Playing hide-and-seek in the massive gardens behind the mansion. How he used to tell his mother he loved her before he went to bed every night and beg for one more story.

The book didn't contain the memories that came later. Chocolate chip pancakes for breakfast in the kitchen. His mother's endless patience as she taught him to read on the comfortable couch in the library downstairs. Playing tag and running through the house, filling the empty halls with laughter.

The only foundation he had for *those* memories was the house itself. The house was what drew him back time and time again. He made an effort to visit at least once a month when he was in town, to walk through the halls and reinforce his memories of his mother, to talk to the staff and ensure that they were taking good care of the place. To remember that he was more than just Nathaniel King's son. He was *her* son, too.

After today he'd no longer have access to Thistledown. He'd have to find a different way to make sure he didn't forget a single thing. To keep the memories from fading over time.

He slid the baby book into the backpack before Samara could ask any questions about it. It was one thing to share a few spare details about his mother. It was entirely another to lay himself bare for this woman who ultimately couldn't be trusted.

Beckett hitched the backpack onto his shoulder. "Let's go."

"That's it?"

He stopped in the doorway. "What's it?"

"That's…" She motioned vaguely at him. "You took two pictures and a baby book. This room…" Another wave to encompass the room. "You don't want anything else?"

He almost didn't answer, but the thought seemed to

bother her so much he found himself explaining. "It's all just…shit. The house is what holds the memories, and I can't take that with me." *Why the fuck did you deed the house to Lydia, old man? Was it some kind of misplaced guilt? Was it one last final "fuck you" to me for not erasing my mother the way you wanted me to?*

If the ghost of his father lingered in these halls, he gave no answer. Just as well.

Beckett walked out of the room and this time Samara followed without protesting. He'd left the container with his father's ashes in the entranceway, so he retrieved it and headed for the back of the house. It would have been just as easy to go around the outside, but he wanted to say good-bye in his own way. He'd fight for Thistledown Villa. It was too important *not* to fight for. But he didn't want to miss his chance to say good-bye all the same.

When his great-great-grandfather had struck oil and gotten rich, the first thing he'd done was have this absurdly massive house built. Three wings, fifteen bedrooms, five stairwells, a ballroom, two libraries, half a dozen other rooms for everything from entertaining to hiding from the family. And for what? The legacy the man had obviously envisioned where a busy family occupied this space…it never came to pass.

After cancer took Beckett's mother, he and his father were the only ones who lived there on a daily basis, and the staff was sufficiently terrified of his father that they weren't willing to respond to any overtures of friendship from Beckett. It was as if his father had extended welcome to his mother, but after she was gone, Nathaniel couldn't stand anyone who wasn't King or staff setting foot in these hallowed halls. Beckett took perverse pleasure out of bringing his friends here, of forcing laughter and chaos into the halls his father wanted silent.

Yet another way he and Nathaniel never saw eye-to-eye.

He took the door from the kitchen into the greenhouse. "My grandfather had these gardens built as a wedding gift to my grandmother." Paths wound through the thick foliage, and there were little signs announcing the various types of tropical flowers planted along them.

"That's one way to woo a woman."

He slowed so she should catch up, and they walked together. "She was the daughter of a pastor, and the man hated my grandfather—probably with good reason—and forbade them to marry. They ran off to Europe, and while they were there, they visited the Palacio de Cristal in Madrid. She fell in love, and so he built this."

Samara reached out and ran her finger along a brilliant orange flower. "That's a beautiful story. It's too bad he was such a horrible father."

Beckett couldn't argue that, so he didn't bother. His grandfather was ultimately the reason why Lydia split from the family. There was probably a time right after the decision to name Beckett's father as the heir when things could have been repaired. But they hadn't been. Pride kept everyone to their own sides and so Kingdom Corp was born, and Thistledown Villa was banned to Lydia and any children she'd have. *Pride is one thing every single one of the Kings have in common.*

He opened the back door for Samara and they walked out onto the fields that were pictured in Lydia's office. He glanced at Samara's shoes. "It might be better if you stay here. The ground is pretty soft right now." Her heels would sink right into the dirt.

"Do you want me to come with you?"

The question seemed straightforward enough on the surface. Truth be told, Beckett *didn't* want to do this by himself. He might never have been on the same page as his father, but in his heart of hearts he'd hoped that one day they'd figure their shit out and admit that if they had nothing else in common, they had a love for his mother. He'd never get that chance now.

But he didn't explain that to Samara for the same reason he didn't tell her about the baby book in his room. He shook his head. "I got it."

Beckett could feel her gaze on him as he walked out into the field. It was too early in the year for the wildflowers to be in full bloom, but that was fitting in its own way. He stopped in the same spot where his father used to come stand after it rained. The same spot where the picture in his pocket had been taken.

"I hope it was worth it," he said quietly. "I hope all the backbiting and bullshit and cruelty was worth it." *I hope you end up with her.* He couldn't say it, though. No matter how much his father may have loved his mother, it didn't make Nathaniel King a better man. He'd had a choice after she died, and he'd gone down the path that was destined to set him and Beckett forever at odds. "Good-bye, old man." He took the top off the container and scattered the ashes into the wind.

CHAPTER FOUR

Samara pulled up in front of her childhood home, her heart heavy. Friday dinners were for her *amma*. The tiny two-bedroom house was clean and tidy on the inside, but anyone walking by could see the peeling paint and desperate need for a new roof. The obviously well-loved yard did nothing to elevate the first impression most people got as they walked past it on the street. Samara had offered to pay for the fixes, but her mother had shot her down so sternly that she hadn't had the courage to offer again.

The building was about as far from Thistledown Villa as it could be and still be termed a house. Before today, that might have filled her with shame—and guilt for feeling shame—but after watching the raw memories play out over Beckett's face, she was reminded forcibly just how lucky she was. Samara may never have met her father, but her *amma*'s love ensured that she'd never felt the lack. This little house might not be picture perfect or have been in her family for generations, but it was filled to the brim with happy memories. Even the bad times were never *that* bad, because no matter how often life kicked her, Samara's *amma* never let her hope flicker.

The screen door had a tear in the bottom half that had been there since she was a kid. She'd always hated that tear, hated the lack of money it represented. It seemed such a petty thing to focus on now. She opened it and knocked.

Amma opened it almost immediately. "Samara, you're here." She enveloped her in a hug that almost took her off her feet despite the fact that her mother was a good six inches shorter than she was. The scent of sandalwood had her smiling despite the weight of the day. *Home.*

"*Amma.*" She hugged her back and frowned. "You've lost weight."

"So have you." Her *amma* clicked her tongue and pinched her arm. "Much more of that nonsense and you'll be more shadow than girl. Come in, come in."

She followed her *amma* into the little kitchen. "You didn't have to cook for me. I'm more than capable of picking up takeout on the way here." The protest was barely halfhearted. Takeout couldn't compare to *Amma*'s cooking, and they both knew it.

"It's not a chore when it's done with love." Her *amma* shot her a look. "And last time you offered to pick up dinner, you brought me raw fish and rice."

Samara laughed. It had seemed like a good idea at the time. "At least let me help you."

"Absolutely not. Sit. How's your work? Has that witch seen the error of her ways and found religion?"

"*Amma*, Lydia is not a witch." She ran her fingers through her hair and absently started braiding a lock. "Things are going well. I'm personally handling the proposal for an important government contract—it's a great opportunity. *Lydia* gave me that."

Her *amma* huffed. "She didn't give you anything. You

worked for it. That's not going to stop her from trying to make you over in her image." She looked up from the samosas she was putting together and narrowed inky eyes identical to Samara's. "Look at you. You walk like her, you talk like her, you dress like her."

"*Amma*, please." She tried and failed to rein in her irritation. They'd had this conversation more times than she could count, and she didn't see this one going any differently than the hundreds before it. That wouldn't stop her from trying, though. "There is nothing wrong with ambition."

"Ambition is like salt—a little is a good thing, but too much ruins the meal."

"I know." It wasn't Lydia King that her *amma* was opposed to—it was the world she moved in. Once upon a time, her *amma* had been on the same path Samara was on now. She'd come from India to attend McCombs School of Business on a full scholarship and had all the hallmarks of going places.

Until she met Samara's father. Devansh Patel was rich and beautiful and charming, the youngest son of a local congressman. It had been a love affair for the ages—at least long enough for her *amma* to get pregnant and drop out of school, losing all her scholarships—and then Devansh unceremoniously dumped her, and his family's lawyers had blocked any attempts to declare paternity.

Left with nothing of the future she'd thought she'd have, her *amma* ended up cleaning the houses of people like Samara's father and the Kings to pay the bills.

All her life, *Amma* had supported her in every way she could. Samara wore secondhand clothes and never had money for school lunches, but she'd kept her eye on the prize. Even after a long day of backbreaking work, her *amma* would stay up late to help her with whatever school-work was giving her trouble. Anything for Samara. She wanted her daughter to shoot for the stars in a way she hadn't been able to.

Just not *this* star.

"Enough of this. I don't want to fight. Tell me what's new in your life."

Samara settled in and gave her *amma* a purified version of what she'd been up to. She kept the stories light and entertaining, and very carefully didn't share any details that could be upsetting. It took more effort than normal, mostly because she was preoccupied with Beckett.

She rarely questioned Lydia. The woman was a genius when it came to business, more than proving she should have been named CEO of Morningstar Enterprise instead of Nathaniel. But this situation with Thistledown Villa didn't sit well with Samara. It was obviously a footnote for Lydia—bragging rights—and it was just as obviously *important* to Beckett.

It's not my business. My job is to follow orders and keep my head on straight—it's not to get between the members of the King family.

Dinner passed pleasantly enough once they got all the bickering out of the way. Samara did the dishes despite *Amma*'s protests, and she slipped a couple hundred dollars into the cookie jar where her *amma* had stashed her savings. It was their little song and dance. They had their ridiculous pride in common, but the truth was that her *amma* needed money, and if she wouldn't take it directly, Samara had no problem hiding it in places where it wouldn't be found until she was safely out of the house.

Amma would find the money and they'd both pretend

it was there all along and she'd miscounted it somewhere along the way. Unnecessarily complicated, maybe, but her *amma* had sacrificed everything to bring Samara into this world and ensure that she grew up in the best life possible considering their financial situation. A few hundred dollars here and there was the least she could do.

Samara made tea and they spent a pleasant couple of hours watching the *Jeopardy!* episodes her *amma* had recorded over the week.

Her phone buzzed next to her. She almost ignored it, but her best friend's name came up. "Sorry, *Amma*."

"Don't worry, *bachcha*. Take your call. I'm on a roll."

She smiled. "You are." She'd never met anyone better at *Jeopardy!* If her *amma* hadn't gotten pregnant and altered her entire life to accommodate her new role as a mother, she would have gone places and changed the world.

Guilt rose, choking her. There was no way to assuage it—over the years it'd become her constant companion within the four walls of this house. Her *amma* was the best of mothers. She loved Samara beyond all shadow of a doubt and never once let so much as a whisper of accusation pass her lips. If she blamed anyone for her life, it was Samara's sperm donor rather than the baby she'd ended up with, but even that anger had faded over time.

Samara's guilt wasn't going anywhere, though

It was almost a relief to step out of the room and take the call. "Hey."

"Hey, what are you doing after you leave your mother's?" It didn't surprise her that Journey King knew where she was—everyone knew that Friday nights were for her *amma*. Even Lydia respected this unless it was an actual emergency, probably because it was the only boundary Samara ever put her foot down about. She moved a little deeper into the kitchen. "Work."

"Wrong answer. We're going out. We've been working crazy hours, and knowing my mother, that's not going to be changing anytime soon. Take a break. Come have a drink with me. Dish about what the hell is going on with my estranged cousin."

"I really don't think that's a good idea." Talking about Beckett would only bring up memories of what they'd been doing in Thistledown Villa today—both the good and the bad. Journey knew her too well for her to hide the truth, and her friend wouldn't hesitate to pry every last detail out of her.

"It's funny. Sometimes you talk, and my mother's voice comes out." Journey laughed. "Come on, Samara. I'm not above pulling the best-friend card and kidnapping you for the night if I have to."

She wasn't getting out of this, and the truth was that she needed the break and the reminder of what was really important in her life. Her *amma*. Her friend. Her job. *Not Beckett.* "I have to go home and change, but I'll be there in about an hour."

"See you then." Journey hung up.

Samara turned and found her *amma* standing in the doorway, a sad expression on her face. "You're playing with fire, *bachcha*."

"*Amma*, we've talked about this. She's my friend." Journey might be Lydia's oldest daughter, but their friendship had grown outside of work into something real and important to her.

She shook her head. "King blood is like Patel blood. You might feel like you're one of them—*they* might even feel like you're one of them—but that can change without warning. If something threatens them, they will close ranks like a shoal of fish, and you'll be left on the outside for the circling sharks."

Just like her *amma* had been.

"*Amma*—"

She grasped Samara's shoulders, her weathered hands aged beyond her years by the cleaning chemicals she used. "I love you, *bachcha*. I don't want to see you hurt."

"Nothing can hurt me. I'm bulletproof." An old joke, but this time it didn't make her *amma* smile.

"You might think you are. You won't realize your mistake until it's too late."

After he got back from Thistledown Villa, Beckett couldn't stay in the apartment. The thought of being closed in by those four walls made his skin crawl. He spent a useless hour trying to wade through his father's paperwork on the proposal, but the words kept running together as he flipped between thinking about how good Samara had felt in his arms...and what plan he could put together to get the house back.

It was no use.

He thought better on the move, so he changed into a pair of shorts and running shoes and headed out. It wasn't late enough for either the foot traffic or the humidity to have thinned, but he welcomed the struggle each breath became as he started to run.

Houston had its ups and downs and the traffic was bad enough to make even the most even-tempered person crazy, but he loved how full of life it was. The Theater District's restaurants were some of the best in the state—in his completely unbiased opinion—and he inhaled the tempting scents as he passed tables full of people eating before they headed to shows down the street.

He ran until his legs started to shake and his mind was finally blessedly clear. Between Samara and Thistledown Villa, he'd let himself get turned around. Ultimately, both could wait. He'd spend the day tomorrow in the office. The presentation to secure the government contract was next week, which meant that had to take priority over everything else.

Back in his condo, he showered, already feeling better, and sat down to pick through the proposal. It would secure majority oil rights in the Gulf of Mexico for the next ten years—rights Morningstar Enterprise had held for generations. The only other company that came close to edging his out was Lydia's, and he'd be damned before he'd let that happen here. If he lost the bid, it would hardly be the end for the company, but it would hit them at a time when they didn't need more uncertainty. If their shareholders thought for a second that they might crash, they'd abandon the company in droves, and *that* could potentially send them into a nosedive they might not make it out of.

It won't happen. I won't let it happen.

His phone rang, and he tensed at the sight of Frank's name flashing across the screen. *News about my father's death.* If there was one thing that would take priority over the company, it was *that*. "Hey, Frank."

"You have time for another beer?"

Not good news, then. He glanced at the clock over his oven. It wasn't early, but it was nowhere near late enough that he'd manage to sleep. "Careful, Frank. You keep asking me out and I might start to think you're sweet on me."

"Never that." Faint noise in the background, as if he was walking down the street. "Meet me at Cocoa's."

Beckett frowned. Cocoa's was a high-end club that catered to Houston's elite. They only served top shelf, all their employees were painfully beautiful, and the whole place was decorated like a speakeasy—or at least how the owners thought a speakeasy should look. "Not really your scene."

"It is tonight." He hung up.

He changed into a suit—Cocoa's had a strict dress code and jeans didn't fit into it. He hesitated. Frank liked his games, but he wasn't into the pretentious bullshit any more than Beckett was.

Only one way to find out what's up.

Thirty minutes later, he walked past the velvet rope—a velvet rope, for fuck's sake—and into the low din of Cocoa's. Throbbing music had the dance floor packed, the crowd moving in a slow writhe that gave the impression of an orgy in progress. The roped-off VIP section was on the other side of that mess. People lounged on the fainting chairs and couches, pretending that eyes didn't follow every little movement they made as they waited for something resembling an invitation.

That was the other reason he hated this place. The club might pretend it catered to the elite, but its true clientele was the masses of social climbers who came here *for* the elite. Whether the aim was one night of bragging rights or some deeper game, if someone wanted a partner with more money than God, they had a good chance to find them at Cocoa's.

He skirted the edge of the dance floor, pointedly ignoring several women who gave him blatant invitations. Even if he wasn't preoccupied with a certain Indian woman, he wouldn't be tempted.

Frank saw him coming and motioned to the pretty brunette manning the entrance to the VIP area. She stepped aside, and then he was just another lion prowling the cage while the crowd watched. *You're here for a reason. Get the info. Have a drink. Get the fuck out.*

Beckett dropped onto the couch next to Frank. "Why here?"

"I have my reasons." Frank sounded distracted, his attention on the dance floor. He could be looking at any one of the scantily clad women grinding to the throbbing beat. But this was Frank, which meant he had a specific one in mind— the woman who was probably the reason he'd set the meeting there to begin with. Finally, Frank shook his head and focused on Beckett. "I bought it last week."

"*Cocoa's*?" He looked around the room with new eyes. It wasn't any more appealing than it had been before. "Why the hell would you—" He stopped short. *Of course.* What better way to gather information than from the elite who came there to drink themselves stupid? They were bound to spill secrets into the right set of ears. "You crafty bastard."

"Man's got to make a living."

Beckett didn't dignify that with a response. Frank had enough money that he wouldn't have to work for the rest of his life—and that his theoretical grandchildren wouldn't have to work for the rest of *their* lives. "What do you have for me?"

"You want to wait for a drink first?"

He tensed. "No, I don't want a fucking drink. Just tell me the news."

"Suit yourself." Frank shrugged. "Your old man's driver

is enjoying a vacation in Brazil right now. He left the day Nathaniel died, and he's been blowing enough money to turn heads down there."

He was paid off.

Beckett didn't know the man. He was someone Nathaniel had hired years ago, and one of his father's conditions for a driver was complete silence. *Be seen, not heard. Better yet, don't be seen, either.* He should have ordered the damn drink. "Who?"

"Not sure yet." Frank flagged down the waitress, a blonde dressed in a black flapper dress that barely covered the essentials. "My friend here needs a double of whiskey on the rocks."

"My pleasure."

He waited for her to move away to lean forward. "Beck, there's something else. Your old man had a meeting that night—a meeting with Lydia King."

CHAPTER FIVE

Y ou needed this. Tell me I'm wrong."

Samara laughed and raised her martini. "You're not wrong." Her life was high stress on the best days, and the last forty-eight hours had hardly been that. She'd always had a very firm opinion of Beckett and Nathaniel King, and spending an hour in Beckett's presence when they weren't banging each other into oblivion was enough to start chipping away at everything she thought she knew. It left her feeling like she was wearing too-tight clothing with an itchy tag just beyond reach.

"Are you going to tell me what's going on, or do I have to start ordering shots?" Journey stretched out long legs. She wore an impossibly short black jumper, which should have looked ridiculous, but she somehow managed to pull it off. Samara could never pinpoint if it was confidence or her model-proportioned body, or some combination of the two, but Journey could probably show up dressed from head to toe in a fuzzy pink bear suit and she'd still rock it.

"No shots. I have to work in the morning." She *should* be

working now, truth be told. "The proposal for the government lease—"

"Is up in seven days," Journey finished. "I know. Between you and my mother, I could probably give you the exact amount of time left to submit the proposal, down to the minute." Her hazel eyes went contemplative. "Maybe the second, too."

"Don't you dare. I already have enough stress without a literal countdown clock." Samara sipped her drink. "I was out at Thistledown today. Lydia sent me to babysit Beckett. I don't know what she thought he was going to do—burn it to the ground, maybe."

Journey snorted. "If anyone's going to do that, it's my mother. I don't know why she's so damn bitter. Nathaniel and his father were dicks, sure, but that was thirty freaking years ago. She won. Kingdom Corp is the single biggest competitor Morningstar has. We own a third of the world's leases for oil rights. At some point, you'd think it'd be enough."

"Maybe once we secure this contract, it will be." She didn't believe the words even as she gave them voice. Lydia was driven by things beyond understanding. Samara got it, at least in part. She'd been spurned by her father, too, albeit in a much different way. He hadn't met Samara, hadn't raised her from birth, only to tell her that she'd never be good enough. Her father had rejected her when she was barely the size of a lima bean. It was different.

She set her drink down. "You're right. I don't want to talk about work. It'll hold until tomorrow."

"That's my girl." Journey grinned. "We'll get through it. My brothers will be back in Houston at the end of the month, and then work will get back to something resembling normal. We just have to hold out until then."

With Lydia's two sons in DC schmoozing senators to ensure that they looked favorably on Kingdom Corp, the bulk of the work they usually handled had fallen on Journey and Samara. It happened twice a year, and she'd been prepared for it.

What she hadn't anticipated was Nathaniel King dying and her being tasked with handling Beckett in addition to the rest of her responsibilities. *One more week. Not even a full week. Once this contract is secured, I can get back to focusing on the rest.*

Samara turned and leaned against the bar. Being in Cocoa's always felt like waking up in a fever dream. Everything was too ostentatious, too over-the-top, in an effort to prove how rich it was. While it brought in good business, the place missed the mark of the top one percent by a mile. Cocoa's was more what normal people thought rich people were than anything resembling reality.

It didn't stop Houston's crème de la crème from coming out in full force every weekend. She studied the dance floor and VIP lounge, picking out two hotel moguls, an heiress, and no fewer than four CEOs. Two men sat with their backs to the bar, and she frowned. "Is that Frank Evans?"

"I wouldn't know."

She glanced at Journey, taking in the tight set of her shoulders. "Uh-huh. Your mom sent you to negotiate with him again, didn't she?" While the Kings might be one of the richest families in Houston, Frank Evans owned half of the city. Anyone looking to expand—like Lydia was—had to deal with him in order to negotiate for the best buildings and property.

"He's a jackass."

Samara had met him only a handful of times, and though

she found him distant and maybe a little scary, she hadn't gotten the jackass vibe. She held up a hand. "I believe you. You hate him, I hate him."

Journey glared at the back of his head as if she could turn her gaze into laser beams. "I bet he's awful in bed. He probably just grunts—a sixty-second man."

She raised her eyebrows. "That's a very...specific thing to speculate on."

"Shut up."

"I didn't say anything."

Journey rolled her eyes. "I'm being irrational. I know it, you know it. Just let me have this moment, okay?"

"Consider this moment had." She turned to catch the bartender's eye and motioned for another round. Shots might not be on the agenda, but this had just turned into a two-to-four-drink night. "Do you want to talk about it?"

"No." Journey caught her look and laughed. "Really, I don't. I'm just frustrated because negotiations are at a standstill and none of my usual tricks work on him. He just sits there and...stares. It's irritating in the extreme. I can't tell if he's actually listening, or if he's indulging in some lucid dreaming while I drone on."

Samara didn't envy her that task. There was nothing worse than giving a presentation and having the main audience look like they were seconds away from falling asleep. "Maybe you should bring an energy drink basket to your next meeting. That would get your point across."

"You know, I think I might do that." Journey went tense. "Uh, Samara?"

"Yeah?" She accepted their drinks from the bartender and glanced at her friend.

"Correct me if I'm wrong, but is that my cousin staring at

you right now? He looks like he's playing a game of Fuck, Marry, Kill, and he's not sure where he's going to land."

She spun around and, sure enough, Beckett was the other man sitting next to Frank in the VIP lounge. The expression on his face was decidedly *not* friendly. Her stomach sank as he shot to his feet, his intentions clear. "He's coming over here, isn't he?"

"Looks that way." Journey downed her drink and squared her shoulders. "Want me to run interference?"

Considering that Journey's version of *interference* often resulted in her photo on the front page of some tabloid, that was the last thing Samara wanted. Any scandal would factor into whether their bid got accepted, and Lydia might skin Journey alive if she thought her daughter caused them to lose it. "No, I got it." She considered her drink for a half a second and then followed her friend's lead and downed it like a shot. A very large, very potent shot. *Shit, that wasn't a good idea.*

Beckett cut through the crowd, and despite the music and general intoxication, people scrambled to get out of his way, a flock sensing a predator in their midst. Frank trailed after him, his expression as closed off as ever.

Journey shifted closer to her. "You sure? He's already drawing attention."

He was. His dramatic path only ensured that whatever conversation he seemed determined for them to have would be in the presence of a hundred witnesses, every single one of them with a camera phone that would record it for posterity's sake. *Damn it. It's not Journey I have to worry about making a scene.* While Beckett wasn't hers to corral, Samara couldn't afford for *her* face to end up all over social media. Lydia would kill her.

"I'll be back in a few," Samara murmured and moved away from the bar. She met Beckett as he exited the dance floor and grabbed his arm when he opened his mouth to speak. "Not here." She didn't give him a chance to argue, towing him down the hallway to where the bathrooms and private meeting rooms were. She briefly debated shoving Beckett into a storage closet, but the only story that would be more scandalous than their co-opting a meeting room was them disappearing into a mop closet. "In here."

The room was blessedly empty, and she shut the door behind them. The manager would probably be pissed, but it was nothing she couldn't handle. She could just shell out the money to rent the damn room for an hour—with a little extra to ensure that the manager kept his mouth shut. "What the hell were you thinking?"

He strode three steps deeper into the room and spun to face her. "What was *I* thinking? You have a lot of nerve acting like the injured party right now."

That brought Samara up short. There was real anger written across his features. She'd registered it before, of course, but she hadn't really expected it to be aimed at *her*. Aside from their ongoing rivalry, she hadn't done anything that should piss him off more than normal. She crossed her arms over her chest and lifted her chin. "Want to enlighten me about the bug that's crawled up your ass?"

"Did you know?" He didn't move, but he seemed to loom over her all the same. "Did you know Lydia met with my father the night he died?"

She froze. "What are you talking about? Lydia had her monthly pamper session that night. I know because I booked the appointments myself."

He searched her face as if trying to dig inside her head and read her thoughts. "You didn't know."

"I'm not sure where you got your information, but you're wrong. Lydia despised Nathaniel. She went out of her way to avoid him. Samara shook her head. "There's no way she would have met him."

If she had... No. Samara didn't believe that for a second. She *knew* her boss. Lydia would rather set herself on fire than spend a single second in the same room as Nathaniel King. She didn't know where Beckett came up with the idea that she had, but he was wrong.

Dead wrong.

Journey could feel him watching her. It was a hot itch at the nape of her neck, and no matter how shamelessly she flirted with the bartender, there was no distracting from Frank Evans's gaze drilling a hole into her back. If it were any other circumstances, she'd say to hell with it and stalk out—but not before she ordered him a shot with an absurd name. Blowjob. Sex in the bathtub. Slippery nipples.

Actually...

"Hey, cutie, I'm going to need another shot. Something special this time." She was being petty, but she didn't care. After the weeks of frustration and dealing with Frank's barely concealed contempt, she was due for some petty revenge. *If ever there was a man who needed a sense of humor, it's this one.*

Shot in hand, she wiggled and shimmied her way around the edges of the dance floor to the VIP lounge. Journey didn't need to look over to know he was still watching her. She put a little extra swing into her step, working it for all she was worth. If he was going to stare, she might as well give him a show.

She recognized the woman manning the velvet rope and gave a cheery wave with her free hand. "Hey, girl! How did things go with that blind date?"

"That douche doubled up his dates and the girl before me was still there when I showed up. He tried to pretend like it was totally reasonable for all three of us to sit down for a drink." The redhead shook her head, her lip curling.

She watched Frank out of the corner of her eye. "I hope you told him to get lost."

"Oh, I did." The hostess grinned. "Right after I drank my weight in top-label gin."

"Good girl." She smiled. "You have a nice night." She hesitated, but at this point all she was doing was putting off the inevitable. Journey sauntered over to the couch where Frank had taken up residence. It was like everything in Cocoa's—a little overdone, a little cheeky. The damn thing looked a bit like an oversized throne made for five people instead of one. *Probably for the orgies.*

An image plastered itself into her brain. Frank's dark skin bare and glistening in the low light. His muscles flexing as he thrust. His cock...

Danger! Under no circumstances are you to think about Frank Evans's cock.

She stopped in front of him, suddenly not sure if she should take a seat on the orgy couch-throne or keep the advantage of standing. *Though standing puts his face right about even with my...* Journey sat, keeping a full cushion between them. She leaned over and offered the shot. "With my compliments."

Frank took it deliberately, his steady dark gaze seeming to categorize everything about her appearance—and then dismiss her entirely. It stung. Every. Single. Time. Journey might not go out of her way to grab the spotlight, but a woman liked to think she wasn't considered a total waste of space. That's exactly how Frank made her feel—like a waste of space. She'd heard the nasty comments enough to know how it went, even if *he* never said them aloud. *Party-girl heiress. Not brilliant like either of her brothers. Not a model like her younger sister. A Lydia King knockoff. Damaged goods.*

He sniffed. "Jägermeister and Red Bull."

Anger as his dismissal made her words sharp enough to cut. "It's called Liquid Viagra. Seems to me that you could use some."

Instead of looking pissed, the corner of his lips twitched up. Coming from Frank Evans, he might as well have boomed out a laugh that deafened the entire room. *It's a wonder his face doesn't shatter from breaking its dour mold.*

Frank leaned forward and she was too proud to retreat. Not after she'd thrown down the gauntlet. Damn it, he wouldn't win this interaction. His gaze dragged over her in another perusal, but there was *intent* behind it this time. He lingered at her sky-high heels, the hem of her jumper that just hit the tops of her thighs, at her breasts pressing against the deep V-neck, before finally settling on her mouth. "Point to you, Duchess."

"Don't call me that." She cursed herself for reacting, but she *hated* that nickname. The media had coined her Duchess after her failed engagement when she was nineteen. It didn't matter that her fiancé had been a baron, or that it was an empty title in the first place. He'd promised to take her away from Houston and to help heal the poison deep within that she never seemed to be able to escape. The media reported snidely on a King finally becoming legitimate royalty until it all fell apart.

And then their meanness had turned into gleeful cruelty at her expense.

That was a long time ago.

It didn't *feel* like ten years with Frank looking at her like he knew every single one of her secrets and would exploit them in his own time. She belatedly realized that she wasn't coming out on top of this interaction any more than she had on their previous ones. "Just give me the damn building, Frank. You aren't using it and we're willing to pay an absurd amount for it." The apartment building wasn't in a prime location, but Lydia had plans to convert it into high-end condos for out-of-town teams that Kingdom Corp contracted from time to time to help with specific jobs.

When Frank didn't respond, she gritted her teeth. "You have absolutely no reason to hold out...unless you're getting off on being the biggest dick in the room?" Journey lowered her voice, forcing him closer. "Because, for real, only one of us has a cock, so it's not exactly a contest at this point. You're just being ridiculous."

Frank took his shot slowly, maintaining eye contact in a way that should have been awkward but instead sent a bolt of need right through her. He was so *focused*. She'd seen him dismissive and distracted and uninterested, but she'd never had Frank Evans's full attention directed at her.

Until now.

He took her hand and pressed the empty shot glass into it. Their skin barely touched, but she felt the contact all the way to her core. He leaned closer yet, not touching her anywhere else, but she swore she felt his lips move against her neck. "You seem tense, Journey. Distracted." He shifted, the phantom touch moving up to the spot below her ear. "Have I done something to piss you off?"

She licked her lips before she could remind herself why it was a bad idea to react. "That would require me to care about you one way or another."

"You do." He inhaled deeply. "You're sitting here, wearing that cocktease of an outfit, and all but begging me to slip my hand up your jumper. We both know I'll find you wet and wanting, and we both know you're wet and wanting for me and me alone."

She shoved him back, fury and something like fear taking the reins. "Oh, fuck right off, Frank. You're delusional if you think I want you."

"I *know* you want me." His slow grin had her fighting not to clench her thighs together. "Just like I *know* you're going to go home alone tonight and touch yourself while pretending it's me."

"I loathe you."

"That's one way to put it." He snagged the glass out of her hand, which was just as well, because all she wanted to do in that moment was throw it at his perfect face. "Have a nice night, Duchess."

Beckett stared at Samara. There wasn't a single damn reason to believe the shock in her dark eyes. She was on Lydia's payroll, and his aunt would use every advantage she could come up with to undermine him. Lydia wasn't stupid, and if her connections were half as good as Frank's, she already knew about him and Samara. She knew that Samara could be a dangerous distraction to him.

Every time he'd seen Samara up to this point, she was... toned down. He didn't know how else to put it. She owned

her sexuality, but it was blunted with a professional edge. It
didn't make her less beautiful, but tonight it was like whatever normally banked her fire had been removed.

She took his fucking breath away.

Her brilliant red dress set off her dark skin and hair,
a flame in the shadows. It barely touched the tops of her
thighs, and the fabric clung to her breasts and hips, the tex-
ture seemingly soft to the touch, a temptation to do exactly
that.

She leaned against the closed door, watching him as if
he was the dangerous one in the room. As if she didn't fray
his control with every breath she took. He started for her,
not exactly sure what he'd do when he finally closed the distance between them.

"Beckett." She licked her lips, her gaze dropping to his
mouth. "We need to talk. Really talk."

He knew that, but desire hijacked his reasoning capabil-
ities and he couldn't focus on anything but Samara and that
tiny fucking dress. "You look good in red." He stopped in
front of her and reached up to sift his fingers through her
hair. *So fucking soft.* "Every time I dreamed of you over the
last six months, you were wearing those tiny red panties that
you had on that night. If I hadn't needed to get on a plane
that next morning, I would have booked us a flight to anywhere you wanted to go and spent the next week fucking
you senseless."

Her dark eyes went wide. "That... You can't..."

He kissed her. She tasted of cinnamon. Beckett brushed
his lips against hers, a soft question he didn't have to put
into words. She went tense for half a breath, and he stilled,
waiting to see what she'd do.

Samara grabbed the front of his shirt and jerked him

against her. It was all the invitation he needed. He gave in to the need to touch her, a demand he didn't know how to put into words. *Touch me. See me.* The dress was soft and slick and brought to mind all the things he wanted to do to her—with her.

She moaned, arching closer. Beckett coasted his hands up her sides, liking the feel of the dress sliding over her skin. It was softer than he expected, but then Samara was as well. She kissed him like she needed his air to breathe. He let go of her hips and slid his hands along her jawline, tilting her head back to give him better access to her mouth, and into the heaven that was her hair. She could put on her power suits and professional dresses and act like a younger version of his aunt, but her hair gave lie to the image. She was wild down to her core.

He tore away from her. Each breath was a razor through his chest, and every muscle in his body clenched with the need to have her against him again, but he embraced the agony. "Turn around, Samara."

"This is a mistake." Her breath was as harsh as his, and he almost groaned at the sight of her nipples through the dress.

"Maybe." He reached around her to flip the lock on the door. They'd walk out of this room when they were damn well good and ready, and he refused to allow an interruption to fuck it up. Beckett traced his thumb over her bottom lip. "Let me see you."

This was the moment when she'd either tell him to go to hell—something he rightly deserved—or she'd obey and prove that they had more than a few things unfinished between them.

Samara dug her fingers into the fabric of his shirt. "I'm going to regret this."

"No, you won't."

She shook her head. "Yes, I will." But she turned and braced her hands flat on the door.

God. She was fire in his arms, the quiver in her body belying her hesitance. He shifted her hair off her neck and kissed her there, taking his time. Her dress dipped low in the back, the entire thing held in place with two tiny straps over her shoulders, and he took full advantage of all that exposed skin. Beckett dragged his mouth down her spine and licked the twin dimples on either side of the small of her back. She was all defined muscles beneath smooth skin. Her ass... *Fuck.* He palmed her there, letting his thumbs dip beneath the hem of her short dress. "Fuck, Samara."

She spread her legs, the tiniest bit, and arched her back in a clear invitation. Even with those signs giving him the green light, he wanted this out there in the open between them. He slipped his hands beneath her dress and growled. "I'm going to taste you now."

Silence for a beat. Two. "Do it."

He hadn't had a plan when he'd started this, but there was no going back now. He might tear this fucking room apart if he didn't taste her in the next breath. He drew a single finger through her wetness, spreading it up and over her clit. It wasn't nearly enough.

Beckett bracketed her thigh with one hand and guided her legs even wider, opening her for him completely. He tilted his head and closed his mouth over her pussy from behind. Her startled gasp turned into a moan almost immediately. He should feel victorious that he'd managed to shut her smart-ass comments up, but all Beckett felt was totally and completely out of fucking control.

One taste wasn't enough.

It would never be enough.

He sucked on her clit once, twice, a third time, until her legs shook on either side of his head and she was trying to move against him to guide his rhythm. He tightened his grip on her thighs, forcing her to hold still.

Too much. Not enough. He couldn't have stopped if he wanted to.

He spread her legs wider and fucked her with his tongue. She tasted...

She tasted like coming home.

Samara couldn't breathe. She twisted to try to see Beckett, but their positions meant she was well and truly at his mercy. *What the hell am I doing?*

He pushed two fingers into her and her brain shorted out. All the very specific reasons she had not to let this get out of control went up in smoke. She *ached* for him. Samara pushed back against his hold. "Beckett, please."

"Tell me what you need." She felt each word against her clit.

"I need to see you." The words were barely voiced when his mouth was gone. He lifted her and half tossed her into the chair next to the small conference table. Beckett went back to his knees in the same move, as if he couldn't stand more separation than strictly necessary.

"You taste so fucking good." He guided her legs up and over the arms of the chair. All the while, his gaze never left her pussy. "Can't get enough of you."

But what happens tomorrow when we go back to normal?

It was just as well that Beckett speared his fingers back into her before she could forget herself enough to actually say the words aloud. Samara arched her back, giving herself a few seconds just to enjoy the sensations.

If you don't do something, you're going to be begging for his cock and then everything you've worked so hard for will be gone for good. Regain control.

She inhaled, trying to think through the pleasure. "Your mouth. My clit. Now."

Beckett grinned at her, more wolf than man. "You keep talking, I'll give you anything you want." He flicked her clit with his tongue and then got down to business. Beckett went at her like she was his favorite flavor of ice cream and he couldn't let a single inch of her remain untasted.

She had no intention of touching him, but her hands were in his hair, holding him in place even though he was obviously exactly where he wanted to be.

For now.

"The dress. Let me see you."

She didn't need to ask what he meant. Samara shimmied enough to get the tiny straps of her dress off her shoulders and push the fabric down so her breasts were free. Public sex wasn't really her thing, but knowing that she was totally and completely exposed, even with a locked door between them and the rest of the club...

Her orgasm rolled over her without warning, bowing her back, and it was only sheer stubbornness that kept Beckett's name from her lips.

He gentled his kisses until she was only barely shaking. "Damn, Samara. If you ever want to leave my aunt's company, I'd hire you in a hot second."

It was a bucket of cold water in the face of her post-orgasm bliss. It was one thing to fuck around. A stupid thing, to be sure, but it was a strictly physical response to an attractive man who she knew could make her feel good. His throwing around words like daggers was something else altogether. *Leave the company you've been at for years because I like the way you fuck, and when I get tired of you— and I will—then you'll be left just as high and dry as your mother was when your father left.*

She used a single finger against his forehead to push him back, and he let her do it, his dark eyes seeing too much. Well, too damn bad. He could see all he wanted, but that didn't mean anything had changed.

It couldn't.

She wouldn't let it.

As soon as he was far enough from her, she stood slowly. There were no words to explain how badly she'd just fucked up. She was supposed to be the one in control—the one who was handling Beckett and avoiding a scandal.

It'd taken him a grand total of five minutes to have her riding his mouth and begging for release. If the door lock had failed and someone had managed to take a picture of them...

Her career would be finished. No one would take her seriously. Lydia would fire her on the spot. She'd lose everything she'd worked so hard for. She fixed her dress, her gaze on the floor.

"You don't have to look like you're on your way to the chopping block. It was a fucking orgasm, Samara."

There was nothing left to do but turn and face him.

Beckett looked as off-kilter as she felt. His breath was coming too fast, his hair standing on end from where she'd run her fingers through it, his entire body clenched like he was fighting between moving closer to her and putting more distance between them.

At this point, she wasn't sure what she preferred.

Stop that. Get your priorities in order.

Once she was sure she wasn't in danger of indecent exposure, she walked to the door. "If you start spreading around lies about Lydia's whereabouts the night of Nathaniel's death, I'll see you sued for defamation."

She didn't hear him move. One minute he was across the room, and the next he was pressed against her back. Every part of him was hard, from his arms bracketing hers to his cock pressing against her ass. Beckett dragged his mouth over her shoulder, the rasp of his whiskers a sensation she felt in places nowhere near where he touched her. "Right here, right now, we're going to be honest with each other."

Not likely.

He released her and stepped back, waiting for her to face him before he continued. "We get close and it's like our connection has its own gravitational pull. It doesn't matter that you work for Kingdom Corp and I'm with Morningstar. You can't resist it any more than I can." He crossed his arms over his chest. No matter how she searched his face, his expression gave nothing away. He just…waited.

"Watch me." She might want him, but it didn't matter. Samara was stronger than her baser impulses, no matter what they'd been doing two minutes ago. She had to be.

Beckett didn't have anything on the line with this. No matter how much his father's death had messed him up, he still had a place within Morningstar Enterprise—*owning* Morningstar Enterprise. Whoever came out on top of this bid for the new contract, he and Lydia would walk away already preparing how they'd win the next one.

Beckett was a King.

Samara was not.

End of story.

CHAPTER SIX

Beckett made a point to go into the office the next day despite it being Saturday. He needed the grounding effect of being inside Morningstar's headquarters to remind him what was important.

He couldn't even blame what happened last night on Samara. It was all Beckett. He'd been so damn off-center since his father died, since he'd lost Thistledown, and the ground only seemed to be growing more unstable with each passing day.

No matter what Samara had said, he trusted Frank. If his friend said Lydia met his father the night he died, then it happened. She might have had appointments elsewhere, but that didn't mean anything in the grand scheme of things. People missed appointments all the time. He *did* believe that Samara didn't know anything about that meeting. Maybe he shouldn't, but his gut said her surprise was real, and he'd learned to trust that instinct over the years.

His gut also said Lydia had something to do with his father's death.

It might be as benign as drinking with him and letting

him get behind the wheel, but Beckett doubted it stopped there. Someone had paid the driver off and sent him out of country, and Lydia had barely waited twenty-four hours before she was trying to convince Beckett to sell the company. It was possible it was a coincidence…

But add in the shock of Nathaniel willing Thistledown to Lydia, and it was too much to explain away. There was only one person who benefited almost uniformly from Nathaniel King's death as things stood now—and it was Beckett's aunt.

He stepped off the elevator and froze. Walter Trissel, Morningstar's attorney on retainer, stopped short in the doorway to his office, a plain brown box in his hands. *Damn it.* Beckett slid his hands into his pockets and leaned against the wall next to the elevator, watching the man closely. "Walter."

"Beckett." The man went red. "I didn't expect you in today."

"I can see that." He nodded at the box. "Clearing out your office?"

Walter's red face took on a purple tone and he seemed to find the floor remarkably interesting. "I'm sorry, Beckett. I would have liked to stay on to see the changeover through, but, well, a man's family has to eat."

"You make over six hundred thousand dollars a year, Walter. And you're single. Don't treat me like an idiot." Beckett's eyes narrowed. "What did she offer you?"

"I don't know who you're talking about."

He kept his posture relaxed through sheer force of will. Venting his frustration on Walter Trissel was like squashing a cockroach—ultimately unsatisfying. But knowing that didn't kill the impulse. "Lydia. That is who you're defecting to, is it not?"

"I…uh…" He drew in a breath and expelled the next sentence in a rush. "I don't feel comfortable talking about this. I'm sorry, Beckett. But I really have to go." Walter skittered past him and onto the elevator.

Beckett might have rolled his eyes to hear the man frantically pushing the door-close button under other circumstances, but he was too fucking furious to care. It wasn't enough that she'd taken his childhood home, but she was going to take one of his key employees in the process?

Unless she didn't stop at a single employee.

A slow-dawning horror had him moving through the floor that held most of the high-level offices for the company. He counted five, seven, twelve empty desks, their personal effects stripped. In the offices, he was missing his COO and his director of media relations.

He could fill the empty positions given enough time, but trying to hold everything together without missing a beat and still being ready for the bid in six days? This might not be totally impossible, but it danced cheek-to-cheek with it.

He took out his phone and considered.

What Beckett really wanted to do was call Samara. It didn't make any sense, but he held a deep assurance that hearing her voice would settle the jagged pieces inside him. *Not her job.* She'd made her priorities clear enough last night, and he couldn't exactly blame her for it. Lydia had bolstered her career and they shared a long history. He might have meant it when he offered her a job, but she didn't know that. Jumping companies wasn't uncommon in their field—or in any field—but if word got out that she'd jumped while they were sleeping together, it could harm her future prospects.

So, yeah, he got why his job offer had pissed her off.

But it also meant that he couldn't call her now to help him. They might match up well in bed, but they'd be a disastrous combo outside it. She was too proud and he was up to his nose in this bullshit surrounding his father's death. Even if they weren't a shitty match, the timing wasn't anywhere near close to right.

He considered his phone. The timing for romance might be off, but that didn't mean he had to cut her off completely. She was Lydia's second-in-command, after all. She knew things about his aunt that no one else did outside her children. If he could get Samara to see that Lydia didn't walk on water, he stood a chance of having an inside man—or woman—at Kingdom Corp.

Excuses.

It's a legit strategy.

Before he could think too hard about it, he pressed the call button.

Samara's phone buzzed on the table for the fifth time in an hour, and she almost threw the damn thing across the room. All the prep work for the bid was done—had been done for days—but she had to present it, and therein lay the problem. She was fine with public speaking—better than fine. But being the one to give a presentation that so much depended on...

It needed to be *perfect*, which would be a whole lot easier to accomplish if everyone and their dog wasn't trying to get ahold of her this Saturday.

Her phone trilled again, reminding her that she hadn't dealt with this particular interruption yet. She snatched it up. "Samara Mallick."

"Samara." Beckett's voice rolled through the line like the

best kind of whiskey. Deep and a little rough around the edges. "How would you like a full tour of Morningstar Enterprise?"

She pulled her phone from her ear and double-checked that it was, in fact, Beckett. *What's he up to now?* She'd made their respective positions pretty damn clear last night. When the sky didn't open up and deliver her answers, she sighed. "I don't have time to play these games with you. You might be able to flit around as you please, but some of us have to work for a living." It wasn't fair. She *knew* Beckett worked his ass off to secure contracts for the company and expand Morningstar's influence, but driving home the difference in their roles was the only option she had to keep him at a distance.

"What would Lydia say if she knew you passed up a chance to see an unfiltered view of her biggest rival?"

She froze. She knew exactly what Lydia would say. *Get your ass over there, distract him, and snoop.* It sounded great in theory, but she got hung up on the *distract him* part. Samara knew exactly how she and Beckett got *distracted.* She'd already more than proven that she couldn't keep herself in check when she was around him. Worse, she craved the way his touch stilled the rapid circling of her thoughts and cut through all the bullshit. When they were together, she wasn't planning her next corporate move, or worrying about anticipating Lydia's needs. She was just Samara, the woman.

That's what made Beckett King so damn dangerous.

"Speechless?" His dark laugh took up residence in her stomach and then lower. She sank onto her couch. *Damn you, Beckett.*

"Never." She bit out. There were only two options at this

point. She could hang up the phone, go back to working on her presentation...or she could agree to meet Beckett and see what information she could gather. Samara doubted he intended to give her anything she could use against him, but just because that was *his* plan didn't mean she had to go along with it. "What time would you like to meet?"

"Now."

She wet her lips, trying to control the pounding of her heart. "Right now?"

"Unless you have something more important to do?"

She looked at the presentation notes spread across her living room. Several notebooks with different-colored writing, more pens than one woman should probably own, and a master timeline for the income she'd projected for Kingdom Corp. Samara closed her eyes. "You can't just crook your finger and expect me to come running."

"I'm not Lydia. I'm not treating you like a pet." Something rustled in the background, and she could perfectly picture him leaning back in his chair and straightening his muscled legs. "I'll order in lunch. Be here in an hour." Beckett hung up, leaving her wondering if she should curse him or admire his ingenuity.

He's got an agenda. I can't afford to forget that.

With that in mind, she dialed Lydia. Her boss barely let the phone ring. "Is this important, Samara? I'm in the middle of something."

"Beckett King just invited me to Morningstar Enterprise for a business lunch."

A meaningful pause. "He's moving fast." Her disdain for Beckett practically oozed through the phone. As far as Samara knew, Beckett had never done anything to her boss personally. She could be wrong, but...

Still.

She straightened. "I'm confident I can gather information that will be useful."

"I have no doubt you will do exactly that. I expect a full report Monday." Lydia hung up.

Monday?

Samara dropped her phone onto the couch. What did Lydia think she'd be doing for the next thirty-six hours that she wouldn't report until Monday? Her stomach lurched.

She almost called Journey, but there wasn't anything more to say. Beckett had issued the invitation, Lydia had supported her accepting it. Overthinking things at this point wouldn't do anything but waste more time.

Samara was ready inside of thirty minutes—a small miracle—and picked a fitted green dress that did wonders for her breasts and ass. Strictly speaking, it was a little too sexy for a business meeting, but she'd already blown the chance to keep her relationship with Beckett professional.

Not to mention, anything that gave her an edge at this point was an asset.

Sure. That's why you're pulling out all the stops. To distract Beckett.

It's sure as hell not because you want to see that look of appreciation in his dark eyes.

Definitely not.

CHAPTER SEVEN

Heaven was Samara in a little green dress.

Beckett watched her walk across the lobby, her mile-long legs eating up the distance with ease. That glimpse of wildness she'd given him last night was in full effect today, her hair a mass of black waves that seemed to curl and snap around her shoulders with each step. Her dress fitted her like a second skin, sloping down over her breasts, her stomach, to her hips and thighs.

But it was her dark eyes that drew and held him. Anger and desire and something like guilt lingered there, and she held his gaze as she stopped in front of him. "Do I meet your expectations?"

"You're beautiful."

She arched a single eyebrow. "I know."

That surprised a laugh out of him. Beckett turned to the elevator bank and offered his elbow. The gentlemanly move was over-the-top for their current circumstances, but he couldn't be this close to her without touching her. Kissing her now, here, was a terrible damn idea, so he'd settle for the small touch. "No false modesty. I like that."

"I think we've established that I don't operate based on what you like." Despite her words, amusement pulled at the edges of her lips, and she set her hand carefully on his forearm. "Every time I think I have your number down, you surprise me. Most guys get pissy pants if a woman doesn't fall at their feet when they call her beautiful."

"I'm not most guys." He waited for the elevator door to open and led her onto it. "You can't fit me into a box and write me off, Samara."

"I'm beginning to see that." She shook her head, her hair brushing against his shoulder. "My life would be a whole lot easier if I could."

He couldn't argue that, so he didn't bother. Beckett took them up to the executive level. He noted the way she studied everything, obviously filing away every bit of information she could lay her eyes on. "What does Lydia pay you these days?"

She dropped her arm and stepped back. "Oh no. I don't think so." She pointed at him. "We went over this last night. I'm not for sale."

"It's an innocent question."

"It is most definitely not an innocent question." She looked like she wanted to take off her shoe and throw it at his head. "I don't care what issue you and your aunt have. I'm not part of it. You don't get to use me as leverage. I'm not a pawn for either of you to sacrifice in this pissing match you have going on."

Shame tried to take hold, but he wouldn't let it. Samara knew the game, no matter how much it apparently offended her. "I'm the bad guy for trying to offer you a job, but I'm sure you agreed to show up here solely out of the goodness of your heart." He pretended to think about it. "Wait, no you didn't—which you already admitted. You're here because Lydia wants to do whatever it takes to sink Morningstar. Full stop." He motioned at the offices behind him. "Wake up, Samara. I'm only playing the game *she* made the rules for."

She took in the empty COO office on the other side of the glass wall. "She poached your employees."

"Convenient timing, don't you think?"

"You're not still harping on that paranoid talk about Lydia meeting Nathaniel." Samara hesitated and then moved to stand in front of him. She pressed her lips together and then very gently said, "Do you think maybe it's a good idea for you to talk to someone?"

Beckett jerked back. "What?"

There was nothing but sympathy in her dark eyes. "I'm serious, Beckett. I've known you a long time, at least by reputation, and this delusion you have going isn't like you. Is it possible that Nathaniel's death is hitting you harder than you realize? That you're fixating on Lydia instead of your own grief because it's easier to deal with an enemy than face the fact you can never make things right with your father?"

Every word flayed him, cutting to the quick. Beckett gritted his teeth against the need to tell Samara that *she* was the one who wasn't thinking clearly. To yell. To expel some of the ugliness that had been brewing in him for a very, very long time. "I didn't call you here to offer you a job, and I sure as fuck don't need a shrink."

She stood her ground as he advanced. Her heels put them at the same height and she still managed to look down her nose at him. "Then why *did* you call me here?"

Because I can't spend another fucking moment alone without going out of my mind.

He didn't say it. To admit how long it had been since he'd

felt a connection with another person was to hand Samara—
Lydia—a loaded gun and invite her to point it directly at his
heart. He didn't answer her verbally at all. Beckett cupped
her waist and slowly pulled her against him, giving her
plenty of time to register his intentions.

"Beckett." Despair colored her tone and she gave a desperate laugh. "What are we doing?"

"I don't know." Using a hand on the small of her back, he
pressed her firmly against him. "I don't want to stop."

Samara hesitated, but finally placed her hands gingerly
against his chest. He waited, letting her decide. Yes or no.
Push or pull. Stay or go. She hitched a breath. "I don't want
to stop, either."

"Thank fuck." He kissed her and dug his free hand into
her hair, tilting her head back and teasing her mouth open
with his lips and tongue. *I need you. Let me touch you.* He
nipped her bottom lip and devoured her gasp. Reality narrowed down to the feel of her tongue against his and the way
she writhed against him, her hips rolling as if she'd take his
cock right there in the middle of the executive offices.

That slowed him. He lifted his head and looked around.
There was no one there to witness, but that didn't mean he
wanted to put her at risk. Beckett might have every intention
of poaching Samara, but he didn't want her or her reputation
harmed in the process.

He looked down at her. Her lips were swollen from his
kisses and there was a hazy expression in her eyes. Because
of *him*. He didn't have a right to the possessive feeling that
soared through him in response, but Beckett didn't give a
fuck.

He scooped her into his arms, ignoring her yelp of surprise, and stalked down the hall to his office. It had more

privacy just by the nature of its corner position, but he still set her on the desk and moved to close the wood-slat blinds covering the glass wall overlooking the rest of the offices. Beckett shut and locked the door and turned to find her watching him. "We're doing this."

"Yes." A wicked smile lit up her face. "Can I tell you a secret?"

"I want all your secrets." His gaze fell to the gold ring on her right hand, the one he'd never seen her without. *A secret.*

Samara laughed. "I might be a little punch-drunk off lust, but not *that* much." She smoothed her hands over his stainless-steel desk and leaned back. The move pressed her breasts dangerously against the bodice of her dress, as if they might spill free at any moment. Her gaze dropped the front of his jeans and she licked her lips. "I've thought about fucking you on this desk."

He pulled his shirt over his head and advanced on her. "Tell me."

"We'd fight—we always fight—and you'd kiss me." Her lips quirked. "Kind of like you just did."

"Mmm." He stepped between her knees, and slid his hands up her legs. Beckett coaxed the dress up under her hips and then all the way off. It left Samara completely naked and he froze. "In this fantasy, did you show up to my office without a damn thing on under your dress?"

"I may have." She hooked her fingers in the waistband of his jeans and towed him closer even as she undid the button and dragged down the zipper. "Though I will admit—in my fantasy, it was in the middle of the day and there were a dozen people around who could hear it if we weren't quiet enough." She glanced at the closed door and windows. "This is better."

"Samara." He framed her face with his hands. "If nothing else, I'll never do something to intentionally harm you."

She shivered. "The proposal—"

"Is business." He let his thumb drop to press lightly against her throat and dragged his other hand down the center of her body to cup her pussy. "This? This isn't business. This is pure fucking pleasure." He pushed two fingers into her, watching her eyes slide half shut and her lips part.

"Mixing business with pleasure is a bad idea."

"We left business behind out there." He jerked his chin to the rest of the world outside his office. "In here, it's just me and you."

"And pleasure."

"And pleasure," he agreed. Beckett spread her wetness up and over her clit and then resumed fucking her with his fingers. "Look at that." He drew almost all the way out. "Look at the way you coat my fingers. So fucking wet for me." He bent and sucked one nipple into his mouth, sucking hard and flicking with his tongue even as her fingers tangled in his hair and she cried out.

"Yes, Beckett! Like that." Samara's hips lifted to take his fingers deeper, but he had no intention of pushing her over the edge yet.

He kissed the underside of her breast and then the valley between them. "What happens next in this fantasy of yours?"

"I suck you off."

He lifted his head. "Describe it. In explicit detail." He kept stroking her between her legs, urging the words from her lips.

Samara blinked and seemed to try to focus. "You're in your office chair. I'm on my knees. But we both know who holds the power."

Her.

His cock jumped and he bit back a curse. "That's what you want."

It wasn't a question, but she bobbed her head in confirmation. Beckett circled her clit and claimed her mouth. He used the tiny circles that drove her crazy, urged on by every moan and shudder she made. As tempting as it was to bring her like that, he wanted her just as wild and desperate for him as he was for her. He took her right to the edge and then removed his hand, still kissing her.

Samara sobbed against his mouth. "You bastard."

"You like these games we play."

She reached between them and tunneled her hand into his jeans to stroke his cock. "I love them and I hate them."

"That makes two of us." He stepped back, forcing her to release him, and strode around the desk to the office chair. Samara turned to follow him with her gaze, and he slowly finished unzipping his jeans and drew his cock out. "This is what you want."

She licked her lips and he fought back a groan. Samara walked to him slowly, letting him look his fill. She was... Beckett didn't have words to describe her. Her brown skin practically glowed with her desire, her full breasts swaying with every step, the curve of her waist inviting his hands, her legs...Fuck, her legs. Perfection did not begin to cover Samara Mallick.

She went to her knees before him and ran her hands up his thighs. "Yes, Beckett. That's what I want." She gripped his cock and guided him between her lips, her gaze never leaving his.

He watched his length disappear into her mouth, felt her wet heat close around him, and nearly lost his fucking mind.

It took everything he had to keep perfectly still and let her control the interaction. As it was, he white-knuckled the arms of his chair. "Suck me hard, Samara."

She released him and flicked the underside of his cock with her tongue. "You aren't driving this bus. Not right now. I am." She licked his cock like her favorite flavor of ice cream was melting right off the cone. "And I'm going to have my way with you...all in good time."

She worked him, alternating between sucking him deep and those playful little licks that damn near made his eyes roll back in his head. Over and over again. Payback for leaving her on the edge earlier. He held out as long as he could, but she took him deep enough that he bumped the back of her throat and Beckett tore the fucking arms off the chair.

Samara didn't get a chance to react to Beckett destroying the chair before he clamped his hand on the back of her neck and hauled her up his body to straddle him. She grabbed his shoulders to steady herself. "You could have just told me to stop. You didn't have to break things."

"Stop talking." He kissed her and grabbed her ass as he pushed out of the chair and set her back on the desk. The cool metal shocked her, but it only spiked her desire hotter.

Samara reached between them to stroke his cock. "I don't want to wait anymore. I need you inside me." *I've needed you inside me for the last six months.*

He yanked open the top drawer and pulled out a condom. Samara raised her eyebrows. "You keep condoms in your work desk."

Beckett set his teeth against her neck and then nipped her earlobe. "Want to know a secret?"

Her skin flashed hot. "Yes."

He tore the condom open and rolled it on, all without taking his mouth from her skin. "We share the same fantasy." He circled her clit with his thumb and teased her with two fingers, pushing them in just enough for her to moan before withdrawing again. "I've imagined you coming in here to yell at me about something. I'd shut the door and then we'd be on each other." He dragged his cock over her clit and pressed against her opening. "I'd shove up your dress and set you on my desk just like you're sitting now. From behind you look downright proper, but here..." He squeezed her thighs hard enough that she hoped she'd have bruises tomorrow. A physical mark to hold the memory of this time together close even when they went back to their default sniping.

"Here." He went to his knees and breathed over her clit. "I'd fuck you with my tongue and no one would be the wiser." Beckett looked up her body and sucked her clit into his mouth. He released her and dragged his mouth across the most sensitive part of her. "No one but the building across from us."

Samara jumped, her gaze flying to the windows behind Beckett's desk. The tinted glass reflected the sun's glare away from the windows, and rationally she knew no one could see inside, but staring at her own reflection in the glass, her nakedness on display, Beckett's face buried between her thighs...

A tremor went through her. "I could come just thinking about that."

"Not yet." He slid his hands beneath her ass and lifted her to meet his mouth. "I don't want it over too soon." He kissed her there, fucking her slowly with his tongue until she had to slap a hand over her mouth to keep her moans internal. Beckett breathed against her clit. "Think about someone watching, Samara. Think about him palming his cock in envy as he tries to get a better view of your pretty pussy. Think about him hating me for knowing your taste when he'll never get to."

She tangled her fingers into his hair and pulled. For a long moment, she thought he might resist her urging, but Beckett finally rose. She dragged her nails down his back, pulling him closer. "Who says it's a man watching?"

His dark eyes glinted with interest, and that was the only warning she got before he lifted her and reversed their positions, leaving her to straddle him on his desk. This time, she wasn't letting him get away with teasing her. Samara guided his cock into her, taking him into her completely. Only then did she start talking again. "Maybe it's a woman with her hand down her skirt." She rolled her hips, biting her bottom lip at how freaking perfect it felt to have him stretching her, filling her. "Maybe she'd pretend she's the one riding your cock where anyone could see, taking you as deep as she's able, your hands on *her* body."

"Fuck her." Beckett shifted farther back onto his desk, giving her leverage to ride him more thoroughly. "Fuck them both. The only ones who matter are you and me." He cupped her breasts roughly. "Ride me, Samara. Take what you need. What we both need."

She gripped his shoulders and did what he commanded. Each stroke dragged her breasts against his chest. Every nerve ending zinged, trying to feel everything at once, every sensation linked back to Beckett's mouth on her neck, his hands on her body, his cock lodged deeply inside her. She ground down on him, seeking her pleasure as much as she wanted to give him his. It was all too much, too quickly.

She came with a cry that she tried to muffle against his shoulder. Beckett kept his hands on her hips, keeping her moving as he followed her over the edge. He growled her name as he came and Samara had never heard anything sweeter in her entire life.

This was such a bad idea.

She didn't have the strength to move, let alone address the way they kept complicating the situation despite their best efforts. Or maybe because of their best efforts. She didn't know anymore. Nothing was clear in the peace after the glorious sex they'd had…except that she wanted to do it again. Samara shifted, but Beckett wrapped his arms around her.

"Just a minute." He kissed her shoulder. "The rest of the world waited this long. It can wait a couple minutes more. And if you're going to bolt out of here as soon as you have clothes on, I might have to throw the damn dress out the window."

She smiled because that had been exactly what she was thinking of doing. "Do you really think that would stop me?"

He leaned back enough to catch her gaze. "Not a chance. You'd steal my shirt and find a way to get out of here without anyone being the wiser." His dark gaze sparked with mischief. "You'd bill me for the dress, wouldn't you?"

"You know it. I love that dress."

"I love that dress, too. I'll buy you seven of them—one in every color."

Though he was still joking, she shook her head. "No, thanks." She could take care of herself—could buy herself pretty much whatever she wanted. Even joking about taking gifts from him set her teeth on edge. She tried to temper her response, but it was too instinctive to deny completely. "I don't want anything from you, Beckett."

The humor bled out of his expression. "You couldn't have made that clearer if you'd tried."

"I'm sorry."

"You keep apologizing to me, but I don't think you mean it any more than I do. I'm not fucking sorry, Samara. This. You. Me. This could be something special if we'd stop getting in our own way long enough to make it happen."

He might think so, but she kept coming back to the inequality of power between them. Beckett didn't see it because *he* was the one with all the power. He wanted her, sure, but if she walked away, the most he had to worry about was a broken heart. Despite so many country songs out there, no one had actually died of a broken heart. He'd be sad. He'd mourn the loss of her—or what she represented—until some other beautiful woman came along and loved away his pain.

If Samara lost her job—and lost it because it came out that she was sleeping with the competition—no one in their industry would hire her. While she might be qualified to work in most corporate settings, that reputation would follow her for the rest of her damn career. She might find another job, but she'd never be trusted the way she currently was.

If she screwed this up, all her mother's sacrifice was for nothing. All the long hours, the endless homework and helping Samara write papers and fill out scholarship applications. The times when she *knew* her *amma* went hungry so she could have what she needed. All for nothing.

"We have to stop doing this," Samara whispered.

"You don't want to stop."

She started to deny it, but here, in this moment, she couldn't lie to him. "No, I don't want to stop. But we *have* to stop."

Beckett stroked a hand down her back. "Trust me to protect you, Samara. Take a leap of faith with me."

She never thought she'd actually be tempted by the offer—and it *was* tempting. Beckett was the kind of man who took care of everyone he considered his. She saw it in the way he fought so hard for this company, and in the sadness lurking in his demeanor because the one relationship that should have been solid—with his father—was anything but. He might not admit it to himself, but he felt it all the same.

If she let him, he might even take care of her, too. Maybe it would even turn into a love for the ages and they'd have a wonderful future together.

It still would have started with her making all the sacrifices and him making none.

She didn't hold that against him, but he couldn't put himself in her shoes, and she couldn't imagine a life like his, either. Not really.

Samara climbed off him, doing her best to ignore the way her body cried out at the new distance between them. "I'm sorry, Beckett."

"Are you?"

She picked up her dress. "I am."

The phone rang, saving them from what would be an undoubtedly awkward postcoital conversation. She shimmied into her dress, watching him out of the corner of her eye. He stood naked next to his desk, not the least bit self-conscious. *Why would he be? He's built like a freaking gladiator.* All lean muscle and barely contained power.

Beckett frowned. "What do you mean, the door's locked?" He turned to look at Samara as alarms screeched through the building. A pulsing, screaming sound, followed by a monotone, "Fire. Fire. Fire." And then it started all over again.

"Call nine-one-one!" Beckett barked into the phone. He snatched up his pants and yanked them on. She'd barely got her dress straps over her shoulders when he grabbed her arm. "Run!"

CHAPTER EIGHT

Thirty fucking floors.

Beckett kept hold of Samara's hand, ensuring that she didn't trip as they raced down staircase after staircase, their bare feet slapping the floor. *Too slow*. In the distance, he heard sirens. With each floor they passed, the temptation to get to a window, to look out and figure out what the fuck was going on, rose.

"Beckett, I can't." Samara stumbled, her free hand pressed against her stomach. "We have to slow down."

The door at the next landing marked the tenth floor. Closer to the ground—to safety—but not close enough. Beckett bit back his frustration. "Keep up or I'll carry you."

Her jaw dropped. "You can't carry me."

"This isn't up for negotiation. You have five seconds. Decide."

She set her jaw and her eyes went steely. "I'll keep up."

"Good."

They ran.

Ninth floor.

Seventh.

Fourth.

The scent of smoke curled through the third-floor landing, though he didn't *see* it. His breath sawed through his lungs, a burning brand in his chest. Samara looked as bad as he felt, her skin shining with sweat, her hair a tangled mass. Beckett slowed, just a little. "Don't touch the doors."

"I know how fires work," she snapped. Real fear lurked in her eyes and she clutched his hand tighter. "Let's get the hell out of here."

If they even could. Without knowing where the fire started or how fast it had spread, they were operating blind. They had two floors between them and the relative safety of the ground floor, but that didn't mean they could reach the emergency exit. Leaving the stairwell was a risk—a big one. Staying was even worse.

He squeezed her hand. "We're almost there."

She choked out an exhale and nodded. "I can make it."

In another life, he might fall head over heels for this woman with her strength and determination, no matter if she was facing down a corporate rival or a fucking fire. "I'm going to get you out, Samara. I promise." He started moving before she could respond, half dragging her down the stairs toward the second floor, and then the first.

The smoke was thicker there, creating a thin haze that left everything looking surreal. It coated the back of his tongue, stung his eyes, burned his lungs. He staggered to a stop. They were in the northwest corner of the building, closest to the park that butted up against the building, rather than the street. The nearest emergency exit was roughly a hundred feet away. He touched the doorknob. Cold. "You ever see that movie *Backdraft*?"

"Beckett, that is *not* funny."

He pulled her close and positioned them behind the heavy door. "Just making conversation." *And keeping you distracted so you're not thinking too hard about how horrible it would be to die in a fire.*

"You're crazy." She tucked herself under his arm, her body shaking despite her even tone. She was faking it just as much as he was.

"You bet your ass." He didn't *think* there was a wall of flames waiting for them on the other side, but he couldn't afford to risk it. Beckett grabbed the door handle. "Fire's bad, we run up to the second floor and take a different stairwell down."

Her shaking got worse. "Beckett..."

"Don't you dare." He gripped her chin and kissed her. "We're getting out of here, Samara. If it means I have to lower you by hand out of a fucking window, we're getting out of here. Do you trust me?"

"Yes," she whispered.

He twisted the handle and yanked the door, keeping their bodies behind it. Smoke poured into the room in a thick cloud, but no flames burst through. Beckett coughed and pulled Samara down so they were crouching. They weren't fully below the smoke, but the air was slightly more breathable there. "Don't let go of my hand."

"*You* don't let go."

"I won't." He shifted around the door and squinted into the lobby. The haze of smoke was too thick to see much of anything, but he couldn't see any flames, either. He could see the front doors from where they were, and there seemed to be a clear path. "Stay as low as possible." Right now, the smoke was more dangerous than any flames.

"Okay." Samara started coughing.

I have to get her out of here. Now.

He shifted his grip to hold her wrist and rushed out into the lobby. *No flames. Just smoke.* It should have comforted him, but it meant there was a fire somewhere else in Morningstar. *Doesn't matter. It's just a building. Samara is a person.*

They hit the doors at a full-out sprint and Beckett registered a thick pipe jammed through the door handles. *The delivery guy said the doors were locked.* He yanked it out and tossed it away. They'd deal with *that* when they were both safe. He jerked open the door and shoved Samara through first, following close behind.

He'd never been so fucking happy to be breathing in Houston's humid air.

A fire truck screeched to a stop in front of them and disgorged half a dozen firefighters. One split away from the others and hurried to them. "You just come out of the building?"

"Yes." He kept Samara against him. They hadn't come this far for him to let her collapse now. "I don't know how many people are in the building. We don't have a full staff on the weekends, so it could be anywhere from ten to a hundred people." There had been no one else on the executive floor, but that still left twenty-nine other ones.

"Do you know where the fire started?"

"No. We came through the front doors. I didn't see a fire. Just a hell of a lot of smoke." Samara started to shake and he held her closer. "We need to sit down. We just ran from the top floor."

The guy nodded. "We have an ambulance on the way. Grab a curb over there and I'll get you set." He motioned to the curb on the opposite side of the street. Another fire truck screamed up, blocking traffic on the other corner of the block, but that didn't stop people from crowding on the side of the street the firefighter had indicated. Half of them had their phones out, and the other half were talking animatedly as the firefighters went to work suiting up.

Beckett shifted to give the onlookers his back, shielding Samara. He took her shoulders and looked her over. Her dress was haphazard from the run and her feet looked worse for wear, but she seemed fine otherwise. "How are you doing?" He pitched his voice low.

She looked over her shoulder as the building coughed out more smoke. "I don't know. That was..." She shuddered. "I never want to do that again."

He pulled her back into his arms and hugged her tight. Little tremors worked their way through her as she clung to him. "You're safe now. It's okay. Everything is okay."

Even as he reassured her, he wasn't so certain. The main lobby was all marble and steel. There wasn't a damn thing that could start a fire there by accident—especially not on a Saturday when there was minimum traffic through the building. *That pipe wasn't jammed to block the doors by accident.*

Things happened fast after that. The ambulance arrived, which made it impossible to watch what the firefighters were doing. Oxygen masks and blankets were pushed on both Beckett and Samara, and he submitted to the care to ensure that she did, too.

Time stretched on, and eventually there was a disturbance in the crowd. A leggy blonde in shorts and an oversized T-shirt shoved through two men muttering with their heads together. Her gaze caught on him, but then she focused on Samara. "Holy shit, you really are here."

Beckett belatedly recognized Journey King, his cousin. "She's fine."

"That's nice. I wasn't talking to you." She crouched down in front of Samara, her hazel eyes worried. "Unless the smoke damaged your vocal cords and you need him to translate?"

Samara coughed out a laugh and pulled her oxygen mask off. "I'm fine. I had more cardio in thirty minutes than I've had in the last three weeks, but I'm fine."

"You'd say that even if you burned all your hair off and needed half your skin grafted." She snapped her fingers at a bemused paramedic. "You—is there something wrong with her? Does she need to go to the hospital?"

The guy laughed, drinking her in. "Nah, she's fine." He made a visible effort to drag his gaze from Journey's legs to Samara's face. "If you get light-headed unexpectedly or have any trouble breathing, come in and get checked out, but you shouldn't have anything to worry about."

"Thanks, handsome." Journey pushed to her feet. "Let's get the fuck out of here. Don't even pretend like you're going home—you're coming with me so I can make sure you don't die in your sleep."

Samara caught Beckett's gaze, but allowed Journey to guide her to her feet. She hesitated. "Give me a second."

His cousin finally deigned to notice his existence. "Beckett."

"Nice seeing you, Journey."

She cocked a single eyebrow. "You're so cute when you're lying. Holler if you need me, Samara."

Samara shrugged out of her blanket and folded it neatly. She gingerly crossed to Beckett. He eyed her bare feet. "I'll return your shoes as soon as they let me back in the building."

"Beckett..." She sighed. "I don't know what to say."

"You don't have to say anything at all." He didn't want her to leave. He wanted her to come home with him where *he* would watch over her. Things might not have been actually as dangerous as it seemed when they were running for their lives, but that didn't change the adrenaline letdown that demanded he take her to bed and hold her until they were both sure everything was okay.

It's not okay. There's no way that fire was an accident, which means someone's gunning for me—and the only real suspect is Lydia fucking King.

Not that Samara will ever believe that.

Keeping their audience in mind, the only contact he allowed himself was to reach out and squeeze her hand. "You'll feel better if you go with her." The selfish part of him might hate watching her leave, but he was still glad she had someone who cared enough about her to bully her into staying over. He tightened his grip ever so slightly and stroked her wrist with his thumb where no one could see it. "If you need anything—anything at all—you can call me, Samara. It doesn't matter what time it is."

She smiled, though the expression was filled with sadness. "Thank you." The two words sounded a whole lot like good-bye.

Samara looked at the spread of food piled on Journey's kitchen island —and burst out laughing. "I'm fine, Journey. I don't need you to feed me back to life."

"Food is the answer for every problem." Her friend motioned to the vat of soup and the delicious-looking round rolls that had come with it. "Chicken noodle soup, specifically, is known to cure a list of problems as long as my arm. I have whiskey and honey and lemons for hot toddies, which will help any residual pain in your throat and give you the feel-goods. And three varieties of cookies because no meal is complete without dessert, and cookies are comforting. Peanut butter, oatmeal raisin, and lemony sugar cookies." She pointed at each item in turn.

Warmth started in Samara's stomach and spread through her, gathering in the edges of her eyes. "What did I do to deserve such a great friend?"

"Ha! We both know you're the better friend, so I have to rack up points where I can." She waved the remote. "Now, are we going to decompress to some *Desperate Housewives* or are you going to tell me what you were doing all alone with my cousin at Morningstar Enterprise in the middle of a Saturday?"

She started to beg off, but the truth was that she desperately wanted to talk about what was going on with Beckett with *someone*. "I don't know if it's a good idea to get into it. You're not exactly known for your love for him."

"Correction—I loathe his father. I have absolutely no opinion regarding Beckett himself." When Samara just stared, she finally relented. "Okay, fine, I don't like him on principle, but that's mostly because I'm toeing the party line inflicted by my mother. Obviously something about him caught your eye." She waggled her brows. "Or caught something else."

"It's not like that." Samara managed to hold it together for a grand total of three seconds before relenting. "Okay, it's exactly like that. Six months ago, when I lost out on that contract in Norway, I drank enough tequila that it seemed like a good idea to let him know all the reasons I found him loathsome." She eyed the whiskey bottle. "And then I slept with him."

Journey seemed to be struggling to keep a straight face. "That'll show him."

"Shut up. I know it was a bad idea."

"Keep talking. I'm putting the hot water on." Journey rounded the kitchen island and moved to the state-of-the-art stovetop. "You keep eyeing that whiskey and you're going to start taking shots instead of drinking medicinal hot toddies. Focus, woman."

God, she'd missed her friend. It felt like they hadn't seen each other much lately between all the work Lydia had piled on their respective positions. As COO, Journey was a master juggler and kept all the moving parts of Kingdom Corp from crashing into each other. For her part, Samara had been kept busy handling the various projects and contracts Lydia set her sights on. They only seemed to grow in number as time went on, and as much as she loved her job, she wished she had the slightest bit more downtime.

Speaking of...

She checked the clock and cursed. "I have to go."

"Nope." Journey set her old-fashioned kettle on the stove and turned it on. "If you go home, you're going to work until your body gives out, and then you'll feel even worse when you wake up." She crossed her arms over her chest and leaned against the counter. "Is twelve hours really going to make or break this presentation? You still have a couple days left, and knowing you, you could give that bid today and they'd be falling all over themselves to sign the contract."

As grateful as she was for Journey's unwavering support, it wasn't earned this time. "The bid is done, but I can't get the presentation right. Something's missing, and I can't afford to botch this."

"You won't botch it." She walked over, grabbed the

whiskey, honey, and two lemons off the table, and went about putting together the hot toddies.

Samara couldn't just sit there while Journey sliced lemons, so she pushed to her feet. She *was* a little light-headed, and her throat felt like she'd chain-smoked a pack of cigarettes. "I'm not having a crisis of faith or anything. I'm just worried. There's a lot of pressure on this one contract." The majority of leasing rights in the Gulf of Mexico was a huge coup to secure, and if she pulled it off, she'd prove that she deserved to be Lydia's second-in-command. "I can't afford to let being preoccupied with Beckett screw it up."

"Are you?"

"Am I what?"

Journey poured hot water into the whiskey concoction in the two mugs in front of her and stirred it. "Are you preoccupied with Beckett?"

She started to deny it, but she didn't make a habit of lying to her friend. "It's not that simple."

"Explain it to me." She pushed one mug toward Samara. "I say that not in a judgy tone—I really want to understand."

"I like him." Saying the words aloud felt like a betrayal. "More than that—I respect him and the way he does business. He cares about the people who work for him." She blinked and saw the betrayal written across Beckett's face when he snarled about Lydia stealing his employees.

The man had no family, not really. His business might not be a true stand-in for that kind of relationship, but he took their defection significantly more personally than anyone else she'd known. He *cared*. "But he and Lydia are heading for a clash of epic proportions and if I get caught in the middle, they'll trample me."

Journey contemplated her hot toddy. "I trust your judgment, so if you say he's not half bad, I believe you. But you're right about being caught in the middle. Mother's been fixated on Morningstar Enterprise since before I was born. With Nathaniel gone, it only makes sense that she's doing everything she can to seize the opportunity."

It made sense, and it was even a good play if she looked at it without her emotions involved. That was the problem, though. Despite her best efforts, her emotions *were* involved. It didn't change the fact that she wanted Kingdom Corp to come out on top, but she also didn't see why Lydia couldn't leave well enough alone when it came to Morningstar. "I know."

"What's stopping you from waiting until this all plays out, letting the dust settle, and then seeing if there's something there with him without the countdown ticking in your ear?"

She almost didn't answer, almost changed the subject to avoid talking about it. Journey and her mother didn't have the best of relationships, and her friend was fiercely protective when it came to anything she viewed as taking advantage of Samara. Since she felt the same way about Journey, they'd come to an agreement of sorts in that they didn't try to fight each other's battles unless requested.

This was different.

She pulled at the edge of her tunic-length shirt. They'd stopped over at her place so she could shower and change before coming to Journey's. *Stop stalling and spit it out.* "I think your mother was implying I should use Beckett's attraction to me to get close to him."

"The fuck she did." Journey slammed her mug onto the kitchen island hard enough that hot liquid splashed over the countertop and her hand. She didn't seem to notice. "That's bullshit. It's one thing to encourage you to flirt up the competition so they'll spill information. We've all done that. She knows you slept with Beckett, doesn't she?" She held up a hand. "You don't even have to answer. I know my mother, and I know how she operates. She suspected you had unfinished business with him and she decided to leverage that to her advantage and to hell with the consequences. God*damn* it. That is such a dick move, and I can't even say I'm surprised."

Samara sipped her hot toddy and waited her friend out. It would do no good to interrupt until Journey ran out of steam, and she didn't have the energy to get into a fight about what she was and wasn't okay with. If their situations were reversed, she would react the same way.

Journey hissed out a breath. "Okay, I'm done."

"You sure? I can sit here and keep drinking."

She laughed. "Yes, O Patient One. You're about to tell me that you can fight your own battles, aren't you?"

"Journey," Samara said seriously. "I can fight my own battles—even when it comes to your mother."

She grabbed a pink dish towel and wiped up the spilled hot toddy. "My mother is good at getting people to shift their boundaries to accommodate her needs."

Samara couldn't argue that. She'd both seen it in action and been on the wrong end of Lydia's manipulations. The worst part was that she didn't always realize it had happened until much, much later. *It's all for the end result, which I support. I haven't done anything I can't live with.* She ignored the uncomfortable twinge the thought brought. "Beckett's a big boy—"

"Didn't need to know that."

"Oh, for God's sake, get your mind out of the gutter." She laughed, but sobered almost immediately. "He walked into this thing with eyes wide open. If anything, he sees me as a pawn to be moved around the board the same way Lydia does."

"That doesn't make it right. You're not a fucking pawn, Samara—you're a person."

She knew she wasn't a pawn, but that didn't change the fact that she wasn't a big player in whatever conflict Beckett and Lydia had coming. She might be damn good at her job and work her ass off, but she wasn't a King. She could work at Kingdom Corp for the rest of her life and, twenty years down the road, she'd still be cut out or moved about by Lydia because ultimately Samara was replaceable. Beckett wasn't. Journey and her siblings weren't. Samara was just another ambitious woman who had her eye on the prize.

Could I be any more depressing?

She shook her head and took a large drink of the hot toddy. It warmed her stomach, a nice contrast to the air-conditioning Journey had cranked on high. "You're right. I can take twelve hours off."

"Fuck, Samara—that wasn't even a good dodge."

"I know. And I'm not sorry." Samara grinned. "You know what would make me feel immeasurably better?"

Journey laughed, the infectious sound rolling through the room. "I bet you're about to tell me."

"Brownies. Brownies would cure all my woes."

"I suppose I could whip up a batch."

"You're the best." Samara tugged on the ribbing of her sleeve. All the thoughts and fears and anger swirled inside her. Things weren't finished with her and Beckett now any more than they had been two days ago. If anything, they were infinitely more complicated. She *should* just walk away from the whole damn thing. It was the smart choice to make.

I don't want to.

Proving yet again that some things are hereditary. Both my amma and I have shitty taste in men.

Journey set out all the ingredients and paused. "I just can't believe there was a *fire*. What kind of ship is my cousin running that his building is spontaneously bursting into flame?"

"Things only spontaneously burst into flames in the movies." She thought back over the mad race down to the ground floor, to the smoke coating everything and making it impossible to see clearly. No flames, though. "I wonder what caused it? There isn't exactly a lot of burnable material in that lobby." She shook her head. "What am I saying? It was probably faulty wiring or something."

"Faulty wiring is another thing that happens a lot more in movies than in real life." Journey went to work making her famous brownies. Well, famous as far as Samara was concerned.

"I suppose it doesn't matter what started it. We got out, no one was hurt, and the firefighters were able to save the building." Not that she cared overmuch about Morningstar Enterprise's headquarters. She definitely didn't.

"I'm glad you're okay."

She looked up to find Journey uncharacteristically sober. "Beckett got me out." She might have managed on her own, but he'd been the one to make sure it happened in the shortest amount of time. She made a face. "I should send him flowers or something. As a thank-you."

"Trust me, honey—if you want to thank Beckett, I'm sure there are half a dozen ways to do it more effectively than sending flowers."

CHAPTER NINE

Beckett met the fire inspector at the office bright and early Sunday morning. The small man was probably one-forty soaking wet, but he knew his shit. They walked through the lobby to the employee break room he'd had installed a couple years ago.

It was damaged beyond repair.

"You're lucky the door was closed. Slowed things down." The fire inspector held out a hand when Beckett started to lean into the room. "We still have to conduct a full investigation, but I can tell you right now that it wasn't an accident."

He studied the blackened walls and the destroyed cabinets. "This is one of the only rooms with flammable shit in it on this floor." The door was usually locked, but there were currently half a dozen keys unaccounted for because of the employees he'd lost. Normally, there were more people in the building on Saturdays—there would have been if Lydia hadn't poached the ranks.

Lydia.

Beckett wanted to blame her for this, but even without

Samara's voice in his head he knew he was jumping to con-
clusions. She'd caused him other grief, and he wanted to lay
this at her feet, too. Someone could have snuck in through
one of the side doors somehow, and there was a spare key
the girls at the front desk kept hidden in case one of them
forgot their own. It was against company policy and they
didn't advertise its existence, but it *did* exist.

The fire inspector pulled a toothpick out of his pocket and
motioned. "That cabinet is ground zero. They left a cigarette
burning down into a bowl of lighter fluid. Not fancy, but it
got the job done." He turned to survey the rest of the lobby.
"If you had a different interior decorator, we might not be
having this conversation at all."

Because the fire would have spread too fast, preventing
escape. Beckett cataloged every single thing about the
burned room and imagined opening the bottom stairwell
door to find the entire lobby on fire. Fear took root in the
pit of his stomach. He could have died. *Samara* could have
died.

She didn't. She's fine.

It didn't kill the impulse to call her to reassure himself
again that she was safe. It wasn't his right. She didn't want
him hovering. He'd see her at the end of the week when they
gave their respective proposals for the government contract.
And then...

Then they'd go back to something resembling normal.
Barely seeing each other. Pretending like he didn't know
what his name sounded like from her lips when she orgasmed.

Focus.

"Will there be a report I can read once the initial investigation is complete?"

"Yeah." The fire inspector hesitated. "Are you filing an insurance claim over this?"

Beckett shrugged. "I was planning on it."

The fire inspector huffed out a breath and nodded. "You have any idea of who might have set this? Disgruntled employee? Pissed-off ex?"

Lydia.

He didn't say it. "Not off the top of my head." He had no damn *proof*. Beckett had no proof of anything. Not of her meeting with Nathaniel. Not that she'd somehow orchestrated his father deeding her Thistledown Villa. Sure as hell not for the fire.

At least one of those things he'd be able to confirm soon. Frank was working on getting provable confirmation for the dinner, and he'd work forward from there to figure out how Nathaniel was on that particular road at that particular time of night.

Samara might be right. It might just be that the old man made a shitty decision and paid the price. I might be hyper-focusing because I can't deal with my grief.

He set it aside. There was no other option. "Thanks for walking me through it."

"No problem." The fire inspector shrugged. "You might want to keep an eye out, though. Someone has it out for you. Doubt they'll stop with a petty little fire."

It hadn't felt like a petty little fire when the alarms had gone off. "I'll watch my back." He walked the man out and stood just inside the door, surveying the street. It was too late for Sunday brunch and too early for dinner, so there wasn't much foot traffic. It didn't matter. He still searched the face of every person who walked past, wondering if they were all as innocent as they seemed, or if there was something deeper going on. He'd been outmaneuvered again and again since he got back to Houston. *Pretty shitty track record for just a couple of days.*

That had to change. Now.

As if summoned by his thoughts, a limo pulled to a stop at the curb outside the building. He knew who it was before a white-clad leg appeared, followed by the rest of Lydia King. She wore another white pantsuit, but the top below the blazer was gold lace. Giant sunglasses shielded her gaze from him, but he knew the exact moment she registered him standing on the other side of the glass doors. Her step didn't hitch, but she seemed to focus in on him.

He moved back as she came through the doors. "Lydia, to what do I owe the dubious pleasure?"

"Beckett." She nodded and made a show of looking around the lobby. "I heard you had a fire. I came to ensure you were unharmed."

Uh-huh. Sure she did. He could tell her to get lost, but they were on *his* territory now. "Walk with me." He didn't want her in the building or near anything important. The gardens were safer across the board.

"Happily."

He strode through the lobby, a little too fast to be perfectly polite, but her long legs kept pace without any visible effort. "Did you know Samara was here when the fire went off? It's a small miracle we got out unharmed."

"Not small, certainly." Lydia allowed him to open the back door for her and stepped out into the sunlight. "I'm profoundly grateful that Samara escaped without any damage done. She's invaluable."

"I know." Though he doubted they meant it in the same way. Beckett suspected that Samara's deep-seated belief that she would be sacrificed as a pawn was at least partially Lydia's fault. He might only know his aunt in the business sense, but she had a take-no-prisoners attitude that seemed to apply to her own people as easily as to the enemy.

Lydia stopped and inhaled deeply. "I haven't been in these gardens in a very long time."

He surveyed the area, trying to see it the way she did. Morningstar owned more of the lot than just what the building sat on. In addition to the gardens he put in at Thistledown Villa, Beckett's grandfather had created a second paradise here. It was all local plants, rather than the imported ones in the greenhouse, but it didn't make it less beautiful. He'd taken solace on one of the two benches situated in the area the same way he'd utilized the gardens in his childhood home. There was something about knowing that love sowed this space that gave him a sense of being anchored. Of peace. "My grandfather must have loved my grandmother very much."

"Hardly." Lydia laughed softly. "My father was a horrible snob. He put in these gardens to shield his precious eyes from having to look at the rabble of Houston. Mother wasn't much better. She always preferred her fantasy gardens to the mess of real life."

Beckett crossed his arms over his chest. "You have a high opinion of your parents." He didn't want to believe it, but what did it matter why the gardens had gone in? *It matters. Damn it, it really matters.*

She raised one shoulder in a shrug. "Can you blame me?"

"No." He could blame her for everything after the split, but he understood why she'd felt she had to leave. Beckett had cut his teeth on the games and manipulations that went hand in hand with being a King, and even he couldn't believe that his grandfather had passed over Lydia for Nathaniel. His father was a good businessman to be sure, but nothing short of genius would have enabled Lydia to be so successful so quickly as she had with a brand-new company. If she'd been the CEO of Morningstar, who knew what she would have accomplished?

Lydia moved to the nearest bench but didn't sit. It was hard to read her expression with her sunglasses in place, but her mouth took on a brittle edge. "You're so much like your father, it's downright uncanny. Born with a silver spoon in your mouth and so incredibly sure of your place in the world that you're willing to steamroll over anyone who gets in your way—though he never managed to fake compassion the same way you do."

He raised his eyebrows. "Every King is born with a silver spoon in their mouth." He could argue that he'd never steam-rolled over someone less powerful than he was, but there was no point. Lydia obviously had the narrative she wanted when it came to him. Why should a little thing like the truth matter?

She tilted her head back and seemed to look at the cloud passing over the sun. "He left Houston once upon a time. Did he ever tell you that? He loved the money but not the re-sponsibility that came with it, and when he turned eighteen, he told our father he wanted nothing to do with being a King and jetted off to Europe."

As Beckett was growing up, his father hadn't talked much about his time before he was CEO of Kingdom Corp. Beckett tried to picture the man who had constantly touted *family first* leaving with no intention of coming back. "Don't you have a daughter in Europe right now? The model? Jet-ting off after graduation is something of a rite of passage."

Beckett had never done it—he'd gone straight into college after high school. There was no need to backpack through Europe to find himself, because he knew exactly what path his life would take, whether he wanted it or not. And after college, he'd traveled more than half the time to further Morningstar's interests.

And to salvage what little relationship I had left with my father. Hard to fight when we weren't even in the same country.

"Eliza knows what she's about. When the family requires her presence, she'll return." Lydia trailed a finger along the back of the bench. "Nathaniel intended to stay until his money ran out—and we both know that wasn't going to happen."

Beckett made a noncommittal noise because he wanted to see what her angle was for this moment of sharing. She seemed to take that as an invitation to continue. "Do you know who our father sent to retrieve Nathaniel when it became clear he wouldn't come back on his own?"

"You." It was an educated guess. For all intents and purposes, Lydia should have been the one his grandfather chose as heir. She was the oldest, and she was more than capable of handling the job. If he'd trusted her with the job of retrieving Nathaniel, he should have trusted her with the rest of it.

"Me," she confirmed. "I pulled my brother out of a high-class whorehouse, sobered him up, and brought him home. And do you know what my father did to reward me?" *Tap, tap, tap* went her finger against the metal bench. "The next week, he named Nathaniel as the next CEO."

"I'm sorry." He'd known she was passed over but not the story behind the events leading up to it. As much as he sympathized with the girl she used to be, that changed nothing about the current situation. They stood on opposite sides of a line that might as well have been the Grand Canyon for all they were going to reach across it. He might understand how she got to this point and the deep well of bitterness that turn of events had to have created inside her...but it didn't excuse a damn thing he suspected her of doing.

"This company should have been mine, Beckett. You know it and I know it."

Dredge up sympathy and then go in for the kill. He studied her. With her white suit, her impeccable blonde hair, and her ridiculous sunglasses, she would have looked more at home in some fancy resort than standing here in a muggy garden with him. "You got a raw deal, but you made the best of it. There's no point in trying to turn back time. You have your company. I have mine." All the posturing irritated the hell out of him. He had better things to do than circling his aunt and trading barbs. "Let this go, Lydia. You won't like what happens if you keep fucking with me."

"Darling nephew, I haven't even begun to fuck with you. Yet." She smiled that viper's smirk. "It's a shame about the fire, isn't it? I hope the repairs won't be too extensive. If you need a loan, don't hesitate to ask."

Alarm bells pealed through Beckett's head, but he kept his expression even. "I'll keep that in mind. Was there anything else? I have things that require my attention."

If anything, her smile widened. "I imagine you do." She strolled toward the doors, leaving him trailing behind her. He still didn't miss her next words. "You've become awfully cozy with my Samara."

Do not react. "I expect you had something to do with that."

Her laugh raised the small hairs on his neck. There was nothing inherently wrong with it, but it set him on edge all the same. "Contrary to what you seem to believe, I'm not responsible for everything going wrong in your life these days."

He wasn't going to touch that. Beckett could number the things that had gone to shit since his father died, but Samara wasn't on that list. He knew he couldn't trust her—and that she didn't trust *him* —but when she was in his arms he wasn't worried about his next move or watching his words. Even with all their respective baggage, what was between them was honest in those moments when they let their bodies do the talking.

He waited until Lydia had her hand on the door to ask, "What did you and my father talk about the night he died?"

She paused, but didn't look back. "I don't have the slightest idea what you're talking about. I haven't seen Nathaniel in months."

For the first time since she showed up, a thread of tension worked its way through her words. *She's lying.* He'd known Frank's information was good, but this confirmed it independently. "Funny you should say that. I have evidence that says otherwise."

She seemed to take a fortifying breath and turned to face him. He would have paid a significant amount of money to see her eyes just then. Lydia raised her hands in the universal sign of surrender. "You caught me. I had a private dinner date in the same restaurant he was at that night. He was already drunk when I arrived, and we shared a few words before I moved on." She shook her head slowly. "I don't know what you thought a thirty-second conversation would prove, Beckett. I'm sorry that your father's gone, if only for your loss. I didn't wish him dead."

"That's the second time you've lied to me today, Lydia." He didn't ask her what they'd allegedly talked about. It didn't matter. She was scrambling to come up with a logical reason why she would be photographed in Nathaniel's presence the night he died, and she'd just keep lying until he had the leverage to get the truth. "The games end now."

"Oh, honey." She smiled. "The games are only getting started."

He waited for her to leave the garden, and then waited some more until he watched her leave the building altogether. Beckett pulled out his phone and brought up Samara's number. Lydia bringing her up specifically was a threat if he'd ever heard one. He needed to see her, to reassure himself that she was really okay, to warn her that his aunt was the goddamn devil.

She won't believe you.

Even if she does, the safest place for her is as far from you as she can get.

No, he couldn't call Samara. He couldn't avoid her indefinitely, but the closer she got to him, the closer she got to the target Lydia had painted on his chest.

Instead, he called his bank. His aunt's comment about finances wasn't in passing. Once he confirmed that no unauthorized charges had been made to his personal account, he ordered it locked down for everything except in-person withdrawals. Then Beckett did the same with his trust fund, the three accounts his father had willed him, and Morningstar's accounts as well. Even with no evidence of any attempts to access the money, he couldn't help feeling a little paranoid.

Either she'd been bluffing to waste his time ... or she was already three steps ahead of him.

Fuck that. Beckett dropped onto the bench and leaned back to stare at the sky. He couldn't go on like this, reacting to the shit Lydia pulled. Eventually, she'd get the best of him and he'd lose yet another thing he valued. No, he had to get ahead of this and he had to do it before the next blow fell.

The government contract.

Beckett hesitated. By all rights, he should wait for the presentation Friday and let the dice fall where they may. Samara had been working her ass off on her bid, and if he played dirty on this, it might hurt her standing with her job.

And maybe that's exactly what Lydia wants. She shoved Samara at me and, while that connection might be real enough, Samara's been very *clear about where her loyalties lie. I can't put her before Morningstar when she's not doing the same for me.*

Whether he liked it or not, his attraction to Samara was a glaring weak spot. Lydia wouldn't hesitate to exploit it, and *Samara* wasn't above using it against him, either. He was in the middle of a game where he was the only one playing by the rules, and there would be no winning if he continued on that route.

There would be no justice.

This is the only way, no matter how distasteful I find it.

He braced himself and made the call.

CHAPTER TEN

Samara spent Sunday with her *amma*. Going through the normal weekend routine of her childhood was like wrapping up in a warm blanket. It transported her back to a time when she believed there was nothing her *amma* couldn't do. When she stood as shield between Samara and the rest of the world.

They cleaned the kitchen from top to bottom, starting with wiping the cabinets down, inside and out, and ending with mopping the floor. Only when they were finished and Samara had rinsed out the mop bucket and set it aside to dry did her *amma* dry her hands and turn to her. "Are you ready to talk about it?"

The dam inside her that held everything in its proper place had been showing hairline cracks since her first night with Beckett six months ago. At her *amma*'s softly spoken question, it burst and words poured out. "I don't know what I'm doing."

Amma considered her. "This has been bothering you for some time."

"Yes." She leaned against the counter and looked out

the back window. There wasn't much to see—a postage stamp-sized backyard that her *amma* kept well groomed. The neighbors whose backyard bordered theirs were within easy speaking distance. She'd always hated that. Condo living might have its downsides, but growing up here had been like living in a fishbowl. Everyone was in everyone's business, and they had no problem snooping and gossiping to get the scoop on whatever petty drama was currently playing out.

"Samara." There was no censure in her *amma*'s voice, but she felt it all the same.

"Ever since I was a little girl, I had a path. It's a good path. I've worked my ass off to get where I am now. I've made sacrifices." She raked her fingers through her hair. It didn't help. "He's under my skin, *Amma*. I thought I could keep my head about him and do what needed to be done, but every time we're together he has me questioning things I know for a fact are true."

"Beckett King." She spat the name.

"Beckett King." Samara took a deep breath and looked at her *amma*. She might have her father's strong nose, but in every other way, she was made in her mother's image. The years had been kind to her *amma*, dealing out laugh lines as easily as they dealt out the pinched stress lines that peppered her forehead. She wasn't smiling now. Samara forced herself to look at her hands, at the weathered and beaten fingers that could have belonged to a woman twice her *amma*'s age.

Those hands had sacrificed so Samara could have every opportunity, could shoot for the stars without anything holding her back.

She forced a smile. "I'm sorry, *Amma*. The stress of this

upcoming bid has me talking crazy. Why don't you get out
the cards and we'll play rummy?"

Amma hesitated like she wanted to dig into this conversation, but finally nodded. "It's not every day my daughter has
an entire Sunday to give me. You'll stay for dinner?"

"Of course." She had to get back to the rat race sooner
rather than later, but it would hold until after dinner. She
needed this reminder of why she couldn't deviate from her
path. Beckett might believe that Lydia was behind every
misfortune he'd been dealt since his father's death, and he
might even be right about part of it, but that had nothing to
do with Samara.

She ignored the tiny voice inside her that disagreed with
leaving them to hash it out. It didn't matter that Lydia had
her children and Beckett had…Well, no one. It *couldn't*
matter. Samara didn't make choices with her heart. She
couldn't afford to. She might not have achieved the level of
ice-queen persona that Lydia cultivated, but what she had
was better than nothing.

In this industry, a thin skin might as well be an invitation
for a knife in the back.

Samara didn't even make it into her office Monday morning
before she was waylaid by Lydia's assistant. "Ms. King
needs to see you—now."

*Of course she does. She wants a damn report on how I
fucked Beckett on his desk and then almost died in a fire.*

Samara wouldn't give it to her. She wasn't willing to
cross that particular line.

Lydia turned from looking out her floor-to-ceiling
windows as Samara walked into her office. She wore a
gold dress that should have looked ostentatious as day-

wear, but she managed to pull it off all the same. "Close the door."

Apparently we're getting right down to it. "Good morning, Lydia."

"Yes, yes." She waved that away. "What do you have for me?"

"It might help if you told me what information you're looking for. Beckett wasn't exactly sharing state secrets when I was at Morningstar Enterprise."

Lydia crossed to lean against the edge of her desk. She motioned to Samara to sit. "Start with why he invited you there in the first place."

"He offered me a job." She made a face. "He didn't come right out and say it, but the offer was there all the same."

Instead of being furious, Lydia's lips quirked up. "My nephew isn't as dumb as his father. He knew losing you would be a serious blow to both me and Kingdom Corp, and he didn't hesitate to leverage your...history."

"I didn't take it."

"Of course you didn't. You're loyal to a fault." Lydia still looked entirely too amused. "He'll try again, of course. He's infatuated with you, and you present quite the prize both personally and professionally. Beckett won't be able to resist attempting to seduce you away from me."

Samara stared. She'd had a couple ideas how this conversation would go, but none of them involved Lydia looking downright giddy at the thought of facing off with Beckett — of continuing to face off with him. "I'm not a toy you two can fight over, Lydia. I have better things to do than to lead Beckett King around by his nose." That wasn't what they were, but she wasn't about to get into the intricacies of the push-and-pull between her and Beckett. They grappled for power within each interaction, but it was as much for their own enjoyment as to pursue their independent goals.

"On the contrary. You're uniquely qualified to do exactly that. He might not trust you completely, but he can't leave you alone." The amusement drained out of Lydia's face, leaving only cold calculation in its wake. "If you're so concerned about handling your various responsibilities, I can off-load the upcoming bid to Journey to free you up."

"You're not serious." She shouldn't have questioned Lydia, but it was too late to take it back now. Samara pushed to her feet. "You're treating me like a glorified whore."

"You're paid significantly better than any whore I know."

She stopped short, half sure she'd misheard. But no, Lydia had actually just said that. Samara took a careful breath and kept her body as relaxed as possible. *Do not scream at your boss.* "Lydia." She spoke quietly, biting off each word to keep from losing control. "Nowhere in my job description does it include seducing the competition, let alone the competition who's grief-stricken from losing his last remaining parent a few short days ago."

"Oh, please. Nathaniel was nothing but a burden on everyone connected to him. Beckett should be grateful he's gone." Lydia tilted her head to the side and studied Samara, leaving her feeling like a bug under a microscope. "You're being uncharacteristically hysterical this morning."

She did not *just*—Samara gritted her teeth. "Well, I almost died in a fire on Saturday, so that might account for my poor mood."

"Honey, you were never in any danger from that fire."

The world seemed to hold its breath around her. Samara went still, her breath stalled in her lungs. "What are you talking about?" How the hell could Lydia possibly know what kind of danger she was or wasn't in? *Samara* didn't even know the true level of danger because the fire inspector had had to wait for the scene to cool down before he could do his job.

"It was just a small fire. No one was in any danger." Lydia must have seen the incredulous expression on her face, because she laughed. "No, I didn't set it. I spoke with Beckett yesterday. Don't look at me like that, Samara. I'm not a monster."

I'm not so sure. She wouldn't know without speaking to Beckett, but Samara didn't see him sharing specifics about the fire with his aunt. It didn't make any sense. But if she contradicted Lydia right now, she was essentially accusing her boss of arson. Without proof.

She'd be fired before the words were fully voiced.

Lydia pushed off the desk and stalked toward her. The concerned expression on her face didn't detract from the menace in her body language. "You look a little peaked, Samara. I'm sure you suffered some smoke inhalation on Saturday. Why don't you take a few days to recover and then we'll talk again?"

A few days. "If I take a few days, that will hamper my ability to give the presentation for the government contract."

"Yes, honey, I know. Stop by Journey's office on your way out and give her the pertinent information. She'll take this one, and we'll field you the next one."

Just like that, all Samara's hard work was shelved so someone else could take the credit. It didn't matter that Journey was her friend and would be as horrified by this turn of events as Samara was. What mattered was she'd been treated like the pawn she'd fought so hard to rise above.

Samara lifted her chin. "I think you should reconsider."

"You're more than capable of handling this, but that doesn't change the fact that I've been leaning on you entirely too much since my boys left." Lydia's hazel eyes were sympathetic, but her words cut through Samara like a knife. "I take care of my employees. This is in your best interest, Samara." Nearly the same words Beckett had used, but for a very different purpose.

There was no point in arguing. She'd just confirm how hysterical Lydia accused her of being. With it framed as being something for her benefit, Samara wouldn't win. "I'll be back on Wednesday."

"Might as well take the full week. Don't look at me like that—you have a month's worth of vacation days. A week will do you a bit of good." Lydia tucked a strand of hair behind her ear. "In fact, it might be just the opportunity to take a real vacation. You haven't had one of those in years. Our Hamptons house is always open to you, of course. I can make the arrangements."

"That won't be necessary." She couldn't keep the stiffness out of her voice. "I'll see you Monday." Samara turned and walked out of the office. It was tempting to keep on walking until she got control of the fury blossoming with each breath, but no matter how pissed she was, she couldn't leave Journey hanging.

She managed to keep her expression under control until she shut the door between Journey's office and the rest of the building. "Fuck. Shit, fuck, god*damn* it." She wished she had something to throw, but she wasn't going to destroy her friend's office just to make herself feel better.

Journey hung up her phone and stood. "What the hell happened? Mother just called and let me know *I'm* taking over the bid? That's your project."

"Not anymore." She stalked from one side of the office to the other, her heels sinking into the thick carpet. "She basically just kicked me out of the office for a week. Forced vacation time."

"That's bullshit." Journey glared at the door. "I'm going to take care of this."

"No, don't." Samara stepped into her line of sight. "If you and your mother get into a fight over me, it will just make everyone else on this floor miserable for the next week." Not to mention the fact it wouldn't do any good. Lydia obviously wanted her out of the office—out of the city—for the next week. In all her years of working for this company, she'd never once been ordered on vacation. *Something is going on.*

"Samara, this is wrong."

"I know." She walked over and took her friend's shoulders. "Can you drop by later and pick up the stuff I have for the bid? It's at my place. You have to pull this off."

"I'll take care of it." Journey turned contemplative. "Does this mean you're going to take over negotiating with that jackass Frank Evans for me?"

"Not a chance." She hugged Journey. "It will be okay."

"You just got shafted and you're comforting *me*." Journey shook her head. "That's so messed up."

"It will be fine. There will be other projects."

She narrowed her eyes. "You're taking this suspiciously well."

"I know when to pick my battles." Several things Lydia had said had her suspicions rising. The woman shouldn't have known about the specifics of the fire, but it *was* possible that Beckett had shared them with her. Samara wouldn't know until she asked him.

Taking a risk.

So be it.

"If you need anything—anything at all—this week, you let me know."

"Yes, ma'am."

Journey gave her another suspicious look, but moved back to resume her seat. "I'll be by later to grab that stuff."

"Actually, I'll have it couriered to you. No reason to waste more time." She smiled to reassure her friend, but Journey just looked more worried. Samara sighed. "Look, I'm angry and upset and I just want to drink too much wine and rage about the injustice of it all."

Journey stared. "Okay," she said carefully. "Tell Beckett I said hi."

She paused. "I never said I was going to Beckett."

"You didn't have to." Journey gave a soft smile. "Might as well make the best of a shitty situation."

That wasn't why she was going to Beckett, but she didn't correct her friend. Samara would never do anything to hurt Kingdom Corp but…If Lydia really *was* behind the arson or, God forbid, Nathaniel's death, then Samara was under an obligation to do what it took to bring that to light. She wasn't a detective, but outside of the King family, no one knew the woman as well as Samara did. "I'll call you later."

"Talk to you then."

She headed home and got everything packaged up and couriered out. Samara stared at her phone. She didn't have to make this call. She could go on the vacation Lydia pressed on her. The Hamptons house was a small slice of paradise. She and Journey took a long weekend there every year and spent three days sunning themselves on the beach, drinking too much, and unwinding. Maybe if she left Houston now she'd get her head on straight and come home with her priorities in order.

But if she left now there would be no answers. Beckett might think the worst of Lydia, but no one else would believe him. He had the disadvantage of being seen as grieving, and while that gave him some leeway with his actions, it also counted against him when it came to his credibility.

I might be wrong.

She couldn't guarantee it, though.

What would she have done in Beckett's place? If it had been her *amma* who suddenly died and there were no answers to be had. If there was someone who had answers, she'd want them to come forward. She'd *beg* them to come forward. Samara might not have concrete information, but she could get it given enough time.

She'd lose her job if she did.

She paced around her apartment, round and round as she argued with herself. There were no answers here. There were no easy answers at all. With a sigh, she pulled the theoretical trigger and called Beckett.

He didn't make her wait. "Samara, is everything okay?"

She blinked, his concern stopping her in her tracks. "Why wouldn't it be?"

A pause, like she'd surprised him. "You may have forgotten, but just forty-eight hours ago, we were running down far too many flights of stairs."

For some reason, she got the feeling that hadn't been what he was originally going to say. Samara forced some lightness into her voice. If there were things she wasn't willing to say over the phone, it stood to reason that he might have some as well. "I'd like to see you tonight."

"I may have to work a little late, but why don't you just meet me at my condo. I'll have my doorman let you in."

She pressed her lips together. "Beckett, that's not necessary. Just text me when you're done at work, and I'll come over then."

"Humor me. You'll be safe at my place."

Safe. Beckett *definitely* knew something she didn't. Samara pictured Lydia's face as she pushed her to leave the city for the week. *Surely Lydia wouldn't hurt me to get at Beckett. That would require him to actually care about me.*

She hated that she even considered it a possibility.

She hated even more the fear that threaded through her.

"I . . . Aren't you worried that I'm going to snoop through your stuff and report back to Lydia?"

He snorted. "I'll see you tonight, Samara."

"See you tonight." She hung up and glanced at her clock. It was only noon. Six hours to go until she saw Beckett.

She had work to do.

CHAPTER ELEVEN

Beckett didn't cut out of work early. Knowing Samara might be in his condo, waiting for him, made staying a herculean effort. He managed. He walked through his front door at five fifty-five to the scent of something spicy cooking.

He closed the door and leaned against it and, just for a moment, imagined this was what his life was like. Coming home to Samara every night. A traitorous thought, maybe, but they matched up more than physically. He liked her determination and the way she handled business. Her ambition and ruthless business sense were balanced out by the softness that shone through when he least expected it. He wanted to know everything about her.

He wanted her to want to tell him.

"Beckett?"

"I'm here." He pushed off the door, paused to make sure it was locked, and then walked down the short hallway to the kitchen and living room. Samara stood at the stove, her hair piled on top of her head in a haphazard bun, wearing a pair of black leggings and a tank top that showed peeks of a bright red bra beneath it.

She glanced over her shoulder. "I hope you don't mind. I was going to order takeout, but today was stressful so I'm taking a page from Journey's playbook and trying to cook some of that irritation out."

He shrugged out of his suit jacket and crossed to look at the covered pot on the stove. He couldn't quite put his finger on the mix of spices. Beckett inhaled and closed his eyes. "That smells divine."

"It's biryani. My mother's recipe." She smiled, but the expression didn't meet her troubled dark eyes. "You look tired."

"It's been a long week."

Samara shook her head. "It's Monday."

"I stand by my statement." He leaned against the counter. "Do you want to talk about what stressed you out?"

"You know, when I called you I thought I did." She glanced down at the pan on the stove. "I'm so conflicted right now. I don't know which way is up, and the more time goes on, the murkier it gets."

He knew the feeling well. He moved closer to her and cupped her face in his hands. "We can talk when you're ready."

She reached over and flipped off the burner. "Dinner will hold for a little bit." Samara pressed her hands to his chest. "I don't want to think for a little while, Beckett."

He kissed her in response. He dug his fingers into her thick hair, enjoying the feel of her as he explored her mouth. She met him stroke for stroke, her wicked tongue flicking against his. Beckett broke the kiss and dragged his mouth along her jawline. "We'll talk later."

"Yes, later." Her hands went to the buttons of his shirt. She undid them at record speed and shoved the offending piece of clothing off his shoulders.

Her gaze landed on the scar that puckered the skin on his shoulder. "This looks bad."

"It was." In the middle of a fight with Nathaniel when he was a teenager, he'd fallen down the stairs and almost destroyed his shoulder in the process. His father had been remorseful and felt guilty, but he'd retreated behind his veil of stony silence right around the time Beckett got out of the hospital.

She traced the crooked edges, and he felt the light touch all the way to his toes. Finally, she met his gaze. Her inky eyes gave nothing away, the soft expression gone as if it'd never been there to begin with. "I'm glad you're here."

This fragile almost-peace wouldn't last. There were still too many obstacles in their path for them to truly make things work. He couldn't even be sure whether she was there because she wanted to be—or if his aunt had ordered her to call him. Beckett cupped her jaw with one hand and dragged his thumb over her full bottom lip. "No business tonight. No fighting or manipulating or bullshit. Just us."

Her breath hitched. "I'm not going to make a promise I can't keep."

He shifted his hold to grip the back of her neck lightly. "No business for the next couple hours, then."

"Deal."

A few flicks of his fingers had the straps of her shirt sliding down her arms and revealing the red bra that had caught his attention earlier. Her full breasts looked like they were straining to get free, so he obliged them, inching down the lace to bunch around the underwire, framing her breasts the way they were meant to be framed. Samara's dark nipples puckered beneath his gaze, an invitation he couldn't ignore.

"I'm fucking you tonight."

She laughed, the sound hoarse and needy. "Or maybe *I'm* the one who's going to fuck *you*."

He managed to drag his gaze back to her face. "Do the semantics matter?"

"Yes."

"Tell me something." He cupped one of her breasts and circled her nipple with his thumb. "Is everything a power game with you? Has everything up to this point been part of it?"

Samara arched her back, thrusting herself more firmly into his hand. Her breaths were coming just as fast as his, even though he'd barely touched her. The chemistry between them was a truth he silently dared her to deny. Finally she shook her head as much as his grip would allow. "Power is important. You have it all and I have none."

"Don't know how you're keeping score, but that sounds all sorts of wrong." He let go of her long enough to pull her shirt over her head and push off her leggings, leaving her in only her underwear. The lace of her panties matched the red of her bra and hid absolutely nothing—if anything, it framed her.

A blatant invitation... if he ignored the threat her thorns presented.

I like the thorns. They made it that much sweeter when she stopped thinking so damn hard and gave herself over to the pleasure.

He took two careful steps back. The picture she presented was almost enough to have him closing the distance between them again, but he managed to hold on to control. Barely. "My bedroom. Go."

Samara blinked, and then shook her head, her hair sliding over her shoulders with the move. "Wait—"

"I'm not going to repeat myself. You want games, we'll

play games. Now, get your fine ass into my bedroom and wait for me." *Trust me, Samara. Let me help you turn off that formidable brain of yours for a little while.*

She licked her lips and he knew he had her. There were other reasons she'd come to him tonight, but she'd come for what he could give her, too. She needed this the same way he did, no matter how bad they might be for each other.

Finally, she nodded. "Don't make me wait long, or I'll take care of myself." She turned and walked out of the kitchen, completely at ease with her near-nakedness—her soft laugh floating over her shoulder. "Then what use would I have for you?"

Samara considered her options as she came through the bedroom door. She wanted to be in a position to really make an impression when Beckett walked in. He'd won the first round in the kitchen through the sole fact that he'd surprised the hell out of her. She'd expected... She wasn't sure. To maintain control. To not be affected by the gentle understanding in his dark eyes when he'd asked about her day.

None of that reasoning held up past the moment when he'd commanded her into the room and her entire body clenched in anticipation. His rough tone and blunt words didn't promise her sex—they promised animal-like fucking on the basest of levels.

Exactly what I need—to get out of my head for a little while.

She climbed onto the bed and leaned back against the headboard. The bed was positioned so that Beckett would walk through the door and see her in profile, so she wanted to make that first look one for the record books. Stripping completely was what he'd expect, so she went in a different direction. Samara let her bra straps fall from her shoulders, but kept it on. She slid her panties down to just past her knees.

She ran her fingers through her hair, and checked her reflection in the mirror across from the bed. She looked like she'd just been fucked within an inch of her life, as if they were so hot for each other they hadn't bothered to strip completely. *Perfect.* Then there was no time left.

Beckett stood in the doorway, his dark eyes drinking her in. She held her breath as his gaze dragged over her from the top of her head to the tips of her toes and back again. He gave her legs the same amount of time he gave her breasts, and he paused on her face the longest of all. "I could get used to this."

"Don't." She shook her head. "I didn't come here to make promises to you and nothing's really changed as far as you and I are concerned." *So many other things have changed, though.* She gulped in a breath and focused on him. "I need this, Beckett. I need *you*. If you're going to demand things I can't give you, then maybe I should leave."

"Not fucking likely." He circled the bed, taking her in from every angle. "Grab the headboard."

Samara liked sex as much as the next person, but she had a clear set of rules—mainly that she was in control at all times. She didn't need to be blatant about the requirement because most men weren't paying enough attention to realize that they had never even been allowed in the driver's seat.

Not Beckett.

He never asked for her submission—he demanded it. More dangerously, right now he was demanding that she trust him. *It's just sex. It doesn't have to apply to any other aspect of life.*

She didn't believe it for a second.

But Samara still raised her hands over her head and gripped the thick wood of the headboard. With her back bowed, every part of her was on display, and Beckett could do whatever he wanted to her as long as she kept her hands where they were. The knowledge made her shake. She pressed her lips together, torn between closing her legs and . . . She didn't know.

Beckett didn't give her the opportunity to think too much. He undid his slacks and stepped out of them in a smooth move. She'd seen him naked before, but it was either through a haze of tequila or in the midst of their frantic fucking on his desk. Not like this, where she could look her fill even as he did. Muscles corded his legs the same way they did the rest of his body, a deceptive strength that his jeans or slacks always masked. So much about Beckett was deceptive strength.

If Lydia had her way, he'd lose everything.

"Beckett—"

"No." He crawled onto the bed. "You were right—we're not going there. Not yet. Not like this. Right now, I'm going to taste you until you beg for my cock in every way that I'm willing to give it to you. When we're too exhausted to move, you're going to curl up against my side and sleep with me. In the morning, we'll sit down over breakfast and have a conversation."

He was asking for a whole lot more than sex. Panic beat frantic wings against the inside of her throat. It took two tries to speak past the feeling. "I'm not sleeping with you." She'd thought maybe they'd have sex, talk, and she'd— what? Do the walk of shame back to her place in the middle of the night?

That's exactly what I thought was going to happen.

"Yes, you are. This is a full package experience." He knelt between her feet and traced the lace of her panties where they were taut between her shins. "You need this, Samara. Let me give it to you."

She stared at him, this tortured god of a man who had no business making her feel things after all this time. She met his gaze, her stomach taking a dive at the conflicting emotions tangled up and on display for her. Beckett wanted her as much as she wanted him, but he carried his past around like Atlas carried the world. That truth was there in the lines bracketing his mouth, in the faint circles beneath his eyes, in the creases at the edges of his eyes.

In that moment, they weren't Samara Mallick and Beckett King.

They were just a woman and a man who needed each other.

It matters who we are. It has to *matter.*

It didn't.

Her true purpose for being there sifted through her fingers like smoke, insubstantial and gone in an instant. Reality faded, narrowing down to a pinpoint—this room, this bed, this man. The entire world ceased to exist in that moment, could be held at bay for the entirety of the night if she'd allow it.

Here, in this place, she didn't have to be stronger, colder, hungrier than anyone else in the room. She could fall asleep in Beckett's strong arms. With him holding her she could believe, if only for the night, that no matter how bad things got, it would all be okay in the end.

Samara dug her fingers into the headboard, the faint pain bringing her back to herself. No matter how tempting the lie, it *was* a lie. She couldn't allow herself to fall prey to the

intoxicating fiction Beckett wove around her. He might not
be the enemy right now, but there *was* an enemy out there
who obviously had no qualms about putting people in danger. Pretending there wasn't was a mistake.

It's only a single night.

"What do you say, Samara?"

Really, there was only one answer. "Okay."

"Good. Then we can begin." He gave her a downright
wolfish grin.

What had she just agreed to? Samara couldn't quite catch
her breath. "It's only tonight. Tomorrow we go back to...all
that."

"I don't give a fuck about tomorrow." He leaned down
and pressed a kiss to one knee and then the other, just above
where her panties were drawn tight by her spread legs.
Beckett stroked his hand up her inner thighs, stopping just
short of where she desperately needed to be touched, and
then back up again. "Don't move your hands. Don't speak
unless it's to scream my name."

She laughed, though the sound was more choked than
mocking. "You can't be serious."

"It's just a harmless game."

It didn't feel harmless. It felt downright dangerous to
give Beckett so much as an inch. *It's just sex.* It didn't matter
how many times she repeated the mantra to herself. It wasn't
any truer now than it had been the first time she thought it.

He shifted down to his stomach and dipped his head between her legs. She might have been having a hard time
breathing before, but the image he presented—his mouth
hovering over her pussy, her panties a bright banner above
his dark hair, the hungry look in his eye reserved for her
alone—sucked all the air out of the room.

And then his mouth was on her.

It had been good in the office—better than good—but it took her all of three seconds to realize that Beckett had been rushing then, as frantic for a taste of her as she'd been for his touch.

Now, he was taking his goddamn time.

Samara kept her grip on the headboard and forced her eyes to remain open so she didn't miss a single second of this. He growled against her skin and pushed her legs wider yet so he could dip down and tongue her. Beckett fucked her with his tongue the way she wished he'd fuck her with his cock.

"You're thinking so loud, it's practically written in neon above your head."

She pressed her lips together to prevent the reply demanding to be vocalized. Beckett, damn him, knew it. He grinned. "Almost had you." And then his mouth was on her again, sucking her clit hard enough to make her cry out. She shifted, trying to get closer to him—if that were even possible—but he pinned her in place easily. Through it all, he never once stopped the onslaught.

She writhed. It was too much. It wasn't enough. She didn't know what it was because her entire world narrowed down to Beckett's mouth on her pussy. "Beckett!"

Samara calling his name was the cue he'd been waiting for, but Beckett was enjoying her taste too much to stop. He wanted inside her so badly he was shaking.

But he wanted to taste her orgasm more.

He flicked her clit just like he knew she liked it. Even if he had unlimited access to her, he'd never get enough of going down on her. He craved her like an addict. Sex was fucking fantastic, but having her on his tongue and her thighs creating a vise against his head? Perfection.

He picked up his pace, responding to her cues, and then she was coming, crying out his name again. As tempting as it was to bring her again and again, Beckett had no illusions—Samara would make him pay for teasing her, with interest. It'd be fun to play with that kind of torture in the future, but that wasn't what tonight was for.

Might not be a future.

Shut the fuck up. You have right now. Make it count.

Beckett sat back and yanked Samara's panties off. Her dark eyes were hazy with passion, but she reached for him immediately. "Now. No more waiting."

He couldn't have said it better himself. He snagged a condom from the nightstand and put it on with quick, concise movements. Ensuring that it was on correctly was the only thing keeping him in check. Tonight was important. If he screwed this up, this would be the last time he and Samara would be together.

He grabbed her hips and pulled her down the bed to meet him. She was so fucking soft it drove him crazy. The woman beneath the skin was as hard-ass as they came, but her body welcomed him even if *she* didn't always. He pushed two fingers into her, ensuring that she was ready, but the time for foreplay had passed.

He needed to be inside her. Now.

Beckett hitched her leg over one of his arms and positioned his cock at her entrance. "Ready?"

"Yes." She arched up to meet him as he thrust forward. The move sheathed him to the hilt and he froze even as she moaned. "Fuck, Beckett."

"You feel so good." He settled his weight on top of her,

bracing himself on his forearms so he could get the angle right. It felt good to be this close to her—as physically connected as two people could be. He kissed her because he craved being closer yet. It was too good. Too fucking perfect.

"You do, too." She wrapped her legs around his waist. "I never want this to end."

It doesn't have to.

He kissed her to keep the words inside. He might want Samara, but that didn't mean she felt the same way. All he'd offered her was one night of escape, and he'd give her exactly that. Trying to talk about the future, even while she clenched around his cock, would violate the terms of their agreement, and he'd be damned before he did something to make her leave.

Needing to feel her coming again, he reached between them to stroke her clit. "This is what you need."

"Yes." Her nails dug into his shoulders. "Yes, oh my God, *yes*. Beckett, don't stop."

"I'm not going to stop. I'm never going to fucking stop."

She came with a sob, her body arching beautifully. Beckett tried to hold on, to hold out, but the truth was he needed this as much as she did. He buried his face in her neck and pounded into her, holding her close as he sought his own release. Pressure sparked through him, the pleasure too intense. He cursed as his strokes went jerky and he orgasmed hard enough to send black spots dancing across his vision. "Fuck."

Samara squeezed him with her entire body and kissed his temple. "You're right, Beckett. I think we both needed that."

He turned and captured her mouth. "I'm nowhere near done with you yet."

CHAPTER TWELVE

Samara woke up to the smell of eggs burning in the kitchen. She rubbed her eyes and tried to make out the blurry red numbers of the clock on the other side of the bed. She froze when they finally came into focus. *Oh my God, I am so late.* On the heels of that, the truth washed over her. *No, I'm not. I'm on forced vacation.*

She threw back the covers and went searching for her clothes. Her panties were trashed, but she managed to find her bra.

Her pants and jacket were still in the kitchen.

She contemplated the door for a full thirty seconds before she dredged up the bravado to walk through it. Grabbing a towel or artfully draping a sheet around her body wasn't an option. She wasn't some demure virgin who was ashamed of being naked, and Beckett had reacquainted himself with every inch of her last night.

No, the reason she wanted something to cover her was because she wanted *armor*.

She and Beckett might have been on the same page last

night, but they had a conversation ahead of them that might put them at odds yet again. *The story of our lives.*

There was nothing left to stall with. She walked out of the bedroom and down the short hall into the kitchen. It was only when she bent over to grab her pants and shirt on the floor that she realized Beckett wasn't in the kitchen alone.

Reclaiming her cold mask was almost a relief at that point. She draped her pants over her arm. "Frank."

Frank Evans very carefully looked only at her eyes. He lifted a coffee mug in a kind of salute. "Samara. Nice seeing you."

"Uh...nice seeing you, too." She tried to keep her face from heating, but there was no way she was pulling this off. *Retreat gracefully...*

Beckett turned from the stove and froze. "What the fuck are you doing?"

His blatant jealousy helped overcome the embarrassment of the situation. She shrugged, starting to enjoy this. "I needed my clothes. As great as last night was, you can't keep me locked up and naked in this apartment."

"My life would be a lot easier if I could." His brows slammed down. "Get your ass in the room and get dressed."

She shot a look at Frank, who seemed to find the ceiling *very* fascinating. "He thinks that tone is going to work with me. Not sure what kind of girls he's dated in the past, but that's not an acceptable way to talk to women."

"Technically, *you* are one of the girls he dated in the past."

"Frank, I don't know what you're doing with your life, but one night of hot sex does *not* count as dating."

"I'm standing right here." Beckett made a sound suspiciously like a growl and turned back to whatever horrific science experiment he was working on at the stove.

As fun as it was torturing him, she had absolutely no interest in standing there naked any longer than she had to. Samara headed back into the bedroom and dressed as fast as she could.

By the time she made it back to the kitchen, Frank was nowhere to be found. "You ran your friend off."

"My friend was only here to drop that off." Beckett nodded at the manila folder lying in the middle of the kitchen island. It had no markings on it, but she could guess what would bring Frank to Beckett's home: evidence.

He leaned against the counter and crossed his arms over his chest. "Let's get this out in the open and stop playing around, Samara. I enjoyed the fuck out of last night. We have unfinished business and I want you in my bed until we figure this shit out."

Her heartbeat picked up even as she called herself an idiot. "By figure this shit out, you mean..."

"I mean Lydia. She's neck deep in this mess, and I mean for her to see justice for any crimes committed."

Lydia. Of course. He wasn't here for Samara, and forgetting that only led to heartbreak. She wasn't about to say that the amazing sex last night had suddenly changed her reservations about Beckett, but orgasms had a way of adding rose-tinted glasses to any situation.

There was nothing rose-tinted about theirs.

He was the CEO of Morningstar Enterprise, and he had hundreds of thousands of workers depending on him for their employment. His family was what passed for royalty in Texas. His net worth was beyond comprehension.

Samara was a woman from a tiny little house on the

wrong side of town. Abandoned by her father before birth, her mother's family wasn't notable in any way. She made good money for a normal person, but it was like holding a plastic fork up for comparison with fancy silverware made of literal silver. They were the same as long as no one started cataloging the differences.

Which was what she *had* to do. She couldn't afford to see Beckett as just the man.

But maybe I can...just for a little while. Just until this situation with Lydia is resolved.

No one has to know but Beckett and me. I'm on vacation, after all.

He was watching her too closely, making her feel like she was showing him more than she wanted to. "Be mine for the duration, Samara."

"Okay." She had to bend over backward and squint a little for this to seem like a good idea, but with Beckett standing before her in a pair of low-riding jeans and nothing else, it wasn't that hard. "For the duration."

He motioned at the stove. "Eggs?"

"Whatever is in that pan, it's neither eggs nor edible." She hesitated. "We need to talk."

"Yeah, I know." He scowled at the mess in the pan and turned off the stove. "I'll order in breakfast, but might as well get started now."

She retreated while he made the call. Samara explored his bathroom. It was just as tastefully decorated as the rest of the condo. A slight lean toward minimalism, which she suspected was more because he didn't care about decorating than any love for the style. The bath was done in white on white, and the massive sunflower showerhead tempted her to get up close and personal with it. *No time.*

She splashed some water on her face and found a box of cheap toothbrushes in the cabinet below the sink. She considered their presence as she brushed her teeth. Did Beckett have so many overnight guests that he needed a Costco-sized box of toothbrushes to accommodate them?

Stop that. It's none of your business.

She didn't *want* it to be her business.

Samara braced her hands on the side of the sink and stared at herself in the mirror. *Real talk time, Samara. Yes, you sure as hell do want it to be your business. You want for all your fears to be unfounded and for this to magically work out. You want Beckett to prioritize you over his company.*

She shook her head. A fool's dream. It didn't matter if she liked how Beckett made her feel when they were alone together. What mattered was the choice he would make again and again. It wouldn't be her. It *couldn't* be her. CEO changeovers were no joke, and combined with Lydia's underhanded stunts, Beckett needed to focus every bit of energy he had on his company and ensuring that it survived.

And Samara needed someone to put her first. She couldn't be in a relationship and be a second-tier priority. She deserved better than that.

Getting ahead of yourself. Beckett said he wants you for the duration—not forever.

She scrubbed her hands over her face and finger-combed her hair. If she was smart, she would have stayed the hell away from him and this entire mess, but the pull between them was too damn strong. *I am so screwed.*

"Samara."

She jumped and then silently cursed herself for jumping. "Sorry. I'm just lost in thought."

"I can see that." Beckett stood in the doorway, his dark eyes drinking her in. "What's wrong? Is it the conversation we're about to have or is it something else?"

She wanted to brush off his question and force him to focus on what really mattered—the danger Lydia presented—but instead Samara answered him honestly. "Both."

He nodded like she'd confirmed something he already knew. "You're still afraid I'm using you in my game against Lydia."

"Aren't you?"

Instead of answering directly, he crossed the distance between them and pulled her into his arms. She tensed, but the heat of Beckett's body was too tempting to fight. He smoothed a hand over her hair. "What happened last night—and every time before—had nothing to do with Lydia. That was all us. I know the situation is hardly ideal, but I'll do everything I can to ensure you come out of this with your reputation intact."

She wanted to believe him. She *did* believe him. But promising that she'd see the other side of this trouble without a scandal was different from saying she'd reach the other side with *him*. Samara rested her head against his chest and focused on breathing deeply for several moments.

This was not her.

She saw what she wanted and she fought hard until she achieved it. She did not waffle or bitch or whine about how life was inherently unfair. Life *was* unfair. It always had been. Instead of railing about how shitty that was, she should be focused on tipping the scales in her favor.

She inhaled the clean scent of him. "I never planned on this getting so complicated. You're the absolute worst person I could be in danger of falling for."

"That's how it always seems to work." His lips brushed the shell of her ear. "It's good that you're in danger of falling for me, because I'm already halfway there for you."

She opened her eyes. "Don't joke about this. I know I'm being ridiculously sentimental. Just give me a few minutes and I'll be back to normal." *With shields firmly in place.*

"Samara." He cupped her face, urging her up to meet his gaze. "I'm not joking." He brushed a kiss against her lips. "Let me take you out on a real date. We'll talk about anything that isn't connected to Morningstar and Kingdom Corp. We'll eat good food and maybe drink a little too much good wine and laugh a little too loud."

It sounded like a perfect night. She frowned. "But shouldn't you be working on your proposal? I know it's three days away and you probably have everything all ironed out, but at least pretend you're a mere mortal who has to practice before the presentation."

Something like guilt flickered over his face, then it was gone too fast for her to be sure. Beckett shook his head. "It will hold for one night."

She wanted so badly to say yes. *Then say yes.* "Yes."

He gave her another brief kiss. "Breakfast is here. Eat with me. Tell me what made you call yesterday."

The reminder of the suspicions she had to deliver damp-ened her good mood. "Okay."

He took her hand and tugged her toward the kitchen. "Whatever it is, we'll figure it out. I promise. You aren't alone, Samara."

Beckett waited to question Samara while they ate breakfast, and then he waited some more. Her conflict was written all over her face, which was all he needed to see to know that

Lydia was the reason she was there. He doubted his aunt sent Samara with false information, which meant she'd done something shitty.

He glanced at the manila folder Frank had left. It had pictures of Lydia sitting at a table with his father in what appeared to be a heated conversation. While he'd half hoped to see some evidence of her spiking his father's drink, there was nothing as damning as that. Judging by the time stamps on the photos, they had been taken two short hours before his father died. There was no evidence of a meal, but they both had drinks at the table. It seemed to give lie to his aunt's story, but there was nothing that couldn't be explained away if she was creative enough.

"I think Lydia had something to do with the fire."

Beckett froze, his mug of coffee halfway to his mouth. "What did you say?"

"Lydia." Samara poked at her omelet. "Did you tell her about the fire?"

"She already knew." The time for holding back information was past. He had to decide now—did he trust Samara enough to tell her everything he knew? Or was he going to keep her close while trying to dissemble? Beckett had his answer before he'd finished the thought. "She came by to see me Sunday as the fire inspector was leaving. We didn't talk specifically about the fire for the most part—it was just more of the manipulative bullshit that the Kings are known for."

"Beckett... you're a King."

He was a King, but that didn't mean he wanted to be lumped in with _all_ the insanity. Some of it was impossible to avoid, but that didn't mean he had to sink to Lydia's level. _Kind of like you sank to her level when you went around_ *the bidding process and secured the renewal of the government contract.* He could argue that it was different until he was blue in the face, but it didn't change the fact that he *had* pulled a shitty-ass move. "Yes, I'm a King."

Samara seemed to chew on that for a moment. "What did the fire inspector have to say?"

"It was definitely started intentionally. If the lobby wasn't mostly marble and steel, it would have spread a lot faster and we might not be having this conversation today. The building wasn't locked up completely—anyone with a key could have gotten in, and that puts the suspect list at over a hundred people." He saw the question forming and answered it. "No, to the best of my knowledge, Lydia doesn't have a key." Unless one of his defecting employees had passed theirs along—or allowed their key to be duplicated.

She seemed to read between the lines of what he wasn't saying. "But several of the people she poached from you did."

"All of them did." There had been only a few short hours between watching Walter walk out and the fire being set, but it was entirely possible that Lydia had started poaching people earlier. Beckett had been gone for six months on his last overseas project, but his father would have informed him of any big changes—and that included changes to the executive staff. There had been none, which meant Lydia had barely waited for his father's body to cool before she started moving in on his employees.

Samara dropped her fork and pushed to her feet. "She knew the fire was started in an employee break room off the main floor, and she acted like she knew exactly how much was—and wasn't—destroyed. How could she know that, Beckett?"

She stalked around his couch, the very picture of fury in motion. "And when I had the audacity to question her, she removed me from the bidding project. I've been preparing *months* for the damn presentation and she just...gave it to Journey."

Relief swamped him, guilt nipping at its heels. He had no business being glad that Samara was currently unattached to the contract he'd taken. She'd been dealt a shitty hand and even if he'd had no part of the crap that morning, he'd still acted against her best interests by making his move.

"Maybe she..." He almost suggested she'd overheard him talking with the fire investigator, but that wasn't right. Lydia hadn't arrived until after. "I don't know. She's got me so damn paranoid, I'm not sure what she is or isn't capable of at this point. Why would she set a fire while knowing you were in the building?"

"Because ultimately I'm expendable." She said it so matter-of-factly, as if it wasn't surprising in the least.

"That's bullshit. You're not expendable. You're a person, and you've been nothing but loyal to her for years."

She shrugged with a sad smile. "Beckett, you think your aunt might have had something to do with your father's death. Compared to orchestrating your own brother's death, what's potentially harming an employee?"

He walked to her and took her hands. "We don't know anything for sure." He didn't know why he was arguing, only that Samara looked brittle for the first time since he'd met her and it scared the shit out of him. She'd allowed herself to be vulnerable with him when they'd had sex and immediately afterward, and she'd trusted him enough the night before to sleep in his arms and then tell him her suspicions about Lydia. None of that could have been easy for her, not with the impressive walls she kept between herself and the rest of the world.

Or just between herself and me.

It didn't matter. What mattered was that she'd let him in and he wanted to keep her safe. "Quit. Even if you don't take the job I've offered you, quit Kingdom Corp. If you're really that disposable to her, then she's not worth your loyalty."

"It's not that simple." She leaned up and kissed him lightly. "And while I appreciate the offer, I'd be just as disposable working for you as I am working for her."

"No."

"Yes," she countered gently. "All employees are disposable to one degree or another. I might be less so than some, but ultimately there are plenty of people out there who can do my job. That's not even getting into the messy complications around the fact that we're sleeping together."

Where the fuck was this coming from? The Samara he'd known up to this point was fierce in her ambition and she'd had no problem taking credit where credit was due. The look on her face, the way she described herself—it was almost defeatist.

Anything he said would be viewed through the lens that she viewed him through—the heir to one of the biggest oil companies in the country. Someone she wasn't sure she could relate to.

"Come away with me."

Samara raised her eyebrows. "That's not a solution."

"It's not meant to be a solution. It's meant to be a reprieve." He hesitated, thinking fast. "I have to take a day trip to LA. I was going to put it off, but the timing is perfect. At the very least, it will get us both out of here for a bit." Beckett leaned down. "And if you're willing, we can make it an overnight trip."

Samara sighed. "It's really not a good idea."

"When has anything between us been a good idea?" He ran his hands down her arms. "If you stay in Houston, what will you be doing for the next twenty-four hours?"

She rolled her eyes. "I'll be sitting in my apartment, driving myself crazy because I don't know what's going on at Kingdom Corp while I'm not there, and probably calling Journey a dozen times and annoying her with unsolicited advice about the proposal."

There it was again, the flicker of guilt. He didn't know if it was better or worse that she no longer helmed the bid from Kingdom Corp. *I did what I had to do.* Strangely enough, that didn't make him feel like any less of a dick. Saying it was just business didn't excuse him, either, because it *wasn't* just business between him and Samara. It hadn't been since they slept together the first time.

Samara sighed, drawing him out of his head. "I suppose there's no legitimate reason to stay."

He stroked her hair back from her face. "If you don't want to—"

"No!" She flushed. "I mean, I do. It just feels...I don't know. Decadent. Forbidden. Like a mistake waiting to happen."

"How about an agreement—we won't talk business for the duration of the trip."

She wrinkled her nose. "I thought this was a business trip."

"It is, but that just means you'll need to entertain yourself for an hour or two while I take my meeting. The rest of my time is yours. We'll go on that date I promised you."

While he trusted that she wasn't fully under Lydia's spell any longer, there were some things Beckett couldn't leave to chance.

Samara looked like she wanted to ask for more details but finally nodded. "I'll go. I just need to stop by my place and pack an overnight bag."

"Perfect." He couldn't resist kissing her a moment longer. Not when they were so close, and not when they might as well have been holding hands on the edge of a cliff, daring each other to jump. Samara melted against him at that first contact. All he had to do was take two big steps back and he'd hit his couch and they could lose themselves in each other for a few hours.

But there was a plane to catch.

Reluctantly, he gentled his kisses until they were the barest brushing of his lips against Samara's. Finally, finally, he lifted his head. "If we keep going like this, we'll never make it to LA."

"Screw LA." She kissed his jaw. "They're all crazy in that city."

He chuckled. "If ever I forgot you were Texas born and raised..."

She went stiff and stepped away. "Yeah, Texas all the way down to my bones." Her laugh sounded forced, though.

"Samara." He waited for her to look at him. Beckett recognized the conflict lurking in her dark eyes. He'd seen it in the mirror often enough over the years. He mentally retraced what he'd said, and it all but confirmed there was some sort of familial conflict. "You can talk to me. If you want."

She opened her mouth, seemed to reconsider, and shut it. "I'm afraid I'm horribly cliché. Daddy issues."

He ignored the attempt at a joke. "If there's anyone in this town who knows daddy issues, it's me."

"And Lydia."

His aunt's name fell like a stone into a still pool, the ripples washing away the rest of his feel-good from the night before. The ever-present reminder that he didn't really have a claim on Samara. Not professionally, that was for damn sure. Not even personally, because Lydia might like to dangle Samara in front of him as some kind of distraction, but she'd lose her shit if she thought for a second that Samara actually cared for him. It would be her father choosing Nathaniel over her all over again.

He didn't like to think what might happen then. If she'd actually gone so far as to kill his father, she wouldn't hesitate to hurt Samara—especially if it would hurt Beckett in the process.

He bit back the demand for her to quit. Samara wouldn't take orders from him now any more than she had a few days ago. Her independence and take-no-shit attitude were things that drew him to her, but the closer they circled, the more danger she might be in.

If Lydia had essentially kicked her out of the office for a week, it was already too late. She was tainted by her questions, by her proximity to Beckett. He couldn't let her be hurt. He had to stop his aunt before it got that far.

Beckett took a measured breath. "If you want to talk—really talk—then I'm here. I can't promise I won't poke at it a little because it's a part of you and I want to know every part of you."

"For God's sake." Samara laughed, a little too high to be natural. "You can't just say things like that."

"Coming on too strong." He grinned and hooked her

around the waist, bringing them chest to chest again. "I hate to break it to you, Samara, but I like you. A lot. If you want to tell me to get lost, I'll respect that, but if you're still making up your mind, I'm going to seduce the hell out of you in the meantime."

Her strong brows came together as she frowned. "I already agreed to go to LA with you. No seduction required."

"I'm not trying to seduce you out of your pants." He kissed one corner of her mouth and then the other. *I'm trying to seduce you out of your heart.*

CHAPTER THIRTEEN

Samara wasn't the least bit surprised when Beckett drove them to a private hangar instead of the main airport later that morning. It stood to reason that, since Lydia had a private jet, the other side of the King family would as well. She marveled silently that this was her life—had been for several years now.

Granted, climbing the steps into the plane with Beckett's presence behind her was a whole lot different from taking a business trip with Lydia or Journey. He hadn't touched her since he'd talked of seduction. He'd been absorbed in his phone at her place when she showered and packed an overnight bag, and she was pathetically relieved not to have all of his attention focused solely on her.

She liked it too much.

She liked *him* too much.

All the careful rules she'd used to guide her life were under one grand umbrella of a rule—do *not* end up like her mother. She loved her mother beyond all others, but it was no secret that a bright star had been dimmed by the damage Samara's father did when he left. There were other single mothers who had gone back to school, who had pushed through to realize the dreams they'd always had. Maybe a bit late, but what did time matter in the grand scheme of things?

Not her *amma*.

Amma seemed content enough with life, but Samara couldn't help seeing what could have been—what *should* have been. If Devansh Patel hadn't professed his undying love and then turned around and dropped her like yesterday's news. If she hadn't been pregnant with Samara when he did. If, if, if.

"You're thinking awfully hard over there."

"It seems to be the day for it." She stroked a hand down the smooth leather seats. The inside of the plane could have been a posh interior room in some resort. So much money and for what? So the King families didn't have to fly with the rest of the rabble.

Samara was the rabble. She couldn't afford to forget that.

Beckett took her hand, his thumb absently playing along her knuckles. "I don't think we're as different as you like to pretend."

Oh, this should be good. "How do you figure?"

"We're both walking middle fingers to our fathers, aren't we?"

She jerked back, but he kept her hand captive. She felt like he'd flayed her first layer of skin away with a few short words, leaving her one exposed nerve in the process. Words crowded against her lips, harsh and petty and guaranteed to slam the distance back between them before he could see how easily he could hurt her. "How?" Was that hoarse, wrecked thing her voice? *Do better.* She cleared her throat. "How did you know?"

He kept up that soothing touch, granting her the relative privacy of staring out the window as Houston dropped away beneath the plane. "Like recognizes like. I was never cold enough for my father. After my mother died, he didn't even mourn. He just systematically erased all evidence of her from our lives—from Thistledown—and he never forgave me for not being willing to do the same." Beckett shook his head. "When I was in college, I had this epiphany. I realized that the whole purge was his grief taking hold, and while I understand that, I didn't know if *I* could forgive *him*. He had a choice after she died. We both did. We just ended up on different paths that never quite met no matter how hard I tried. So I stopped trying."

"Then what happened?" The words were dragged from her by a curiosity she couldn't quell. A *recognition*. She realized she already knew the answer. "You resolved to be better than he'd ever been—and to do it your way instead of his."

"Yeah." Beckett chuckled. "Pissed him off like you wouldn't believe. We became the immovable object and the unstoppable force. It didn't matter if we both wanted the same future for Morningstar—we wanted it to come about in different ways. It took all of three months of working in the office together to realize we'd bring the company down if we didn't get some distance from each other, which is why I took over the overseas areas of the business. It worked out better that way."

"I'm sorry, Beckett." She'd said it before, and she suspected she'd say it again more than a few times. Samara wasn't sure if it was better or worse that he'd recognized that his father was just a broken and angry man instead of some monster without feeling—or if he'd walked her path instead.

He brought her hand to his lips and pressed a slow kiss to her knuckles. To the ring she wore on her right hand. "No reason to be sorry. If he'd been less determined to forge me in a fire of his choosing, we would have had something resembling a normal relationship." His tone took on a wistful note. "We both loved her. There was no damn reason that I had to be left squirreling away evidence of her existence in that house like a damn smuggler. We should have been able to remember her together—to have a bond because of shared loss." Beckett shook his head. "But that's a child's plea. It doesn't matter anymore."

She stared at the seat in front of them. The white leather was stitched together with gold thread, a reminder that Lydia was a King, and had been raised with the same playbook Nathaniel had. There was such a thing as a bad egg, but Samara wasn't blind enough to her boss's faults to assume that was the case in this situation.

She very determinedly set thoughts of Lydia aside and focused on the here and now. "I never got the chance to know my father."

"I'm sorry."

She pressed her lips together. "Oh, he's not dead. He lives in Dallas with his wife and three daughters."

Beckett's thumb paused before it resumed its path on the back of her hand. "Ah."

Samara had expected his sympathy to sting, to feel like pity, but there was a deep understanding in that single word. A kinship. It was enough to keep her talking, digging into the past and that soul wound she'd never quite gotten to the other side of despite so many years of trying. "He and my *amma* met in college. He was handsome and rich and from a prominent Indian family with a long and honorable history. It was love, at least on her side of things." She glanced down at the ring on her right hand. "Maybe it was even love on his side as well. He proposed—a secret engagement that they didn't tell either of their families about. But love has never been enough. I don't know which version of the story is more tragic—that he played my *amma* and as soon as she got pregnant he lost interest in the game and moved on. Or that he really loved her, but was too weak to stand up to his family when they demanded he break off the engagement."

"Shit, Samara."

She kept going because to stop now was to leave the story unfinished. If she didn't keep talking, she might never start again. "Her family disowned her when they found out she was pregnant. Spurned by the blessed Patel family and pregnant with a bastard child? Unacceptable." Some days she put serious thought into tracking down her *amma*'s parents just to prove to them what horrible people they were for leaving their daughter to hang in the wind. Ultimately, though, they didn't matter any more than her sperm donor did.

She laced her fingers through Beckett's, not looking at him because even if he understood, she couldn't risk seeing pity in his eyes. "She gave up her future so that I could have one. She worked her ass off under god-awful conditions to make sure I never went without. This..." She motioned at everything and nothing. "I can't fail, because if I fail then I'm failing her."

"And the ring?"

Of course he'd noticed the ring. She stared at it, at the simple gold band and the shiny emerald that she'd always loved as much as she'd hated. "My *amma* kept the ring he proposed with. She let me take it when I graduated. I think she wanted it to be an apology of sorts, even if it wasn't my father doing the apologizing. I wear it because it's a reminder of what's at stake."

"Have you ever thought about trying to meet him?"

She shook her head even as her stomach dropped. "No. He hasn't shown any interest in my life up to this point. Even if I could forgive him for what he did to my *amma*—and I can't—then what respect do I have for a man who hasn't been there for thirty-two years? No." She shook her head again, more firmly this time. "He's not worth the time we took for this conversation, let alone the effort it would require to attempt a meeting."

"Monster fathers and saintly mothers." He squeezed her hand. "See, I told you we had plenty in common."

Samara loved him, just a little, in that moment. For dispelling the tension, for taking her messy past without pointing out all the holes in her ambition. For just... being there. If she didn't think too hard about it, she could lean on this man when the world became too heavy to bear.

They could lean on each other.

Dangerous, tempting thoughts.

For the first time, she didn't shove them away as soon as they entered her mind. Instead, she turned them over, examining them from every angle. Beckett wasn't her father—he wasn't *his* father, either. Samara was most definitely not a college student with no power of her own. Were they equals in the world's eyes? No. Definitely not.

But if they were equals— really equals—when they were together, then who cared what anyone else's opinion was?

"Take me out tonight, Beckett."

He shifted to face her, still holding her hand. "Anywhere you want to go."

"I don't want to pick. Surprise me. A real date."

His slow grin had her stomach doing a somersault. "Consider it done—on one condition."

Give him the benefit of the doubt. She took a steadying breath. "Okay. What condition?"

"For the night, we're not Samara Mallick and Beckett King. It's you and me as we are—none of the other bullshit."

It wasn't as easy as that, but the picture he presented was still so incredibly attractive. She leaned forward and ran a single finger down the center of his chest. "Deal." She stopped at the top of the band of his slacks. "How much time left in this flight?"

His gaze went white hot. "Long enough."

"Good answer."

Beckett didn't stop grinning all the way from the airport to the hotel. Every time he'd get himself under control, he'd take in Samara's swollen lips and the satisfied look in her eye and know he'd put it there. Then he'd start grinning again.

"Get control of yourself." But she was smiling, too.

The car pulled up to the curb outside the hotel, and Beckett moved quickly to climb out and open the door for Samara. She raised her eyebrows at him, but she didn't comment. He got their bags and guided her through the doors into the lobby. "I'll get you set up with the room and then I have to head to my meeting." He glanced at his watch. *Plenty of time.*

She looked around as they walked into the main lobby. "Do you usually book five-star hotels for a twenty-four-hour business trip?"

"Fuck no." He slipped an arm around her waist. "I usually use one of the Morningstar condos." Beckett kissed her temple. "But this trip isn't all about business."

"I see."

He let her process that while he checked them in. Next stop was the suite. They took the elevator up, and he caught her watching him. "What?"

"Are you trying to impress me?"

He grinned. "Nope. We both know you could book this place as easily as I could." He leaned down and kissed her bare shoulder. "Want to know a secret?"

"Always."

"The reason I chose this place specifically is because I love the ocean. It feels different than the Gulf. Wilder. Less contained. The views from this room are amazing, and the last time I decided to take a break from work and spend some time here, I sat on the balcony for hours and watched the tide come in."

She reached up and touched his face. "A secret for a secret?"

"Always," he said, echoing her earlier response.

"The ocean scares the shit out of me. All open water does. I could live in a swimming pool, but the second I can't see the entirety of the body of water I'm in, I'm out of there."

He liked this game, liked this careful peeling away of their defenses as they shared little details. The conversation in the plane had been heavy, and that was important, too. But this was something special. Something they did only with each other.

Beckett shifted closer. "Did you watch a lot of *Jaws* as a kid?"

"When I was eleven, my *amma* decided I was old enough

to fend for myself while she worked Saturdays, and one of those weekends, there was a monster marathon. *Jaws*, *Piranha*, *Anaconda*. Back to back."

He barked out a laugh. "I could see how that would leave a mark."

The elevator doors dinged and opened. They walked out arm in arm, turning as one down the hallway to the suite he'd booked. *This is how it could be with us. The small moments and the big. Facing down each obstacle as a single unit.*

He couldn't offer her a job again. She wouldn't say yes now any more than she'd said yes up to this point, but at least now he understood why. In Samara's mind, taking a job with him while they were sleeping together put her at his mercy the same way her mother had been at her father's mercy when she got pregnant. It wasn't even close to the same situation, but he understood why it felt similar.

The suite was similar to ones he'd used in the past—a very high-end airy feel with large windows overlooking the beach. The ocean stretched as far as the eye could see, and even that one glimpse settled something inside him. He felt Samara's gaze and spoke without looking over. "Some days, I really consider leaving it all, buying a little house on a beach somewhere, and starting over."

She came up behind him and slipped her arms around his waist. Samara propped her chin on his shoulder. "What's stopping you?"

"It's the coward's way out. I didn't choose this life, but it's mine. I'm uniquely qualified to make changes within Morningstar, and it's my responsibility to see it done." He could sell the company—had threatened to do exactly that once in a fight with his father—but it wasn't the right call. Most days, Beckett even loved his job.

He didn't love what would come next in this conflict with Lydia, though.

With a sigh, he turned and took Samara's hands, dropping a kiss to first one and then the other. "I have to go if I'm going to make my meeting." He paused. "Why don't you take advantage of the superior spa they have onsite? It'll be a real vacation." It was the least he could do after the insanity of the last few days.

"I might just do that." She gave him a playful push. "Text me when you're done and we'll go somewhere for dinner."

"Deal." He forced himself to release her and headed for the door. The car was waiting for him, as requested, and he took a short drive parallel to the beach to Marina del Rey. Following the instructions he'd been given, Beckett made his way to a massive yacht tied to the end of one of the docks. Its name was written across the side in classy blue font. *The Queen Bitch.*

This is the place.

Movement on the top deck caught his attention. A thin man in a pair of swim trunks and boat shoes leaned over the railing. Judging from his tanned skin, he spent most of his time on the yacht. Silver seeded through his hair, peppering the dark brown, and though his eyes were hidden by sunglasses, Beckett knew they were blue. *Elliott Bancroft, Lydia's husband.*

"Beckett King."

"Uncle Elliott."

The man burst out laughing. "Don't start with that family bullshit. Come on up."

Beckett studied the interior of the yacht as he made his

way up three floors to where his uncle waited. He'd only ever been on one once, years ago, and everything had been gold plated and decorated within an inch of its life. In such a small space, it left Beckett feeling claustrophobic and wanting to put as much distance between himself and the yacht as possible.

This wasn't the same at all. Everything from the floor beneath his seat to the trim lining the windows to the furniture in the rooms he passed were all top of the line. Their understated luxury screamed money, but only if one knew where to look. *Part of the inside joke in the perpetual bullshit between new money and old.*

Elliott had acquired a cocktail—a Manhattan from the look of it—and he toasted Beckett. "What do you think of the old bitch?"

"Nice place. You live here?" He already knew the answer, but lording his knowledge of the man over Elliott wasn't going to win him any favors. He needed his uncle on his side, and from the research he'd done on the man, all evidence indicated that Elliott Bancroft liked to consider himself the smartest person in the room at all times.

"For now." Elliott took him in. "You have the look of your old man. Same stubborn expression and that jaw that makes the ladies weak in the knees. Shame to hear he died." The sheer glee in his voice gave lie to the words.

There isn't a damn person in this world actually sad to see Nathaniel King gone.

"He left Lydia Thistledown Villa."

Elliott straightened and whistled. "Well, shit. She actually pulled it off." He grabbed a pack of cigarettes from a little cubby next to the captain's chair. "You mind?"

"Go ahead." Beckett waited for him to light up. "What do you mean she pulled it off?"

"Lydia always said she'd get that damn house back." He inhaled deeply, held the smoke for a few moments, and exhaled through his nose. "She couldn't handle being cut off all those years ago. It drove her out of her mind, and she wasn't completely sane to begin with."

Beckett could think of a few choice words to describe his aunt, but crazy didn't come into the equation. There was nothing uncontrolled or insane about her actions—she was cold and calculating and perfectly aware of what was at stake every step of the way. "How do you think she managed it? The will was changed right around the time my father died." It was one thing he couldn't make fit in the rest of the puzzle. Lydia wanted Morningstar or, barring that, she wanted to bring it down brick by brick. Every single one of her moves up to this point had been inching them toward that goal. But if she'd somehow managed to manipulate Nathaniel into handing over his family home, why not go for the company as well?

"That's the question, isn't it?" Elliott dragged in more cigarette smoke. He tipped his sunglasses back onto the top of his head and stared at Beckett. "Let me paint you a scenario and you tell me how far off I am."

He bit back his frustration. He hadn't come there for more games. He'd come because Elliott Bancroft had a bone to pick with his wife, and even with their spending more time apart than together, they'd been married thirty-two years. If there was anyone who knew Lydia, it was her husband.

Beckett dropped into the seat across from the man. "I'm listening."

"I imagine she's been seeding malcontent with someone within your company for years, dropping little bits of poison in their ears until they're sure night is day and day is night. She's good at playing roles to get what she wants." Something dark flickered over his face, and he tapped the cigarette into an ashtray. "This man—and ten-to-one it was a man—slips something into Nathaniel's drink during a meeting. Nothing serious. Just something to make him a little more *agreeable*. Then they change the will and make it official with two witnesses, both of whom she owns."

Beckett went cold. He pictured Walter Trissel's stammering, red-flushed face when he read the will. *No point to contest it. I stood as witness.* Fast-forward to two days later when Walter left the company for Kingdom Corp. He'd known the man was disloyal, but drugging Nathaniel crossed so many lines. There hadn't been anything in his system but alcohol the night he died, but this would have happened up to a week beforehand. Plenty of time for any evidence to disappear. "Why not just take the whole company at that point?"

"She only fights when she knows she can win. It would be logical for Nathaniel to will her that damn house, but if he gave her everything, that would raise too many red flags. I'm sure she's got some kind of backup plan in place."

A backup plan like convincing Beckett to sell the company.

He sat back. "That's quite the story, but it doesn't mean a damn thing without proof." He had theories for days, but a theory wasn't enough to help him at this point. The photos Frank provided didn't mean anything in the long run now that Lydia had changed her story. He could—and would—

put pressure on Walter, but that meant he had to get the man alone first.

"It's how she operates. If you look back through her history, there are a trail of people—again, mostly men—who have been at her mercy because of events she orchestrated. I was always surprised she didn't try the same song and dance on her father, but maybe he was on to her games." Elliott shrugged. "Or maybe passing over her for CEO was punishment for the shit she'd stirred up with my family."

He frowned. "What do you mean? I was under the impression the Bancrofts and Lydia were on good terms." *Except for Elliott's near-constant affairs.*

"Who do you think her first victim was, Beckett?" Elliott snubbed out his cigarette. "We were friends, once upon a time, but she wanted more and I didn't. She took matters into her own hands, and when it came out that she was pregnant, there was nothing to do but marry her."

Beckett stared. What he was saying...what he was accusing Lydia of? "But you stayed married."

"Bancrofts aren't quitters, nephew. If I walked out on her, I stood to lose everything. Over the years, we fell into what passed for a comfortable arrangement, but I still can't stand to be in the same room as that woman."

There were two sides to every story. Beckett might think his aunt was damn near evil, but he seriously doubted that Elliott was some babe in the woods who'd fallen prey to her. It was far more likely that he'd always been a philanderer and his family had jumped at the chance to make him someone else's problem. But if even part of what he said was true, Beckett needed to have a conversation with Walter Trissel—sooner rather than later. His former attorney might be brilliant in court, but he was a weak man with weak impulses. If

Beckett found something to leverage against him, he could get the man to talk. He was sure of it.

"Thanks for your time." Beckett stood and considered his uncle. "If you were going to hit Lydia where it hurt, where would you aim?"

Elliott threw back his head and laughed. "Good luck, nephew. That would require Lydia to have a fucking heart."

CHAPTER FOURTEEN

Samara put her time to good use while Beckett was gone. If this was going to be a break from reality and a date at the same time, she wanted it to be a damn good date. The *best* date. She chatted up the bellman and got the best restaurant within easy traveling distance—a place just up the beach— and then she went shopping.

It was frivolous and silly to want to wow Beckett, but she couldn't just sit in the hotel room and wait for him to come back. As she flipped through dress options at a little boutique the bellman had recommended, she gave in to the temptation to call Journey. Just to check in.

Right.

Her friend answered as if she'd been waiting by the phone, "Thank *God*. Samara, I swear to all that's holy, you scare me sometimes."

Samara considered a red dress and set it back on the rack. "You're looking through the notes for the bid."

"Of course I'm looking through the notes for the bid. I've been doing nothing but wading through your notes since I picked them up this morning. Seriously, honey, we have to talk about your research habits. You have *two* binders full of information."

"There's a 'CliffsNotes' version in the smaller of the two. I put all the pertinent information there for easy reference." She frowned at a sequined gown that looked like it belonged in a bridal shop. "If you need me to come back—"

"Nope. I don't care what my mother's reasons were for forcing you to take a break, but I do support the end result. You work your ass off for Kingdom Corp. You might as well enjoy those vacation days you've saved up and let your hair down." She paused and lowered her voice. "Are you still with Beckett?"

"Not currently, but yes." Her gaze landed on a dark purple dress and she lifted the hanger to get a better look at it. *Perfect.* "I . . . I kind of like him."

"Honey, I know you do. Just be careful, okay?"

"I will," she promised, though it felt like lying through her teeth. Samara had left careful behind days ago. She was in a full free fall and she couldn't bring herself to care about the fast-approaching ground.

Journey snorted. "Somehow, I just don't believe you. But that's neither here nor there." The amusement disappeared from her tone. "Mother has leveled the direst of threats against me if I screw up your presentation—her disappointment. She's in danger of micromanaging, but you'll be happy to know that I've kept my temper in check. Mostly."

If they hadn't been friends for so many years, Samara wouldn't have picked up on the thread of tension in Journey's voice. Everyone had their hot-button issues. For Samara, it was her father. For Journey, it was *both* her parents.

She glanced around, but no one was paying her the slightest bit of attention. "You can do this. You're even better at this job than I am, and I'm fucking great at my job."

"This isn't my forte, Samara. I'm better at telling people what to do and managing the bullshit that crops up when the different departments start butting heads. Hell, I'd rather deal with the media than *this*."

Samara drifted toward the back of the boutique, her dress in hand. "Are you at home?"

"...Yes. Though if you're about to ask me what I'm wearing, we're going to talk about your phone sex skills."

She laughed. "You know that giant atrocity of a mirror in your front hall? Go stand in front of that."

"Kinky."

"Shut up and do what I say."

"Yes, mistress." Heels clicked in the distance as Journey must have stood and walked to the mirror. Samara could picture the mirror perfectly. It was easily seven feet tall and three feet wide, and its one-foot-wide metal frame only made it seem more massive. Journey huffed out a breath. "Okay, I'm staring at my mirror and feeling like an idiot."

"Repeat after me."

"Oh, no. Samara—"

"I am a badass, capable woman and I'm going to make this bid my bitch."

Silence for a beat. "Do I have to scream it like Jerry Maguire?"

She laughed. "I don't think that will be necessary. Now, stop stalling and say it."

"I am a badass, capable woman and I'm going to make this bid my bitch!" Journey dissolved into giggles. "Okay, I don't hold to the positive affirmation stuff, but I feel slightly better. Thanks. This thing has me all twisted up. It's wrong that I'm doing this, Sam. It should be you."

It should *be me.* She wouldn't say it. Not to Journey. It wasn't her friend's fault that Lydia had pulled this bullshit a couple days before the presentation date. Lamenting about how upset she was to lose her place would only serve to make Journey feel like shit and cause conflict between the two King women. There would be other bids and other contracts to secure.

She hoped.

If she didn't get fired.

If Lydia wasn't implicated in Nathaniel's death or the fire set in Morningstar Enterprise's building.

She gave herself a shake. *Stop borrowing trouble.* "You're going to do great."

"Nice dodge." Journey sighed. "I guess I should get back to it." Her tone perked up. "What are you doing right now? Something interesting? You should tell me all about it."

"Not a chance. Kick ass in your presentation and I'll share all the illicit details over drinks. My treat."

"Actually, on second thought, if those illicit details involve my cousin, I don't think I want to know."

Samara laughed. "Bye, Journey. Call me if you need anything."

"Have fun!"

She slipped her phone into her purse and eyed the jewelry display at the back of the store. The dress she'd picked had a plunging neckline that just begged for some kind of adornment. For shoes, her black heels would work perfectly, and she could take her time getting ready.

Beckett wouldn't know what hit him.

*   *   *

Samara was gone when Beckett got back to the hotel suite. He found a note set out on the table. *Meet me at 1898. 7 pm. Don't be late.* It was signed with the imprint of her lipstick in a perfect kiss. He checked the time. Six thirty. 1898 was a ten-minute walk from the hotel, which gave him enough time to take a quick shower and change.

It didn't explain why Samara wasn't here, though.

He sent a quick text as he pulled out another suit. *You okay?*

Yes. Why wouldn't I be?

The same way she'd responded when they spoke on the phone last. Beckett exhaled his tension. Samara was fine. She wasn't in any danger just because he couldn't see her. She'd been alone for a couple hours and she hadn't come to any harm. He typed out a quick response. *See you at 7.*

I'll be there.

He got ready in record time and actually enjoyed the walk. The humidity that plagued Houston was nowhere to be found here, and the ocean breeze actually felt refreshing. Despite his meeting with Elliott Bancroft, he found himself smiling and picking up his pace. As he came up the stairs to the restaurant's deck, he caught sight of Samara and stopped short.

She leaned against the railing, watching the waves roll toward the beach. Her black heels made her legs look even longer than normal, and he let himself look his fill. The dress was a deep purple that set off her brown skin and it hugged her ass in a way that begged to be touched.

A board creaked under his shoes, and she glanced over and smiled at him. "Beckett."

The dress was even better from the front. It dipped low between her breasts and she wore a long necklace of several knotted strands of pearls. Her hair drifted in the breeze and he didn't bother to resist the urge to walk to her and sink his hands into the dark waves. "Hey."

She ran her hands up his chest. "Hey."

"I like the dress."

Samara smiled. "Good."

"I'll like it even better when I'm peeling it off you as I kiss every inch of your body." He brushed his lips against hers. "Let's get dinner to go."

"Ah-ah. No way. You can spend all night sexing me up. Right now, I want to eat food that I've been assured is amazing and talk with you."

Beckett considered kissing her again, but she was right—he wanted to talk to her. They'd already proved they matched up in the bedroom. He wanted to *know* her. "Tell me another secret."

She laughed. "New Year's Day is my favorite holiday."

"I'm going to need an explanation." He shifted back and slid his arm around her waist. They walked easily toward the front door.

It wasn't until they were seated at a table overlooking the beach through a large window that Samara spoke again. "I never drink on New Year's Eve. It's a silly superstition, but I think what you bring into the new year becomes a self-fulfilling prophecy. I get up early on the first and drink my first cup of coffee out on my balcony and try to be mindful about what I want the next year to be. Then I go to my *amma*'s for breakfast, and around the time I'm finished with dishes, Journey is rolling out of bed, so we spend the rest of the day together."

"That sounds like a great tradition." When he'd first met her, he'd assumed Samara was like a pillar—strong as fuck and separated from everyone around her. It comforted Beckett to know that she had a good friend in his cousin. That she had roots as deep as his, if different.

"It is." She toyed with her water glass. "A secret for a secret?"

He liked this game. It was theirs and theirs alone, another thread linking them together. "What I wanted most in the world when I was in kindergarten was to be a trainer at SeaWorld."

"Orcas or dolphins?"

He loved that she asked it with a straight face. Beckett answered just as seriously. "Orcas, of course. My mother took me there one weekend and I was convinced that the trainers were magic. It seemed like the most amazing thing in the world for them to work with such massive, majestic creatures." He made a face. "That was before I grew up enough to realize what a tragedy it is to keep those animals in captivity."

Samara pressed her lips together. "You donate to PETA, don't you?"

"I can't abide by some of their policies." When she just stared, he huffed out a breath. "I donate to a small group of scientists that are funding research to prove how harmful captivity is for orcas."

"Oh, Beckett." She smiled. "You really are a white knight, aren't you?"

He didn't know what to do with that look on her face, as if he was someone admirable. "What's the point of having all this money and influence if I just sit on it and watch it multiply? The oil industry is problematic in a whole different way. I can't change things all at once, but keeping the status quo is a mistake." It was something he and his father never quite saw eye to eye on. Nathaniel wasn't opposed to clean energy, but he only saw the money to be made—he didn't worry about their planet or what life might be like for future generations if they continued down this path.

If anything, the admiration in her eyes grew. Samara leaned forward, fully engaged in the topic. "What changes? Are you thinking of making the lateral move to clean energy?"

"Eventually. It's not realistic to get out of oil completely, no matter how shitty I think the downsides are. But it's a finite resource and eventually the world is going to wise up to that fact. Renewable energy is one of the fastest-growing industries out there, and I want Morningstar to be on the cutting edge of that wave." He stopped short. "Shit, I'm sorry. I promised we wouldn't talk business, and that lasted a grand total of five minutes."

"This isn't business. This is hopes and dreams." She lowered her voice. "And secrets."

He searched her face, but there was nothing but honest curiosity there. "Are you interested in clean energy?"

"Only distantly. I've been so focused on doing my job that there's not much room left for the kind of research you're talking about." She shrugged one shoulder. "Beyond that, it's not my call to make. I don't head up any departments, and I'm not even part owner in Kingdom Corp. Employees might be the lifeblood of the company, but we don't have much control about the direction it goes in."

He started to press her, but stopped. *No business tonight.*

The waitress appeared at their table. As she went over the specials and wine selections, Beckett's attention kept drifting back to Samara. The dying sunset painted her in shadows, making her beauty look otherworldly. He wanted to touch her, to bring her back to earth, to keep her with him always.

Slow down. You don't have a right to ask her that, and if you do, it'll ruin the night.

Tomorrow they would go back to the viper's pit that Houston had become. He would track down Walter and put pressure on him in an effort to persuade the man to talk. Lydia would undoubtedly have some nasty surprise waiting for him. He'd doubled security on Morningstar before he left, but there was nothing stopping her from trying to bribe them away as well.

"Sir?"

He'd been staring instead of listening, but asking the waitress to repeat herself would just waste everyone's time. "I'll have the special with whatever wine you think would pair best."

She hesitated but seemed to understand that he didn't give a fuck what kind of wine she brought. "Sure thing."

Samara took a sip of her water. "Where did you go this afternoon?"

"I went to see Elliott Bancroft." It felt good to say it aloud, like he'd just removed a weight that had settled over him from the moment he decided to track down his aunt's husband. It was a low move, something his father would have been proud of. He told himself that fact didn't matter, but Beckett wasn't sure if he believed it.

"*What?* You're joking." She set her glass down and leaned closer. "Oh shit, you're not joking."

"I need more information on her—and I'm not going to keep putting you in the middle."

"News flash, Beckett—you're putting me in the middle right now." She picked up her cloth napkin and then set it down again. "Maybe this was a mistake."

"No. Wait." He held up a hand. "I'm sorry. That was out of line and I shouldn't have shared it."

"Don't you see? It's not about sharing or not sharing. You and she are diametrically opposed, and if you ask me to choose sides, you have to know which one I'm going to land on."

He did. He wished it wasn't the truth, but he did know. Beckett took her hand. "I'm sorry. Let's pretend it never happened."

"Fat chance of that."

The waitress swooped in with their wine, not a moment too soon. Beckett's was a bold red with faint spicy undertones. He waited for the woman to leave again before focusing on Samara. "When you were a kid, what did you want to be when you grew up?"

She hesitated, but finally relaxed. "I wanted to be a flight attendant." She took a hasty sip of her white wine. "There was this commercial that played all the time when I was . . . I don't know. Six or seven. I can't even remember what airline it was for, but the flight attendants were pictured visiting these exotic locales and traveling around the world. It seemed like a dream come true for me—to travel and be paid for it." She made a face. "And then I turned twelve and realized that flight attendants don't make much money and they spend all their time being harassed by asshole people on the plane, which pretty much killed that dream."

"That would do it." He chuckled. Beckett took another drink of his wine and turned the conversation away from anything resembling their current troubles. No business. No Lydia. Nothing too close to what put them on this path to begin with.

It was easy being with Samara.

So fucking easy.

Without their roles as rivals standing between them, he found her humor just as tempting as her intelligence and her drive. They traded embarrassing stories from their formative years. Her sewing her own prom dress and going stag when her date didn't show. His one and only game on the football team that ended with him getting into a fight with his own team's quarterback. By the time they'd finished their meal, both were relaxed and he'd actually managed to stop thinking about the shit show waiting for him back home.

After he paid, they made their way to the deck overlooking the ocean. Beckett took Samara's hand. "Walk with me."

"I'd like that."

CHAPTER FIFTEEN

The ocean spread before them in an endless dark swath that stretched to the horizon, hiding any number of mysteries. Overhead, the sky had darkened to a deep purple that edged on blue and the first stars winked into existence. With the sand cool beneath her feet and the soothing shush sound of the waves, something deep inside Samara relaxed.

She kept her gaze on the ocean, on the sky, on the beach. Anywhere but at the man beside her. If she looked at Beckett, she might take him up on the promise written across his face. She'd known this thing growing between them wasn't just the shadow of the inferno of chemistry created by their first night together. It was new and different and all the more dangerous because of it. That knowledge didn't seem to bother him in the least.

She was still deciding if it bothered her.

Liar. It was everything you could do not to throw yourself into his arms and confess that you never really got over him.

She could chalk her failed relationships up to her devotion to Kingdom Corp. She *had* done that. Every time she sat through another talk about how it wasn't working, or she pulled the trigger on ending a dying relationship, there was a niggling little voice in the back of her mind that said there was more to it. That she was waiting for someone.

That she was waiting for Beckett, even if she hadn't been aware it was *him* at the time.

None of her exes held a candle to the man holding her hand and seeming on the verge of telling her things she'd convinced herself she never wanted to hear from *his* lips. The racing of her heart gave lie to that. She wanted to hear it.

It just scared the shit out of her. To want it was to hope, and to hope was to set herself up for heartbreak.

You can't let yourself think like that. We've trusted each other with bigger things than our hearts in the last few days.

Samara moved to him and slipped under his arm. The darkness created a false sense of privacy, and the quiet shushing sound of the waves enclosed them. As long as they didn't look at the city sprawling out at their backs, they could pretend they were truly alone here. They could have been the last two people in the world.

It would have been a relief to have her choice taken away, for it to be just them and no one—nothing—else to interfere. They could have a life. They could spend years getting to know each other again and filling in the blanks of their pasts. There would be no crisis or anyone depending on them. No stakes in any game.

That wasn't their reality. It would *never* be their reality.

She had to either make her peace with that truth, or cut this thing off before it went any further. "I don't know what's happening. I don't know where we go from here."

"Why do we have to have a concrete plan?" He set his chin on the top of her head and cuddled her closer. "Life has a funny way of proving that we're not in control—we never will be. We can fake it, and lie to ourselves and say that we've got it all figured out, but then life comes along and flips the table to prove how wrong we were."

She stared into the night. "Thank you for that rousing pep talk."

"I wasn't done." Beckett chuckled. "My point is that any plan worth having *isn't* concrete. It's adjustable and has alternatives and backups to ensure you don't get caught with your pants down by the enemy."

She huffed. "You make it sound like we're going to war."

"War is life—at least the life we chose. There's no such thing as peace in the energy industry—oil or otherwise. There are always fights that require us to step to the line. That won't change, no matter what else does."

"Shouldn't we be striving for peace?" It seemed the question to ask, if only because she was still chewing on his words. Tasting them to see how they jibed with her worldview.

"Samara." He shifted so he could look down at her. "You can't bullshit a bullshitter. You wouldn't flourish in a peaceful environment any more than I would. We need the battles, whether it's in the boardroom or facing down the competition over a bid. We get off on it."

She opened her mouth to argue, but stopped. She'd never made a habit of lying to herself. She *did* enjoy those battles. Outmaneuvering problems as they arose and working through a situation to get what she needed. There was nothing else like it. "I'm not ashamed of that."

"Why would you be?" He traced her bottom lip with his thumb. "Some people were built for peace. They are comfortable in it, and they seek it out at all costs. We're not those kinds of people, which is a damn good thing because neither of our companies would last long if it was run by people who want to avoid conflict."

"How do two people who thrive in conflict even try to be together? Wouldn't it be a total shit show?"

His slow smile had her entire body warming. "Only one way to find out."

"Yeah, maybe." She didn't know. There was too much she didn't know how to deal with, but the one thing she *did* know was that this moment with this man felt right.

She turned her face into his chest and let him stroke her hair. It was time to admit that Beckett *saw* her. He knew her. He wanted and cared for her despite all her dark corners and emotional scars.

Or maybe, just maybe, he wanted and cared for her—at least in part—because of them.

Beckett wanted to bottle that moment and keep it with him always. He and Samara, standing on the beach and just…being. *It could be like this all the time if we'd let it.* He wouldn't convince her of that tonight, but she was slowly coming around. They had time. He wasn't wavering, and he had no problem waiting until she felt comfortable enough to give him the benefit of the doubt.

He shifted her hair off her neck and kissed her there. "Come to bed with me."

"That's my line." She spoke softly, as if already half asleep.

"If you're tired—"

Samara slid her hands up his chest and pressed herself firmly against him. "I'm tired, Beckett. I'm not dead."

"That's reassuring." He gripped her hips, guiding her motion. They weren't nearly close enough, but he loved the glazed look that bled into her dark eyes. "Someday, when the smoke has cleared, I want to come back here."

"Come back."

"Yeah." He dipped beneath the hem of her dress and dragged his fingers across the backs of her thighs. "Just us. I want to press you against that window in our room and fuck you as we watch the sun set." Her little gasp only spurred him on. "And that hot tub? I can't look at it without seeing you sitting on the edge, the flickering light kisses your skin, your pussy wet and aching for my tongue."

"*Beckett.*" Her fingers dug into his arm.

He lowered his head until his lips brushed hers in answer. "Yeah?"

Samara released him and took two large steps back. "The room. Hurry."

Perversely, that made him dig in his heels. "You like those ideas?"

"What I'd like is for you to put that mouth to better use than talking."

He laughed. God, even when he was so hot for her he couldn't see straight, she still made him laugh. It shouldn't be possible. He could barely think past the need to get her out of her dress and sink between those sweet thighs, but her smart-ass comment warmed him in ways that had nothing to do with desire. *I'm falling for you, Samara.* He couldn't say it now any more than he could say it last time they'd been in bed. She'd either bolt or blame it on sex muddling his head.

There was nothing to do but take his woman to bed.

"Let's go." He kept his hand on the small of her back, the curve of her ass, the long line of her spine, as they strode up the beach and into the hotel. Tension radiated from her body, and every look she sent him had Beckett reconsidering his plan to get her back to the room. Surely there was a storage closet around there somewhere...

Samara dragged him inside the elevator as soon as the doors opened. His back hit the wall and she took his mouth in the same move. Her hands were everywhere, running down his back, up his arms, to his shoulders. Beckett responded in kind, grabbing her ass and hauling her even tighter against him. She tasted of wine and decadence, and he felt more than heard the little noises she made as she ground against him.

The elevator dinged.

He walked her backward out the doors, barely registering the wide-eyed couple waiting on their floor. He and Samara weren't moving fast enough, though, so he swung her into his arms. She kissed his jaw, her hands already unbuttoning his shirt. "Hurry, Beckett."

He hurried.

Even with her in his arms, he got the door open and kicked it shut behind him as he strode into the hotel room. Beckett paused to lock the door behind them and only then did he set Samara on her feet, sliding her down his body. "You want me to put my mouth to good use."

"I did say that—just a few minutes ago." She pulled his shirt up and over his shoulders, and then dropped it on the floor. Just like the last few times they'd been together, she found his scar with her fingers, but this time she followed it with her lips. The kiss was light and almost innocent, but he felt it all the way down to his soul.

As if she recognized that the scars of his past went beyond the skin and she accepted them.

He laced his fingers through her hair and tugged her up

until she pressed against him from chest to hips. The fabric of her dress slid against him, but it might as well have been sandpaper. He wanted her skin on his with nothing between them. "You want my mouth? Demand it."

Her eyes widened even as she smiled. "I want your mouth here." Samara traced the line of her neck with a single finger.

Beckett wasted no time following its path with his tongue. He kissed her neck as if that was all he'd ever get of her, the only touch she'd ever allow. She went soft in his arms, and he nipped her earlobe. It seemed to jolt her a little, because she reached down and unzipped her dress. A tiny wiggle, and it hit the floor, leaving her in only a bra and panties, both a deep purple. "My breasts. I want you there."

"Gladly." Instead of going to his knees, he hooked the backs of her thighs and lifted her to him. She wrapped her legs around his waist, and he felt the heat of her pussy even through his slacks. He captured her nipple through the lace of her bra.

"Harder," she gasped. "Don't be gentle with me."

He walked them through the suite to lay her on the bed, using the change in position to shove her bra down, trapping her arms against her sides. He cupped her breasts, pinching her nipples and kissed one and then the other, laying into the sensitive bud with tongue and teeth, driven on by her moans and writhing hips.

"Lower. I need your mouth lower."

He left her bra where it was, liking the picture it created. It reminded him of the way she'd waited for him in his bed. On display. And what a display it was. Her high breasts shook with each breath, her dark nipples at attention, her skin flushed from desire. *For him.* He licked down her stomach, stopping just shy of the band of her panties. "Here?"

"Not funny." She lifted her hips. "Kiss me, Beckett. Kiss me like you mean it."

He obeyed, pressing an open-mouthed kiss to her silk panties. She was so wet he could taste her through the fabric, and he sucked on her clit hard enough to have her back bowing off the bed. It wasn't enough. It would never be enough as long as there was a barrier between them. He caught the band in his teeth and dragged her panties down slowly.

Her eyes flew open and she bent up to watch him, her lips parted. "Oh. My. God."

He moved slower, revealing her inch by inch, until her panties hit her knees. There, they restrained her the same way her bra did, the pseudo bondage seeming to do as much for her as it did for him. "Someday, I want you tied in red silk...No, in purple the exact shade of your panties." He parted her with his fingers and used his thumb to circle her clit. "Spread for me. Wet and wanting and desperate for whatever pleasure I'm willing to give you." He pushed a single finger into her. "I wouldn't make you wait long, Samara. I'm as desperate for you as you are for me. No power games, no matter how intoxicating, can hold up to that desire.

"I changed my mind."

He froze. "What?"

"I don't want your mouth." She sat up and disentangled herself from her bra. "I want to give you mine."

Samara pushed Beckett onto his back. She craved the feel of his cock in her mouth. She wanted to make him lose control. Even when he was inside her, driving her out of her mind with pleasure, he kept a part of himself tightly wound. Contained.

She wanted everything he had to give. He'd already seen and accepted her shadows—she wanted to grant him that same gift.

She moved between his thighs and lightly raked her fingers down them. He was as muscled there as he was everywhere else—lean and in fighting shape. She took his cock in her hand and squeezed. "I see you, Beckett King. I accept you." *I think I love you.* She couldn't say it. Not now. Not while so much still hung over their heads.

"Samara..." A muscle twitched in his jaw as she gave him another stroke. "You don't have to."

It didn't matter if he meant giving him head or accepting whatever sins he carried within him. Neither of them was perfect, but that might just be what made them work. "I have you. Relax. Give it all to me."

He huffed out a strangled laugh. "There isn't going to be much relaxing with my cock so close to your mouth."

"Mmm." She leaned down and sucked the head of him into her mouth. Even if Samara hadn't planned on giving Beckett the show of a lifetime, the look in his brown eyes would have inspired her to do exactly that. He looked like a drowning man clinging to a life preserver and watching a mountain of a wave descend upon him. Lost. Found. All at the same time.

She lifted her head enough to repeat, "Give it all to me." And then his cock was between her lips and she sucked him down, down, down. Beckett's thighs tensed beneath her hands, and he sifted his fingers through her hair, pulling it back from her face.

"Fuck, Samara, you should see the picture you make. Suck me hard."

The command sent a bolt of lightning through her. She loved this, loved the push and pull between them, loved handing over control, if only for a little while. Beckett's cock was wide and long enough that she had to concentrate to take all of him. She relaxed into it, running her tongue along the underside of him, reacquainting herself with every centimeter. Sheer pleasure threatened to send her spiraling and it was only his hands in her hair that kept her anchored in that moment. With him.

His grip tightened and he lifted her off his cock. "You keep sucking me so sweetly, I'm going to lose control and start fucking your pretty little mouth."

She licked her lips, loving the way he followed the movement. It made her thighs clench together and pleasure throb through her clit. "Maybe that's exactly what I want." She needed him wild for her. She needed him to lose control.

"Samara—"

She was tired of talking. She flicked the tip of his cock with her tongue and sucked him down again. Before, she'd been playing—enjoying giving Beckett head for the sake of being able to do it again—but if he had half a chance, he'd stop her before she was finished. She sucked him hard, using her hand to counterstroke in the way she knew he loved. With her other hand, she cupped his balls, gently squeezing in counterpoint to what she did with her lips and tongue.

"*Fuuuuck.*"

The word was her only warning. One second she was going for broke, the next she was on her back with Beckett's mouth on hers. He wrenched her legs wide and thrust against her, his cock sliding over her clit. "Wicked woman." He lifted her hips to fit them more tightly together. "You want my cum? You have to fucking earn it."

She couldn't catch her breath. She wasn't sure she wanted to. Samara raked her nails down his back, urging him closer. "I *was* earning it."

"Not yet." He nipped her neck and then sucked the spot hard. "I love the sight of you taking me deep, but it's not your mouth I'm craving right now." He reached between them and shoved two fingers into her. She clamped around him instinctively, and he groaned. "It feels like you're trying to hold me to you."

"I am." She couldn't think past his fingers filling her. It was good—so good—but nowhere near enough. Beckett had been right all along—there was only one thing she craved and anything else was a poor substitute. "I need you. Now." She snaked her foot down the back of his leg and pushed up with her hips. "I can't wait any longer."

He cursed again. "Samara, I'm trying to do right by you and you're making it fucking impossible."

"The only thing I want fucking is us."

He chuckled against her neck. "Yeah, I got that." He shifted them closer to the edge of the bed and reached blindly into the nightstand. He pulled back and ripped the condom open, but Samara snatched it out of his hand.

"Let me." She kissed his jaw as she rolled it over his cock, taking her time. As much as she wanted him inside her, teasing him was totally worth waiting a little bit. Once he was sheathed, she gave him another stroke.

"You're killing me, woman." Beckett settled back between her thighs and framed her face with his hands. He kissed her like the kiss itself was the main event and his cock wasn't poised at her entrance. The slow slide of his tongue against hers held a promise that encompassed more than this moment.

A future.

He thrust into her in a smooth movement, as natural as her next breath. Pleasure and promise built with each stroke, and still the kiss went on and on. Beckett held her as if she were the most precious thing in the world, as if nothing else mattered but her happiness. Dangerous, fanciful thoughts, but she wrapped them up and held them close even as she clung to him.

"Yes. Yes. *Yes.*" Each word punctuated a thrust, an answer to a question he hadn't given voice to. It didn't matter. Words were superficial compared to the connection they built there and now.

Beckett's tempo increased, and she rose to meet each stroke. He wrapped his arms around her, so she lay in his embrace instead of on the bed, holding her as close as two people could be. "I don't give a fuck what the world throws at us. I'm keeping you, Samara."

She came with a soft cry, pressing her face against his shoulder, telling herself the burning in her eyes was orgasmic bliss and not anything resembling tears. "Yes," she whispered. "Yes to everything."

CHAPTER SIXTEEN

Journey made it into the office before anyone else on Wednesday morning. Even her mother hadn't graced the building yet, which was just as well. Nothing ruined a day like dealing with Lydia before they both had their morning coffee. In the twenty-four hours she'd spent going over Samara's information on the bid, Journey had racked up over a hundred emails.

Sixty of them were marked as needing urgent responses.

Journey dropped her head to her desk and groaned. *I should have fought harder to keep Samara on this project. Or at least demanded that either Anderson or Bellamy come back here to help with the workload.* She knew better than to ask for help from her little sister. Her brothers both held executive roles within Kingdom Corp, but precious Eliza was off finding herself or some bullshit in Europe. Oh, that wasn't what anyone was calling it—she had a *modeling contract*, after all—but that's exactly what she was doing. Dodging her responsibility to the family.

None of it mattered right then. There was no one to help,

and Journey wouldn't ask them for help even if they *were* in Houston. To ask for assistance was as good as admitting she wasn't capable of doing her job, and her mother would never let her live it down.

The phone rang, and she spent three seconds seriously considering crawling under her desk and pretending she wasn't in the office yet. Just long enough for her to drink her damn coffee in peace and conquer the overwhelmed feeling taking root deep inside her.

But the phone just...kept...ringing.

Journey angled her head to look at her watch. Six a.m. Who the hell was calling her at six in the damn morning?

There was no help for it. She answered. "Journey King." It was too early to fake a smile, so she sounded downright surly.

"Hey, sweetheart."

She went cold. *Not this. Not today. Oh God, make it stop.* It took everything she had to make her voice cool and disinterested. "Elliott."

"Don't be like that, sweetheart. You don't sound happy to hear from your old man."

She stared blankly at the photograph across from her desk, trying to draw strength from the vivid autumn tree standing alone in a misty field. *As alone as I am right now.* "I'm *not* happy to hear from you. It's been..." She shuddered. "Eight? No, nine—nine months since I heard from you. I would have preferred to have gone another nine *years*. What do you want, Elliott?"

All the playful wheedling disappeared from his tone. "Your mother's in a shitload of trouble. If you're not careful, she's going to bring you down with her when she crashes and burns."

Journey pulled the phone away from her ear. "Where are you right now?"

"Los Angeles."

She did some quick math. "You're drunk, aren't you? That's the only reason I can think that you'd be calling me at four a.m. your time and spouting some bullshit about Mom. If you want to fight with her, leave me out of it." She leaned forward to hang up.

"Don't you dare end this call, sweetheart. You won't like what comes next."

Journey froze, and hated herself for reacting to that tone in his voice. She closed her eyes. *He's not here. He's not even in the same state.* She wasn't a scared little girl anymore. She had her own power, and with hundreds of miles between her and her father, she *should* be able to handle a single conversation. *Except even hearing his voice makes me feel like I've been doused in sewage.* "If you were in a position to do something with that big talk of yours, you would have done it by now. Good-bye, Elliott."

"You tell that bitch mother of yours that she's bit off more than she can chew with Beckett King. That boy isn't going to roll over the same way his daddy did."

Journey opened her eyes. Questions bubbled up. *What the hell do you know about Beckett King? What did Lydia do this time? How do* you *have anything to do with it?* She didn't voice any of it. Questioning her father was like feeding internet trolls—once he got a little taste of power and attention, there was no getting rid of him. Better to ignore his bullshit until he found someone else to terrorize. "You'd be better served to sleep that drunk off than calling me issuing threats. Don't call here again." She hung up.

Her hands shook so hard when she reached for her coffee

that she abandoned the motion halfway through. *Fuck me.* She shot a look at her open door, half sure she'd heard her mother's heels clicking down the long hallway from the elevator to her office. But no, it was all in her head.

It was just a phone call. The man was two time zones away. There was absolutely no reason for her heart to be kicking in her chest like she'd just run a marathon. She wrapped her arms around herself, but that only made her shakes worse. *Damn it.*

Before she could talk herself out of it, she grabbed her cell phone and hurried to shut her office door. Journey locked it for good measure, but it didn't make her feel any less exposed. *Stupid. Irrational. Crazy.* She shut the blinds next, blocking out the lightening sky. It wasn't enough.

Her chest hurt, and no amount of trying to count her way through her inhales and exhales helped. It got tighter and tighter, until the only thing she could do was huddle on the little sofa situated in the corner farthest from the door. She pulled her knees to her chest and rocked back and forth. *He's not here. He can't get to you. You are not this fucking weak. Get ahold of yourself.* It didn't help.

It never did.

She unlocked her phone with numb fingers, even as she told herself it wasn't necessary, that it was wrong to call her big brother. It didn't stop her this time any more than it had stopped her every other time. The phone rang and rang, the seconds spiraling away from her in a whirlpool she could almost see.

"Journey?"

"Anderson." Her voice was barely a whisper of an exhale.

The background noise faded and she could hear him moving away from wherever he'd been. *Probably an impor-*

tant meeting that your crazy ass is dragging him away from.
A door closed and then he was there, extending a lifeline
through the phone to her. "What's wrong?"

"It was him." No need to specify. There was only one
him in their lives.

"He's not there." Anderson spoke sharply, as if he could
command his words to be the truth rather than the inquiry
they actually were.

She shook her head. "No. He called. I...I'm sorry. I
should be able to handle this on my own." She was so damn
capable in so many damn ways, but one call from Elliott
Bancroft and she was a whimpering mess reaching for her
real-life teddy bear.

"Don't be sorry. I'm here. Do you need to talk, or do you
want me to?"

The question felt just as formal this time as it had every
time before now, starting when she was a little girl who
would hide in her big brother's room to escape their father.
"Can you? Just for a little bit." She loathed the weakness,
loathed leaning on him. "Wait—Anderson, don't. I'm okay.
I...I'll be okay."

He ignored her pathetic attempt at bravado just like he
always did. "I'm hoping we'll wrap up the last of these
meetings today and reach an agreement with Senator Mc-
Murphy. He's coming around, but he's taken a disliking to
Bellamy, so it's hampering the progress."

"Poor Bellamy."

"No 'poor Bellamy.' The first thing he did when he saw
the good senator was to drop the names of *both* the man's
mistresses in conversation. He's so damn smug I want to
toss him out a moving car sometimes."

She cracked a smile. "Poor Anderson."

"That's right. Poor Anderson. And you'll never guess who I saw yesterday..." He went on like that, talking about nonconsequential things until her panic retreated and she finally stopped shaking.

Journey inhaled deeply. "I'm okay now."

"Do you need me to come back?"

He would if she asked. To hell with their mother's plans and the important business meetings and political agendas. If Journey told her big brother she needed him, he'd be on the next flight out of DC and winging back to Houston to save her.

I need to be able to save myself.

"I'm fine. I'll see you next week?"

"Yeah, we should have things wrapped up by then." He hesitated. "Hang in there, Jo. I know that asshole doesn't call often, but if you need me to..."

He didn't have to finish that sentence for her to know where he was going with it. "No." She straightened and put as much of a command into her voice as she could. "No, Anderson. Don't you dare." Her brother had been protecting her for too long, and she'd be damned before he put another stain on his soul on her behalf. "I'm fine."

"I know."

It couldn't be more obvious that he didn't believe the words any more than she did. She had to get off the damn call before he changed his mind and *did* come back. "I'll call you soon—a real call. Not me freaking out over nothing."

"It's not nothing."

"Yes, it is," she said firmly. One of these days, it might even be the truth.

Not today, though.

Today, nothing was fine at all.

What the hell had her father meant about Beckett and her mother?

As the plane touched down, Beckett reluctantly turned his phone back on. It was tempting to tell the pilot to keep circling or, better yet, to fly him and Samara somewhere far away from Houston. It would only postpone what came next, though. If the thing growing between them couldn't survive the reality of their respective lives, then spending more blissful time together would only make the hurt worse when it inevitably fell apart.

Nothing inevitable about it. I said I was keeping her, and I damn well meant it.

His phone buzzed in his hand, and Beckett frowned as voice mail after voice mail appeared. Three from the superintendent of his building and five from Frank. "What the fuck?"

Samara set down the magazine she'd been idly flipping through. "What's going on?"

"I don't know, but I'm about to find out." He bypassed the voice mails and called Frank directly.

The phone didn't even ring before his friend was on the other line. "Thank fuck. I thought you were supposed to be back in Houston last night. I was just on the phone with the damn airport, threatening my way into getting your flight plans."

Samara shifted closer, her dark eyes worried. *Beckett* was worried. Since they'd known each other, Frank was always the calm and measured one. He'd heard the man raise his voice only a handful of times in a decade. "Frank, what happened?"

"Someone broke into your apartment. The superintendent called me right after he called the cops. You weren't home and I'm apparently your emergency contact."

A break-in.

Beckett frowned. A break-in was bad, but it wasn't any worse than the damn fire. "I don't—"

"It wasn't just a break-in, Beckett. There's blood everywhere. I thought..." He paused, and when he spoke again, his voice was closer to normal. "It was a gut reaction. I couldn't reach you, the police aren't sure if it's human blood or something else, but they're treating it like a potential homicide."

"A *homicide*." Beckett pulled the phone away from his ear and put it on speaker. Samara could hear most of the conversation either way, but he wanted her fully looped in. "I have you on speaker. Samara is with me. Tell me what you know."

"It's not much yet. The police barely let me get a look at your apartment. I have a guy at the station waiting for an update, but it takes time for the tests they did on the blood to come back."

Blood. In his apartment.

Was it meant as a warning or was he being framed? Only time would tell. "I'm assuming the police want to talk to me."

"That's a safe bet." Frank hesitated. "There's something else."

For fuck's sake. He braced himself, and nearly flinched when Samara covered his hand with hers. Beckett turned his over and laced his fingers with hers, taking her silent support. "Might as well spit it out."

"Whoever got into the apartment got into the garage as well. They trashed your Harley. After the cops cataloged the scene, I had it sent to a mechanic I trust, but the guy said it's a lost cause. They put sugar in the tank, and if that wasn't enough, they set the fucking thing on fire. It was the bike that first prompted security to check your apartment out. The superintendent knew it was yours and wanted to make sure you were okay."

Beckett wasn't okay.

The plane taxied toward the private hangars and Beckett allowed himself a full thirty seconds of mourning that bike. He'd had it since he was sixteen, and he'd rebuilt it himself and upgraded it over the years. Countless hours had gone into that vehicle, both with tools in his hands and with the road flying beneath him. Gone. All gone. There would never be another bike like it, if only because of the sheer history.

First Thistledown Villa.

Now my bike.

The apartment . . . His breath stopped in his chest.

Everything he'd taken from Thistledown was in that apartment. The baby book. The pictures. The other things he'd brought with him when he'd moved out after high school. It was all he had of his history, the only reminders that wouldn't fade with time and distance. *Fuck.*

"Beckett?"

"Give him a minute," Samara said.

Beckett realized he had her hand almost in a death grip, but he couldn't make himself let go. She didn't seem particularly worried about it. Samara shifted and rubbed his thigh with her free hand, offering what comfort she could.

He appreciated the gesture even if it changed nothing about what he was about to walk into. "We're pulling up to the hangar now. We'll be at the apartment inside of an hour."

"I'll meet you there."

"Appreciate it." He hung up and forced himself to let go of Samara's hand. "I can drop you on the way."

"What?" Her brows slammed together. "No way."

He recognized the hurt that flickered over her face and reclaimed her hands, being careful to hold her lightly. "I'm not rejecting you, and I'm not trying to spare your delicate woman sensibilities or some bullshit. I don't know what I'm walking into, and the acts against me are escalating. There's no telling what they'll do next." But he could hazard a guess. As threats went, Lydia's were textbook. First she took his childhood home. Then she proved she could get to him both at work and at home if he didn't bow to her will. Next it would be Beckett or the people he cared about getting into unfortunate accidents.

Right now, the people Beckett cared about numbered at two.

Frank could take care of himself.

Samara likely could as well, but she wouldn't be expecting danger from Lydia. Her eyes might be opening to what Beckett's aunt was capable of, but she'd worked for that company for a decade. That was a whole lot of time and experience to be overridden, even when faced with mounting evidence.

"You think it's Lydia."

He picked his words with care. "Even without her pulling that stunt with you and basically flaunting her knowledge of the fire, the timing would be more than suspicious. My sparkling personality might piss people off sometimes, but I haven't been back in town long enough to inspire murderous rage in anyone but my aunt."

The plane jolted as it stopped completely, and Samara pushed to her feet. "Beckett, this is serious."

"I know." He had to put a stop to it and do it now, but if he didn't deal with the apartment first, he'd have to handle both the police and his plans, and that would only hold Beckett back. He stood and grabbed their bags. "I don't want you in the middle of this, Samara."

"I'm *already* in the middle of this. I have been since it started."

He couldn't argue that, so he didn't bother to try. The door opened and he headed for it. They could stand around talking about this all day and get nowhere.

Samara followed closely, frustration rolling off her in waves. She didn't speak, though, as he tossed their bags into the trunk of the waiting car and drove them away from the airport. Beckett gripped the steering wheel and tried to find the right words to say. There *were* no right words. Until he knew the extent of the damage—and whose blood the police had found—he didn't have any answers for Samara. It was entirely possible that Lydia had decided to frame him for some crime, though *murder* seemed going a bit far, even for her.

Except it wasn't going too far when it came to my father.

"Beckett." She spoke softly, not looking away from the windshield. "Promise me that you won't do anything in retaliation for this until we know for sure who's behind it." When he didn't respond, she continued. "If, by some chance, it *isn't* Lydia, then you risk creating two enemies instead of one."

What she said made sense, even though her determination to point the blame at someone else aggravated him. Most of the time, the simplest answer was the real answer. Lydia had the most to gain by ruining Beckett's life and effectively running him out of town. Even if this was all to keep him distracted while she put something else into play, it all revolved around their competing businesses and, even more so, around the split in the family thirty years ago. It obviously didn't matter to her that he was a nephew—he was an obstacle to be removed by any means possible.

The chances of the perpetrator of all the acts against him being some shadowy villain who hadn't been revealed were astronomical. It didn't make any sense.

Telling Samara that wouldn't change her mind, though. She might not be blindly defending Lydia any longer, but she was just as obviously resistant to the idea that the woman she'd trusted for so long was capable of this level of attack.

"I promise that I won't retaliate unless I have to." It was all he could give her. Beckett had no intention of sinking to Lydia's level. A war between them would hurt more than just his aunt. It would hurt his cousins whom he hadn't had a chance to know. It would hurt employees at both companies.

It would hurt Samara.

No, Beckett would do this *his* way.

And he'd remove Lydia as a threat. Permanently.

CHAPTER SEVENTEEN

Samara barely stayed home long enough to shower and change. She didn't trust the wild look in Beckett's eyes as he'd driven away. There was a confrontation between him and Lydia coming—and coming soon—but he'd be occupied for the next few hours at least dealing with the police and figuring out what was salvageable in his apartment.

She hurried down the sidewalk toward Kingdom Corp, feeling like a spy sneaking into the enemy's camp. It didn't make a bit of sense. Kingdom Corp was *her* territory. There was no reason for the guilt gnawing away at her stomach.

No reason except she was up to no good.

Samara took the elevator up to the twenty-fourth floor and then used the stairs the rest of the way to the executive level. She checked her watch. Noon. Lydia should be out to lunch with her "friend" right about now. She disappeared every Wednesday like clockwork for an hour, and since Samara handled her calendar, she knew Lydia took *lunch* in a hotel room a few blocks away.

An hour wasn't much time for what she'd set out to do, but she'd make it work. She padded out the door and down the hallway, her flats not making a sound on the floor. The door to Journey's office was shut, and the whole floor felt almost deserted. Samara used her key to unlock Lydia's office and shut the door behind her. She tensed, waiting for alarms to blare or someone to rush in and demand to know what she was doing there.

Nothing happened.

Stop wasting time being afraid of getting caught and do what you need to do before you actually are *caught.*

She hurried to Lydia's desk and typed in the password to the computer. Thanks to her years working directly under the woman, what passwords she didn't know she could guess. It seemed counterintuitive that Lydia would keep something incriminating on her computer, but the woman's entire life was synced electronically. She abhorred traditional mail, paper notetaking, and anything she considered too luddite. *Technology is the future, Samara.*

She signed into both of Lydia's email accounts and did a few quick searches. Nothing popped up for Beckett or Nathaniel's names beyond a couple of old documents from last quarter about Morningstar Enterprise's reported holdings. The company itself was in more emails, but they were all directly business related and not any more sinister than normal.

Samara sat back. This was getting her nowhere. What had she expected? A smoking gun with Lydia's name engraved on the side? Even if she was involved, her boss wasn't an idiot.

On a whim, she brought up Lydia's calendar. It was synced with Samara's system so she knew where her boss was at all times, and anything important was flagged accordingly on both hers and Lydia's account.

Except...

She frowned and leaned forward. There was a tab at the bottom of the screen, similar to the ones used in her spreadsheet program. Samara clicked it and blinked. New appointments appeared over the top of the ones she recognized. *What the hell?* She grabbed her phone and snapped a picture, pausing to make sure it came out clear, and then she shut everything down the same way it'd been before she got into the office. There were only ten minutes until Lydia got back into the office and she wanted to be long gone before she had to explain her presence there.

She took one last look around the room to make sure everything was exactly how she'd found it and then slipped out of the office and locked the door behind her. She made it halfway down the hall before Journey's office door opened and her friend stuck her head out. She frowned. "Samara, what are you doing here?"

"I—"

The elevator dinged and she watched the doors open in slow motion to reveal Lydia herself. *Oh no.* The woman paused, a frown marring her face as she took in Samara and then Journey. "What's going on here?"

I'm done for.

Journey sighed dramatically. "What does it look like, Mother? We're plotting your downfall, of course." She rolled her eyes. "Get a grip. I asked Samara to stop by and explain some of her notes to me."

If anything, Lydia's frown grew more severe. "I specifically sent her on vacation. If you're not capable of handling this bid—"

"You'll find someone else," Journey finished. "Considering the bid is *Friday*, that threat doesn't work on me right now. Come on, Samara." She grabbed her hand and towed her into the office.

Journey shut the door and held up her hand. They waited in silence as Lydia's heels clicked down the hallway and then her office door opened and shut. And then they waited some more. Finally Journey let out the breath she'd been holding and turned to Samara. "Since we both know that was a crock of shit, do you want to tell me why you're *really* here?"

Samara opened her mouth, but the words wouldn't come. Journey and Lydia already had a tumultuous relationship, but there was real love there when they stopped fighting long enough to acknowledge it. All she had right now was suspicions, and if she laid them out for her friend it would look like Beckett had gotten into Samara's head and poisoned her. "I don't know if I can."

"Honey…" Journey pointed to the couch. "Sit. I think we need to have a conversation about what's going on, because even with your superior lying skills, you have guilt written all over your face. If my mother wasn't so distracted from her *lunch date*, she would have noticed."

"I do *not* have guilt written all over my face." She strode to the couch and dropped onto it. "Things are so damn complicated."

"Yeah, tell me about it."

She twisted to look at her friend. There were shadows under her hazel eyes and she looked a little pale. "Are you okay?"

"Oh, no, we're not switching things around to me. Even if I didn't know you weren't supposed to be here, the fact you're wearing *those* proves you're up to no good." Journey pointed at Samara's ballet flats. "Spill."

When she still hesitated, Journey's open expression closed like a flower retreating into itself. "You don't trust me with whatever it is."

She could beg off and walk out. Journey wouldn't like it, but when things fell out one way or another, Samara would make it up to her friend. *Except...* She made herself meet Journey's gaze directly. "I think Lydia has something to do with the attacks against Beckett."

"*What?*" Journey dropped onto the cushion opposite her. "You can't be serious." She frowned harder. "Of course you're serious. You wouldn't be here right now if you weren't pretty damn sure my mother was behind it. Beckett doesn't have much to lose accusing her, but *you* do."

She hated the reminder that, no matter how tempting the fantasy they'd woven, she and Beckett *weren't* really equal. Maybe they never would be. She steeled herself against that truth. It wouldn't help now. "Lydia also knew details about the fire at Morningstar Enterprise that she shouldn't have known."

"The media has been trying to sniff out the details, but everyone is keeping really closemouthed about it." She shrugged. "Don't look at me like that—you were in that fire. I want answers about what happened just as much as you do. I don't know if you noticed it, but you're kind of only mostly my best friend and I care about you."

Samara warmed even as she felt sick to her stomach. "I don't want to get between you and your mother. If I'm right...if Beckett's right...it could mean bad things for Kingdom Corp—for Lydia." No matter how strong their friendship was, she didn't like being the one having to break this potential news to Journey. "She could be facing jail time."

"If that's where the answers fall out..." Journey looked away. "She wouldn't be the first member of my family that deserved to be behind bars."

"Journey—"

"I'm okay." She shook her head. "That's a lie. I'm not okay." She pushed back to her feet. "But don't you dare let that stop you from finding the truth. Kingdom Corp can weather the fallout. *We* can weather the fallout."

Something was seriously wrong. The loyalty among the King family was legendary. No matter how crappy a mother Lydia was, Samara had fully expected all her children to close ranks around her at the first sign of trouble. For Journey essentially to give Samara the green light to continue digging... "What's going on?"

"You've been here a long time, and you've seen a lot of the inner workings of this place and our family." Journey walked to her desk and sat in her chair. "But even you haven't seen everything, Samara. Some skeletons are just too ugly to see the light."

The suspicion dug deep that they weren't talking about Lydia's theoretical attacks against Beckett. Samara walked to the desk and leaned down, forcing her friend to look at her. She spoke slowly and clearly, wishing she could imprint the words on Journey to chase the darkness from her friend's face. "I don't care how ugly your skeletons are. You are my best friend, and you always will be."

Journey's smile was a ghost of its former self. "I don't deserve you."

"Let's be honest—we're both messes. But at least we have each other."

"Until you admit that you're head over heels for my cousin."

222   KATEE ROBERT

Samara froze. There was no point in arguing, because it was the truth. She'd gone and fallen for the one man who would complicate her life the most. She still wasn't convinced it wouldn't blow up in her face, but she...cared for him. "Whatever happens with him, that doesn't change our friendship."

"Glad to hear it." Journey shooed her. "Now, get out of my office and get back to your investigating."

"Call me if you need anything."

"I will."

Samara left. She did her best to look like she wasn't fleeing, but she didn't want to get cornered by Lydia before she escaped. *What am I going to do on Monday?* It defied comprehension that they could maintain this level of tension for another five days, but there was no reason to think the situation wouldn't be resolved one way or another by that point.

Wishful thinking.

She ignored the little voice inside her and headed for home, her phone and the evidence it contained clutched in her hand the whole way.

"It's pig blood."

Beckett stared at the destruction in his condo. Nothing had been spared. Not the kitchen, where every single plate and glass he owned had been shattered. Not the living room, where the couch cushions had been ripped to shreds. Not his bedroom, including the locked cabinet where he'd stashed the things he'd collected from Thistledown Villa.

He walked to that cabinet in a haze and picked up the baby book, drenched with blood. Ruined. Completely ruined. *It wasn't enough that she took the house. She had to try to ruin the memories, too.* He set it carefully back in its place and noticed that one photo had been spared, tucked as it was just out of the spray. The one of him and his mother in the field behind Thistledown. He tucked it into his suit-jacket pocket and turned to the detective. "I'm sorry, what did you say?"

The wiry redhead—Detective Purcell—looked distinctly uncomfortable. He didn't exactly shift in place, but he had a nervous energy about him that implied being still wasn't in his nature. "The blood tests came back. It's not human—it's pig blood. We've cataloged the scene and taken pictures to document everything, but if you find anything missing of note, we'll need to know."

Beckett couldn't think past the blood marring everything of value he owned. He fought down the desire to throw open every window as if that would cleanse his home of the taint the intruder had left behind. "This building has extensive se-curity. How did this person get in here?"

"Inconclusive. The tapes show nothing—we've checked—so it looks like they were hacked and put on a loop." Detective Purcell clenched and unclenched his fists as if taking that dead end personally. "Until we have more in-formation, it would be best if you stayed somewhere else."

Unable to look at the disaster of his bedroom a sec-ond longer, Beckett turned and stalked back toward the front door, where Frank waited. His friend's calm mask was firmly in place, and he eyed the detective as if the man was wasting both their time. "I trust Beckett isn't under suspi-cion any longer."

"His alibi checks out." Detective Purcell didn't sound the least bit sorry that he'd been under investigation to begin with, no matter how briefly. He glanced at Beckett. "Don't leave town, though."

"I have no plans to." Everything he needed to deal with was in Houston.

"Good. That's good."

Frank looked at Beckett, then turned for the door. "Let's go."

He turned and took one last look at the ruin. Lydia might not have really taken everything from him, but he couldn't disentangle from the grief lurking just beyond his aura of numbness. He didn't give a fuck about the furniture or the condo, but losing the baby book and pictures felt like losing his mother all over again.

He couldn't do it. "Just a moment," he murmured to Frank.

Beckett crunched over the broken glass to the drawer where he stored the plastic bags. He retreated back to the bedroom and carefully enclosed the baby book in a bag. There was no saving it, but he wasn't ready to give it up yet. *She knew how to hit you where it hurt, again and again, and she didn't pull her punches.*

On the heels of that: *The old man would be pleased that I'm finally losing the last bit of evidence that my mother ever existed.*

Once the bag was safely sealed, he stalked out the front door, past Frank, and down the stairs. The thought of being enclosed in the elevator for the few minutes it would take to get to the ground floor was too much.

Frank kept pace easily. "You want to talk about it?"

"No." Not now. Not while the wound was so raw it was practically throbbing. If he let go now, he would be worthless until he worked through the rage rising up within him. He stopped on the next landing. "I want you to know I appreciate that you're here—that you looked into my father's death. It's not your job, and you've put in way too much time on this." He didn't offer to pay his friend—it would be an insult, and Frank wouldn't hesitate to let him know.

"I've worked hard to ensure my company can function without me for short periods of time." Frank hesitated, like he'd leave it at that, but finally pushed forward. "You're my only fucking friend, Beck, and I know all too well what it's like to have unanswered questions about a parent's death. You need me—I'm there. End of story."

"Same goes, though I'm not much use at the moment."

Frank stared at something over Beckett's shoulder, as if the whole moment made him uncomfortable and wish he was a thousand miles away. "This isn't forever. You'll deal with the threat and be back on your feet, with one less enemy to face down in the process. Keep your chin up."

Keep your chin up.

Frank's awkwardness almost made him smile. Almost. "Thanks."

"Don't mention it."

They turned as one and resumed their descent. Beckett waited to speak again until they reached the ground level. "I need one more favor. Could you to find Walter Trissel?"

"Consider it done." Again, there was a minute hesitation. "If you need a place to stay—"

"I'm good." In all the years they'd known each other, he'd never been to Frank's place. Beckett had given it up as a mystery that would never be solved a long time ago. He wasn't going to allow it now out of pity.

"I'll call you as soon as I have Walter nailed down." Frank picked up his pace and pushed through the doors to the street. In seconds, he'd disappeared into a waiting car and was gone.

Beckett took five minutes to speak with the superintendent to assure the man he wasn't going to sue or raise a stink
about the break-in. With every second that passed, the walls
inched a little bit closer, until he almost ran out of the fucking building.

The street was no better. Out there, he was too exposed,
and even though he knew it was paranoia, it didn't stop
the feeling of being watched from making his skin itch. He
pulled out his phone and dialed before he could think better
of it.

"Beckett?"

The sound of Samara's voice hit him like a punch to the
solar plexus. He closed his eyes and tried to breathe past it.
He could hang up, pretend the call was an accident, force
the barriers between them back into place. It was the smart
choice—both for him and for her.

But he found himself speaking without having any intent
to. "I need you."

"I'm here," she responded instantly. "I'm in my condo
right now. Do you want to come here or should I come to
you?" No questions. No requests for clarification. Nothing
but a quiet acceptance of his need.

"I can be there in ten."

"I'll be waiting."

CHAPTER EIGHTEEN

Samara met Beckett at the door. She took one look at the shell-shocked look on his face and the horrible burden he carried in his hands and threw her arms around him. "I've got you, Beckett. I have you."

It took several long seconds for him to bring his arms around her and hug her back. He squeezed her and exhaled as though *he* was the one compressed. "Samara." Just her name. Nothing more.

He didn't have to say anything else.

She'd been there when he walked through his childhood home and picked up the few things that mattered to him. She'd witnessed the intimate window into his past that he'd offered that day. She recognized the bagged baby book for the depth of the loss it represented. It was not just an item. Nothing so simple as that.

Samara hugged him tighter, trying to offer comfort with her body that she didn't think he'd take from her words. *I'm here. You aren't alone. I won't leave.* She stroked her hands up his back and down again, soothing in the only way she knew.

A shudder worked through him and he took a slow, haggard breath. "It was bad."

I'm so sorry. Let me share this burden. More words she couldn't voice. She just kept touching him, pressing as much of her body against as much of his that she could reach.

Another breath. "I'm not under suspicion of anything, but the apartment is unlivable."

"You'll stay here." She didn't form it as question, didn't give him an option. Beckett was more than capable of setting himself up in a hotel for the time being while he figured out his next step, but Samara couldn't bear the thought of him being alone. He was already too isolated. Untethered. She couldn't shake the irrational belief that he'd float away if she let go of him. "Stay with me, Beckett," she repeated.

He stirred as if registering where they were for the first time. "You don't have to offer."

"I want you here, so I'm going to have you here." When he made no motion to move, she slipped back and led him into the kitchen.

It was only then that she noticed the blood on his cuffs and marring his hands. "Beckett?" Samara worked to keep the alarm from her tone. "What's this?"

He shook his head as if shaking off a dream. "Pig blood. You'll be happy to know no one was murdered in my place. It was all for show."

She'd bet whoever trashed his place didn't realize he'd be gone all night. They probably knew about his trip to LA and they'd planned on him coming home, tired after a day of meetings and traveling, and walking into that scene unsuspectingly.

Fury roared through her, turning any doubts she had to

ash. Beckett hadn't done anything to deserve this level of
hate. Even if he *had* been the biggest piece of shit in existence, it didn't justify this systematic dismantling of his life.

She tugged him over to the sink and turned the water on.
"Let's get you cleaned up."

That got a reaction. He disentangled himself from her.
"I'm okay. It was shocking and upsetting, but I'm okay. I
don't need you to handle me."

Words he'd spoken to her after the reading of his father's
will. It felt like a hundred years ago instead of less than a
week. She met his gaze directly. "Some days we all need
a little handling. You already bear the weight of so much,
Beckett. Let me help shoulder the burden, even if it's only
for tonight."

She took the bag from his hands and set it on the counter
in clear sight, and then unbuttoned his shirt. He watched her
like a hawk as she slid it off his shoulders, but Beckett made
no move to touch her. She nudged him closer to the sink and
pointed at the soap. "I'm going to make a quick call, and
then we're going to sit down. If you want to talk, we can
talk. If you want to do something to check out mentally for
a while, we can do that, too."

"Therapeutic sex?"

She snorted. "I was thinking more of renting a movie on
demand, eating good food, and letting me cuddle your tension away."

Beckett considered. His frozen expression had thawed a
little since he arrived, but he was nowhere near normal. It
scared her. He'd never appeared more like his father than
when she opened the door and found him looking at her
from behind an icy wall. That wasn't the Beckett she
knew—the one she'd come to care about entirely too much.

Her Beckett was fire and passion and a healthy dose of attitude.

She walked away before he could answer, hating the way her throat closed, refusing to be upset in front of him when it was Beckett who had been hurt. Samara made two quick calls—one to order several changes of clothes for him to be couriered to her condo from a shop about a mile away, and the other takeout from two different places.

By the time she made it back into the main living area, Beckett had finished washing his hands and was prowling around the space. Snooping. She paused in the doorway to take in a shirtless Beckett in her living room. The muscles in his back flexed as he leaned over to read the titles on her bookshelf.

"Regency romance, thrillers, and a startling selection of classic horror novels." He spoke without looking over. "Every time I think you can't surprise me, you go and prove me wrong."

He sounded more normal, which made her smile a little. "Which of those is the most surprising?"

"Definitely the horror. Thrillers and romance are just two sides to the same coin, so they go hand in hand to some extent." He glanced at her. "Don't tell that to men who like to read the damn thrillers, though."

She recognized the subject for a desperate bid not to talk about what he'd just seen, so she played along. For now. "Do tell."

"Both tell stories that are emotion-driven. Fear and love aren't that different when it comes right down to it."

He spoke with the kind of familiarity that drew her several steps closer. "You sound like you've read a romance or two."

"My mother had a subscription to the old Harlequin novels at one point. I found them in a box in the attic when I was thirteen. She must have read them multiple times each, because the spines were exceedingly abused." He grinned unexpectedly. "I read them all."

She could just picture an adolescent Beckett holed up with those stories, reading them to feel close to the mother he'd lost. "That's really sweet."

"It was." His smile fell away. "Though my father didn't think so. He realized I'd hidden them away when I was fourteen and he made me watch as he burned them all." He caught her expression and shrugged. "He was proving a point."

God, her heart ached for him. He'd lost so much, and he just kept moving forward, barely missing a step.

You don't have to be alone anymore.

She didn't even know if she had any business promising him that. She couldn't fill the void of so many missing people inside him. No one could but Beckett himself. But he didn't have to stand as a pillar of solitude, protecting everyone under his wing without falter.

That was why he'd never left, no matter how shitty his father had been. Why he wouldn't leave no matter how little his heart was in the oil business or the legacy of his family. He had people depending on his leadership, and he'd see it through to keep their lives secure.

Oh my God, I love him.

"What's got that look on your face?"

"Nothing," she answered quickly. She couldn't tell him now or he'd accuse her of saying the words out of pity. No, they had to get through this mess and walk out the other side, and *then* she could confess what she felt for him. *Or maybe I'm just a coward.*

Beckett turned in a slow circle, seeming to take in her place. She tried to see the room from his point of view. Her condo was about half the size of his. Flowers bloomed on her windowsill, and she had pots set up on either side of her balcony. They made her feel closer to her mother, even when they didn't get to see each other as much as she'd like. Her living room was cozy enough, with a reasonable-sized television and a deep gray couch that was deep enough for two people to sleep on side by side. Her mother had crocheted the throw blanket haphazardly folded across the back of the couch, the only bright thing in the room with its happy oranges, reds, and yellows that made her think of a sunset.

"A movie...would be nice. We have to talk but—"

"It can wait," Samara said firmly. She hadn't had a chance to study Lydia's calendar, but she needed to tell him about it. "I ordered dinner. We'll eat. Decompress. And then we'll talk about what happens next."

He hesitated, but finally nodded. "Deal."

Samara handed him the remote and put on the hot water while Beckett flipped through the movie options. The bloody bag on her counter drew her gaze. The baby book inside looked saturated, but if there was a way to save even part of it, it wouldn't happen while the thing was air-locked in a bag. "I'm going to see if I can dry this out."

"If you want to."

He didn't sound exactly encouraging, but she didn't let that stop her. Samara grabbed some towels and scissors and a pan. She carefully set the bag in the pan and cut down the sides. The metallic scent made her stomach clench, but she gritted her teeth and gingerly parted the cover to see what the damage was inside. Blood stained the edges of the pages and the first few were completely ruined, but most of the middle ones were still readable. She just needed to keep them that way. She blotted the wet spots with one of the towels, making sure not to smear it. The front cover was beyond saving, but she propped it up and spread the pages as best she could. She was considering getting her hair dryer and using the cold setting to try to dry it faster when the buzzer sounded.

"I got it." Beckett's voice sounded closer behind her than she expected.

She jumped and twisted to find him leaning against the opposite kitchen counter. "I didn't hear you."

His gaze settled on the spread baby book and the red marking her hands. She didn't know what to say, so she blurted out. "I know it's important to you. I couldn't not try."

He took two steps to her, pressed a quick kiss to her temple. "Thank you. For all this. For being there."

Beckett set the food Samara had ordered out on the coffee table—Indian and Italian—and then took the garment bag into her bedroom to change. He noted the price tags on the suit and lounge pants, fully planning on repaying her the cost. Beckett changed into the lounge pants and paused to take in Samara's bedroom.

He'd expected more of the same from her living room—cozy comfort. But it was downright girly. No less than a dozen throw pillows were artfully scattered across her bed, in gold and red and orange. The bedspread itself was red with a floral border. The gauzy gold curtains let in the early evening light, and the two prints on either side of the window were close-up photos of flowers that reminded him of that painter he'd studied in school. The overall effect was busy, but welcoming. A little sanctuary for Samara alone.

And anyone she's been serious with over the years.

He shut that thought down. Samara hadn't been a saint any more than he had. If she'd had a recent serious boyfriend, there was no evidence of the man in this room. Even if there had been…Beckett was here, not some ex of hers.

You're focusing on something that doesn't matter instead of the hulking elephant in the room.

Beckett sat on the bed and dropped his head into his hands. Seeing Samara trying to salvage the ruined baby book…He hadn't expected it of her. He'd taken the damn book only because he couldn't stand the thought of leaving it in his ruined condo for another moment. He'd called her because being alone was the worst thing he could contemplate while he dealt with the emotional fallout. Knowing someone had broken into his apartment—his safe space—and methodically destroyed anything and everything he valued.

The door opened and he looked up to find Samara standing there.

Not everything I value was destroyed.

But it could be.

She gave a half smile. "You should eat something."

Taking care of him, even when he didn't deserve it. He couldn't let it go without telling her the truth he'd been avoiding for half the week. "I took the contract."

Samara blinked. "What?"

"The contract—the one you've been working your ass off to put in a bid for. I pulled strings behind your back and took the contract before the date to give the proposal." It was selfish, his need to get this out, to drive her away now before she kept piling kind act upon kind act onto him. Before he found a reason never to tell her so that he could keep this thing going between them longer.

Samara leaned against the door frame and considered him. She wore a simple black dress that did nothing to downplay her curves. Sometime after he'd arrived, she'd pulled her hair back into a messy ponytail, and it struck him that this was what Samara Mallick looked like without her many walls in place. Relaxed and a little rumpled and more beautiful than he'd ever seen her.

Look your fill now. This ends soon.

She finally sighed. "Okay."

"What?"

"Okay. It's a dick move, sure. But I get it. It's business. And given that Morningstar already had that contract so long, it doesn't surprise me you were able to bend the rules. I would have done the same thing in your position." She crossed her arms over her chest. "It was still shitty, though."

"I'm sorry that it was you I was up against, but I'm not sorry I did it." Losing out on that bid would hurt Lydia. Not enough and not for long, but it allowed him to retaliate in *some* way.

She threw up her hands. "Beckett, you've been systematically attacked multiple times in the last week and those attacks show no sign of slowing down or de-escalating. Right now, the bid is the last thing I'm worried about." She hesitated. "But you should still call Journey and tell her not to spend the next twenty-four hours cramming for it."

He could barely believe what he was hearing. "You spent a lot of time putting together that proposal."

"Yes, I did. And I'm mad at you for pulling such an underhanded move, but I also know how to prioritize. Your safety—physical or otherwise—is more important than either Morningstar Enterprise or Kingdom Corp." She crossed to him and crouched in front of him, putting their faces closer to level. "My job is important to me—really important to me—but losing that bid won't change my life overmuch. What you're dealing with *will*." She gave him another of those sweet little smiles that he'd started to crave. "But the next time we go head to head, I'm going to kick your ass if you pull a stunt like this...if I don't pull it first."

He gave a faint smile. "Deal."

She took his hand and rose, tugging him to his feet as she did. "You need to at least try to eat. I have my own bombshell to drop."

It wasn't until they were seated next to each other with plates of food that she took out her phone and showed him Lydia's secondary calendar. "I haven't had a chance to look at it too closely and compare it to the one I have."

He zoomed in on it, noting the reflection from the monitor. "You were in Lydia's office?"

"Yeah. How else would I have gotten this?"

Beckett's stomach dropped and he had to fight not to raise his voice. "That was dangerous, Samara. No one knew you were there. Anything could have happened to you."

She raised her eyebrows. "I've worked in that building for ten years, Beckett. Lydia would have been furious if she caught me, and she might have fired me on the spot, but it's not like she'd shove me out a window."

He wasn't so sure. He'd had certain beliefs about his aunt since as long as he could remember, and it never would have occurred to him that she was capable of murder until his father died and so many strings connected her back to what might have happened that night. "There were no drugs found in my father's system, but that doesn't mean he chose to drink that much."

"Wait a minute—you think she actually orchestrated that *entire* night?"

"My father's driver was paid off. He's currently somewhere in Brazil as best I can tell. Even with the guy gone, Nathaniel had three others who worked as backup to accommodate his schedule at any given time. My father drank often enough that his being shit-housed wouldn't raise red flags, but his not having a driver *does*. She was at the restaurant that night—I have pictures proving it. How hard would it be to ensure he got behind the wheel? If it's not murder, strictly speaking, it's still criminal."

Samara poked at her food. "Okay, I'm not saying she's not capable of doing something like that. She wasn't where her schedule said she should be that night."

"Wasn't she?" He zoomed in on the night of his father's death and flipped the phone around to show Samara.

She frowned. "The spa appointments are there, but so is one with…N.G."

"Nathaniel George King—my father's full name."

"She lied." She didn't sound surprised, exactly, but definitely perturbed. "Okay, let's say this played out exactly like you described. I still can't picture Lydia sneaking into your building to set a fire, or breaking into your condo with a bucket of pigs' blood."

He couldn't, either, but that didn't mean a damn thing. "Then she hired someone else to do it."

Samara took several bites and he followed suit. They ate, both lost in their own thoughts, until she set down her fork and turned to face him. "What happens now?"

"Now I find Walter Trissel and see what he knows." At

her questioning look, he explained. "This all goes back to the changing of the will. The only two people who definitely know what happened with it are my father and Walter. If Lydia managed to manipulate my father into giving her Thistledown Villa, then she used Walter Trissel to do it."

"That makes sense. There's a thread that runs through all this, so if you find it, you can trace it back to her."

He forced a smile. "You almost sound like you believe me."

"Well, it's getting impossible to ignore. I don't know that Lydia's personally responsible for every bit of this, but she's definitely the one gaining the most from it." She pressed her lips together. "What's her endgame?"

"I imagine she's got alibis for every single attack against me."

She motioned for him to continue. Beckett leaned back against her couch and sighed. "She tried to buy Morningstar from me."

"She had to know you wouldn't take that offer."

"I'm sure she did. She's not stupid." He stared at her bookshelves, not liking the direction of his thoughts. "I don't know what happens to Morningstar if I die."

"*Beckett.*"

He shifted closer and put his arm around her shoulders. "I'm just musing. I have a will set up, but it mostly concerns my trust fund and Thistledown, the latter of which is a non-issue at the moment. The company is set up differently. Normally, it would be up to the board to determine a new CEO and distribute shares from there, but Morningstar is ultimately a King operation. It has its own procedures when it comes to how the family works."

"What are you saying?"

"I'd have to consult our friend Walter Trissel, but it's entirely possible that if I die without an heir, the company reverts back to the nearest King—either to Lydia or Anderson, her oldest child."

She blanched. "If that's not motive for murder, I don't know what is."

CHAPTER NINETEEN

Beckett wanted to soothe away Samara's worry for him. All he had to do was kiss her, and the magnetic pull between them would take care of the rest. He'd tow her into the bedroom and neither one of them would think too hard about the threats they were facing down for the rest of the night. With his body dragging against hers, her taste on his tongue, her cries in his ears...the rest of the danger would cease to matter.

But the danger would still be there in the morning.

It would still be there no matter what they did, but he wanted her to choose to let him stay without his steamrolling her. He wanted her to choose *him*.

Samara shifted a little and laid her head on his shoulder. "You're staying here tonight."

He should just let it go, but he wanted her to want him there—not to be offering because she thought he didn't have anywhere else to go. "If you're sure. You're probably safer if I leave."

"That's a joke, right? You're not doing this alone. I'll have to deal with Lydia eventually, but for the time being

I'm on vacation because she commanded it. There's no reason I can't go with you to talk to Walter Trissel tomorrow." She nestled closer. "And you shouldn't be alone tonight. Before you get your back up about it, that's not pity talking. Don't let your pride make you act like an asshole. Stay. We don't have to have sex, but you're sleeping in my bed tonight."

Relief surged, the jolt so strong it nearly sent him to his knees. *It's not over between us. Even after everything we've seen in such a short fucking time, it hasn't ruined the possibility of a future together.* "I'd like that." He reached over and scooped her into his lap. The sensation of having Samara in his arms soaked into him one heartbeat at a time. Her mass of dark hair pressed against the side of his face, soft and smelling of lavender. The subtle strength of her arms where they were wrapped around him, holding him as tightly as he held her.

Home.

Samara felt like home.

Beckett rested his chin on the top of her head. "Movie or bed?"

She tensed, but it barely lasted a single breath. "Bed."

It felt strange to walk hand in hand to her bedroom. She dug around under her sink and came up with a spare toothbrush. He raised an eyebrow, but didn't comment. It struck Beckett that this could be his life—brushing his teeth next to Samara every night. Watching her wash off her makeup and strip off her armor as she got ready for bed. Knowing that he'd be able to hold her for hours without having to worry that one of them needed to leave.

Beckett unzipped her dress, his gaze glued to the long slice of bare skin revealed as the black fabric parted. His hands shook with the need to follow the path, to drag his thumbs over the lean muscles lining her back, to find the dimples on either side of the bottom of her spine.

Tonight is supposed to be about comfort. Not sex.

He stepped back before he could do something to damage the fragile balance tonight required. He walked out of the bathroom and into the bedroom before he could come up with a bullshit reason to stay and watch her finish undressing. It didn't help calm his suddenly racing heart. The bed invited him to imagine her laid out there, naked and beckoning him to join her. The closet was filled with bright dresses that had him remembering what was like to press her against that door and go to his knees before her, or how tempting she'd been when she rode him in his office. *Control is overrated.*

He *should* have stayed out of the damn bathroom until he could be sure Samara was covered again, but the sound of the shower running was too much of a temptation to ignore.

She stood with her face tilted up to the spray of water, something resembling peace in her expression. The shower was the only sign of extravagance in the condo. It was a good six feet with varying grayscale tiles and three shower heads—two normal and a sunflower one in the center. Samara had all three going, and with her brown skin slicked with water and the steam twisting through the enclosed space, she looked like some kind of divine creature who'd wandered into this place by mistake. The sight hit him right in the gut, even stronger than before. *I want this.*

Her. Us. The dinners and the comfort and the sex and the conversations. A future together.

I want it all.

She smoothed back her hair and turned to look at him. "I changed my mind."

He forced his body still, using every ounce of his control not to take a single step toward her. "This isn't about sex. Or the shit we're dealing with both tomorrow and in the future. This is about us. I'm not here because I had nowhere else to go. I'm here because you're here."

"I know." She pressed her hand to the glass. "Shower with me, Beckett." Her wicked grin had his cock rising to attention. "You look like the best kind of dirty."

He could no more resist her than he could make the sun rise in the west. Beckett shucked off his pants and stalked to the shower, never taking his gaze from hers. She stepped back as he walked into the shower, and the appreciation he found on her face warmed him even more than the steam, chasing away the last bits of numbness clinging to him like cobwebs.

The water was a temperature just shy of scalding. Beckett rolled his shoulders and ducked his head under the spray. When he opened his eyes again, Samara was right in front of him. She slid her hands over his chest, pausing at his scar. "You're not alone, Beckett. Not anymore."

He wasn't alone because she was there. Because she might...keep being there. Longing nearly took him to his knees. "Samara, I—"

She kissed him as if she knew how close he was to saying something neither of them could take back. It was soft and bittersweet, and it made his chest ache all the way down to his soul. He laced his fingers through her thick hair and tilted her head back, the angle allowing him a slow exploration.

He licked down the long line of her neck and nipped

the sensitive spot where it met her shoulder. Not enough. Never enough. He guided her to lean against the cool tile and cupped her breasts. "If I live to be a hundred, I'll never get enough of you."

"I'm familiar with the feeling." She arched into his touch, her eyes half closed.

Let me keep you.

He ducked his head and captured one of her dark nipples in his mouth. Too many things left unsaid between them. Too much uncertainty in their future. Tonight, they could use touch to comfort each other, to convey all the things they weren't ready to put into words. Beckett ruthlessly smothered the desire to claim her in every way that counted. "Let me take you to bed," he breathed against her skin. *Let me show you all the things we aren't allowed to say.*

She tugged him up and kissed him hard. Samara's cinnamon taste teased him as much as her body sliding against his. She smiled against his mouth. "Beckett, *I'm* taking *you* to bed."

The words were barely out of Samara's mouth when Beckett moved. He scooped her into his arms, his hold sure. Her stomach erupted in butterflies, and she didn't have a chance in hell of keeping it out of her voice when she said, "What are you doing?"

"No time like the present to settle the debate on who's taking whom to bed." He grinned. "For tonight, at least."

He's talking like he means more than tonight. Hope unfurled cautious wings inside her. Even as she called herself seven different kinds of fool, she *wanted* him to stay. To carve out a future with her.

To love her.

You are in the middle of a crisis and that *is where your focus should be.* She swallowed hard. "You're going to break your leg trying to get out of this shower, and then we'll have to spend the night in the ER."

"You know what your problem is, Samara?" He opened the glass door and snagged two of her fluffy pink towels.

"I bet you're going to tell me." She dried off absently, watching him do the same. Beckett was . . . Beckett was obscenely attractive. He'd always been handsome, but grief had created a rough edge that called to her like a siren song. It was more than the seemingly permanent scruff on his jaw or the fact that his muscles were ridiculously defined. The events of the last week had honed the steel within, leaving him as something stronger. More determined. Infinitely sexier.

"Damn right I am." He grabbed her around the waist and hauled her over his shoulder. Her world turned upside down, and the spectacular view of Beckett's muscled ass wasn't enough to detract from the fact that *her* ass was in the air.

"Hey!"

"Oh look—I'm taking you to bed." He dumped her on the bed and snatched her ankle when she raised her foot. "I think that settles that argument."

She glared, but a grin kept slipping through. "Pretty sure you're not playing fair."

"Pretty sure you're right." He grabbed her other ankle and flipped her onto her stomach. "I'll tell you a secret."

Samara shivered and tried to keep her mock anger going. "Fine, I guess I'll settle for a secret."

His low laugh rolled down her spine. "I'm never going to play fair where you're concerned, Samara. Not if it means

I have you like this." The bed dipped as he leaned onto it. "*Especially* if I have you like this."

He adjusted his grip on her ankles and pulled her until her hips hit the end of the bed. "You are so fucking beautiful, it takes my breath away." Beckett lifted her hips with firm hands. He dragged his mouth along the curve of her ass, pressing open-mouth kisses every inch or two. *Worshipping.* "You were there for me tonight. Let me be there for you right now. I've got you."

"*Beckett.*" The comforter muffled her saying his name, but he seemed to hear it despite that.

He shifted down to lick her clit, long and slow. Again and again, as if he was savoring her taste. That, more than anything else, had her fighting not to move. She wanted to arch into him, to ride his mouth to orgasm, but he was in the driver's seat—for tonight.

He didn't make her wait long.

Beckett's mouth disappeared, and she couldn't hold back a moan of protest. And then his hands were on her hips, urging her up and spreading her legs wider to take him. Through it all, he didn't say a single word, and she couldn't see his face to gauge his mood.

"No condom."

His grip tightened on her hips. "I wouldn't ask that of you."

"I'm on birth control and clean." It was easier to take this jump with him when she couldn't see his face. "Please, Beckett."

"I'm clean, too." Still, he hesitated. "You're sure."

"I'm sure." She wanted this closeness, this truth between them. Rationally, she knew this wouldn't be some magic thing that sealed them together, but she craved the connection all the same. *You are not alone, Beckett. I'm here. Feel me. Let me feel you.*

She held her breath as he notched his cock at her entrance and pushed into her, inch by inch. His hands trembled against her skin, just a little, and his breathing hitched as if he was fighting with himself for control. "Samara." In that tone of voice, her name became something more. Something profound.

His cock filled her, stretching her, and she gripped the comforter, fighting for her own control. To not slam back and take him fully. To savor every second of this. To memorize the feeling of his hands sliding over her hips and up her back as if he sought to imprint his own memories with this moment. As if he cherished her.

Beckett withdrew, and she couldn't stifle her cry of protest. He didn't make her wait long. One moment she was facedown on the bed, the next he'd grabbed her right leg and lifted it to prop her calf on his shoulder, turning her onto her side. He slid her further on the bed and knelt between her legs. As he slid his cock into her again, the new position had his thigh rubbing against her clit with every movement.

Better yet, she could watch his face as he fucked her.

No, not fucking. It stopped being fucking when we were in LA.

This was more. So much more. The truth was written across Beckett's face as he watched her. Possessive, yes. But it was the thread of tenderness that did her in. As if he wanted to take care of her the same way she'd taken care of him tonight.

He leaned down and kissed her. His tongue seduced her slowly even as his moves became rougher. He slammed into her again and again, each stroke hitting her cervix and driving her pleasure higher. All the while he kissed her slowly, softly.

She writhed for him, soaking in the feeling that she was the most important thing in the world to him. *Even if only for tonight.* Pleasure sparked and crackled through her, almost painful in its intensity. The heat of his hands on her. The long line of his thigh sliding against her clit every time Beckett's thrust jolted her body. His tongue sliding against hers as if savoring the taste of her.

Her orgasm took her by surprise. She cried out, her nails marking paths in his thighs. He kept going, pursuing his own pleasure even as he watched hers. She kept her eyes open through it all, memorizing every line of his face, the vulnerability of his brown eyes as he lost control, the way his lips curved when he said her name as he came.

No matter what happened in the future, she would always have tonight, and the unnamable thing that lay between them. He slid down next to her, his arm a comforting weight across her stomach and his harsh breaths making the sensitive skin on her neck tingle. She couldn't quite catch her breath. There was no chalking her reaction up to the amazing orgasm. This went bone deep. "Beckett—"

"Not tonight." He pressed a quick kiss to her lips. "We'll have that conversation soon, but not tonight."

He was right. She knew he was right. But that didn't change the fluttering in her chest. She didn't recognize the sensation, couldn't tell if it was hope or despair. He'd blasted through every boundary she'd thrown in place between them, and now she felt like she was wandering in an endless fog without a signpost in sight.

I love you, Beckett King.

She couldn't say it now just like she hadn't been able to

say it last time. "You're right. Not tonight." She kissed him. The orgasm had only sharpened the edge of her need, her desire to show him exactly what he'd come to mean to her. "You took me to bed. Now it's my turn."

"Insatiable."

"Only for you." She nudged him onto his back and straddled him. "You called me beautiful, but I think you might be more beautiful than I am." She leaned down and kissed his scar, tracing its edge with her tongue.

Samara took her time exploring his body the same way he'd done to her in the past. She nipped the carved muscle of his pecs and trailed open-mouthed kisses down his stomach. His abs clenched with every swipe of her tongue, and she grinned against his skin. "Ticklish?"

"Woman, if you think I'm worried about being *ticklish* in our current position, then you're out of your damn mind." He cupped the side of her face with one big hand. "Come here, Samara. Let me make love to you again."

Make love.

She held his gaze as she turned her head and captured his middle finger between her lips. Samara sucked him deep, flicking his calluses with her tongue. His eyes narrowed. "Get your ass up here."

She released him. "Beckett—"

"Don't care. Need you." He hauled her up his body and took her mouth. She forgot all about arguing as he reached between them and eased two fingers into her. He stroked her as leisurely as he'd kissed her before. She quivered with the need for *more, more, more*. Beckett gently bit her bottom lip and then soothed the ache with his tongue. "Stay with me, Samara."

She could almost hear the rest of what he wasn't saying.

Stay with me after this is all over. Stay with me forever. Or maybe it was her own feelings talking. "Yes."

"Ride my fingers. Take what you need."

"What I need is *you*."

The only warning she got was him removing his hand, and then he flipped them. And then he was inside her again, thrusting slowly as he framed her face with his hands. "Have me, Samara."

She twined her legs with his and rose to meet each stroke. Their earlier frenzy allowed for something slower, deeper. They shared breath even as their bodies moved in perfect co-ordination. Sweat slicked their skin, adding to the decadent feeling of friction between them, and she fought the plea-sure spiraling through her, wanting to make this last as long as possible.

That moment. That place. Them together.

Perfection.

"Let go," Becket murmured against her neck. "Give it all to me." He slid his hands beneath her ass and lifted her against him, controlling the rhythm. It was too much and it might never be enough. Her desire for him—her love for him—rose from a well with no end, engulfing Samara com-pletely.

She came with a soft cry, clinging to him even as he fol-lowed her into oblivion.

Samara would have given anything in that moment to make the night stretch onward for an eternity. If the sun never rose, they'd never have to take the next steps that led out of her home, into the dangers awaiting. They never had to deal with reality crashing into the fantasy they'd built to-gether, never had to fight to keep from having everything fall apart around them.

Time marched on, whether she wanted it to or not. The sun would rise and they would rise with it. Tomorrow, for better or worse, everything would change. She was sure of it.

But tonight wasn't over. Not yet.

CHAPTER TWENTY

Beckett managed to slip out of bed without waking Samara. A quick glance at the clock proved it was early, but not indecently so. He poked around her kitchen until he found coffee, and got a pot going. Then he sat down to check emails.

Three from his bank, all notifying him of attempted charges that had been denied, thanks to the holds he'd put on the accounts. He smiled grimly. *Gotcha, Lydia.* She hadn't been able to resist that little dig the other day, and he was glad he'd trusted his gut.

Next up, he answered the few emails that were urgent, and had his HR director post internal job openings for the employees Lydia had poached. It would take time to fill those positions, and it couldn't wait until he'd had it out with his aunt.

He heard Samara stirring and poured a second cup of coffee. A few minutes later, she padded out of the bedroom, wearing a short robe that left her long legs bare. "Morning." She yawned.

"Morning." He set his phone down and watched her cradle her mug in both hands and inhale deeply. *God, this woman kills me.* "Samara."

Her eyes flew open. "Oh, no. What else happened?"

"What?"

"You have a serious tone and it's not even six thirty in the morning. That means something horrible happened."

He grinned despite everything. "I love you."

"You..." She gaped at him. "You can't just say things like that. This is...I'm not...Damn it, Beckett! I love your contrary ass, too."

His heart leaped in his chest. It was one thing to make the declaration himself, to see evidence of her feelings in how she treated him and did her best to offer comfort in what was both the shittiest and the single best week of his fucking life. It was entirely another to hear her say the words aloud. He took a slow sip of his coffee to center himself. "Should I have waited for a romantic dinner and bought you a dozen roses beforehand?"

She rolled her eyes. "I don't even like roses. They're bitchy little flowers. Lilies are better. Or even daisies."

"Noted."

She glared into her coffee mug. "It's so damn early in the morning and I'm not even fully awake and you just spring it on me. It's rude. Thirty minutes from now would have been appropriate." Samara finally looked up and grinned. "But I do love you, Beckett. It's too soon and it's crazy and I don't know how this is going to work. It'll probably blow up in both our faces."

He couldn't help it. He burst out laughing. "You kill me."

"No one needs to be killing anyone. You can't joke like that given your current predicament."

That sobered him when nothing else would have. *Samara*

loves me...and my aunt likely wants me six feet under.
"Life's complicated."

"You can say that again." She touched her hair and grimaced. "I need another shower and a small vat of coffee after last night. What's the plan for today?"

He held up his phone. "Frank found Walter. He's holed up in a little hotel just outside of town. I figured we'd go have a nice conversation with him and then see where the day goes from there." Beckett wasn't too keen to haul Samara around with him, if only because he couldn't guarantee her safety, but he couldn't guarantee it across the board without knowing Lydia's exact plans. But if she wasn't with him...

She scrolled through her phone, a frown appearing. "Actually, I'm being called into the office for an emergency meeting."

Alarm bells rang through his head. "Is that normal?"

"It doesn't happen often, but it does happen. Considering Lydia sent me off on a fake vacation to get me out of the way and is now summoning me back to the office..." She shrugged. "She's always operated under her own set of rules. I don't see why this would be any different."

"Don't go." The words were out before he could think better of them, about what they would mean in the current situation.

"I have to."

"Fuck that." Again, he spoke without thinking, but the stubborn lift of her chin told him everything he needed to know about how this conversation would go. "You can't honestly tell me that you think Lydia is innocent."

"I don't think she's innocent. If I did, I wouldn't have snuck into her office and photographed her calendar."

Frustration grabbed him by the throat and he set his mug down hard enough on the counter to make them both flinch. "Why go, then?"

"Because it's my job." She held up a hand before he could say something more. "This isn't a debate. I'm telling you that I'm going, because that's what I'm doing."

He didn't care *why* she was going, only that she was putting herself in the path of potential harm for a set of principles that didn't make any damn sense. "You know, you're not reenacting your mother and father if you just listen to me for once. You joked about Lydia throwing you out a window, but what's to stop her from doing exactly that when she realizes that I love you?"

Samara stared at him and then slowly shook her head. "I'm fully aware that I'm not my mother and you're hardly my father. But while that might be the case, I'm also my own person, Beckett. Lydia hasn't struck you directly yet—and she won't. She's too crafty for that. She also won't threaten me directly just because we're sleeping together."

She might say that, but she didn't know for sure. *If I lose you right when I found you . . .* He crossed his arms over his chest, fighting against the words that would drive the wedge deeper between them. He gritted his teeth. "Please don't go."

Something like sympathy appeared in her dark eyes. "Beckett, I know this is coming from a place of caring, but you can't bottle me up and stick me on some shelf to take out at your convenience. I have to live my own life, even if it's a life I'm potentially sharing with you. That's not going to change, no matter what else does. If you can't handle that . . ." Another shrug, this one stiffer. "I don't see how this could possibly work."

"I don't like ultimatums, Samara."

"Neither do I." She turned and walked through her bedroom door, shutting it softly behind her. He stared hard at the pale wood, as if he could will her into understanding that he wasn't trying to be an overbearing ass, but taking foolish risks just to prove she was independent was stupid. *Not a fight I'm going to win. Not right now.*

Instead, Beckett changed and wrote a quick note to Samara. He didn't trust himself not to say something to make their current standoff worse, but he didn't want to leave without some kind of good-bye. That done, he headed down to the street and to the lot where he'd parked his car the night before. It was blessedly unharmed. He'd half expected to show up and find it on fire. He climbed into the driver's seat, locked the doors, and called Frank.

"What's up?"

"Thanks for finding Walter for me." He caught movement out of the corner of his eye, but when he turned, the lot seemed just as empty as it had been when he arrived.

"Check your glove box."

Frowning, he obeyed and huffed out a laugh. "How the hell did you manage to get his hotel key?" It was in a sleeve with the room number written neatly on it.

"A gentleman never tells."

He slipped the key into his wallet. "I'm going to owe you my soul at this point, but I have one last favor."

"We're friends, Beck. You'd do the same for me if our situations were reversed."

He would, but he didn't like the ominous tone in Frank's voice. "Everything good?"

"Yeah." And that was that. "What's the favor?"

"Can you put someone on Samara? Lydia's pulling her

in unexpectedly this morning for an emergency meeting or some shit, but it doesn't feel right to me. I think she knows about us and she's going to try to use it to try to leverage some kind of benefit."

"Sounds like her."

Samara doesn't think so. Or she thinks she can handle herself. That was the problem, though—Samara *could* handle herself in most situations. But she still didn't quite believe the kind of evil bullshit his aunt could bring to the table. *He* still barely believed it and Beckett had been targeted repeatedly. "That's what I thought."

"I'll handle it personally, Beck."

Now was the time when he should have said it wasn't necessary for Frank to be the one to keep Samara safe, but he couldn't deny the relief that cascaded through him at the offer. "I appreciate it."

"You heading for Trissel?"

"Yeah, leaving now."

"Good luck."

That was really all there was to say about it. "You, too." He turned on the car.

Beckett hesitated, considering. He scrolled through his contacts to one he'd called maybe once in living memory. Calling Anderson King was a risk. He knew his cousin by reputation more than anything else, and by all accounts he had been raised just like Beckett—to be cold and ruthless and do whatever was necessary to protect the King name and his company.

And yet.

He pressed the call button. This would play out according to Beckett's plans, and that meant he needed Anderson in town.

The man himself answered, sounding irritated. "You've got a lot of nerve calling me."

Guess we're not acting the loving family. It was almost a relief. Lydia played the family card when it suited her, but it didn't mean anything coming from her mouth. "It's in everyone's best interest if you're back in Houston today."

Anderson paused. "Is that a threat?"

"It's a declaration of intent." He hung up. They could circle round and round for hours and it wouldn't prompt his cousin into action. Thinking he needed to be back in Houston to negate a threat? His ass would be on the next plane out of DC.

There *was* a threat. It just wasn't leveled at Anderson.

It was aimed completely at Lydia.

Satisfied he'd gotten the appropriate pieces in motion, he backed out of the space. Beckett searched the cars in the lot as he drove through it, but there was no one there. *Must have been imagining things.*

He couldn't afford to ignore any possibility that he was being followed, so he took a circular route through the city, cutting back and forth across downtown until he hopped on the freeway heading east. Best he could tell, no cars had made the journey with him, but he still kept one eye on the rearview as he followed Frank's instructions to the place where Walter had chosen to hole up.

The chic hotel wasn't *quite* inside the city limits, but it was close enough to the Gulf to list it as one of the main attractions. Its claim to fame, though, was the spa it boasted with a list of services longer than Beckett's arm. *The same spa where Lydia goes for those appointments Samara makes her.*

He walked through the lobby with purpose and no one

bothered him as he took the elevator up to Walter's floor. A quick look down the hall found it empty, and he strode to the door and let himself in, closing it quietly behind him and throwing the deadbolt.

A groan from the bed had him striding over and yanking the covers off the man. Walter Trissel cursed and covered his face with his forearm. He opened one eye and then shot up in bed and crab-walked backward until he hit the headboard. "What the hell are you doing here? You can't just come into my room like this!"

Beckett grabbed a chair and swung it around so he could straddle it. "Morning, Walter. It's time you and I had a nice little chat."

Despite her bravado, nerves fluttered in Samara's stomach as she walked down the hallway to Lydia's office. She'd picked a pair of slacks and a simple blouse with sensible shoes. *Being paranoid. Beckett has me thinking I'm going to have to run for my life, which is just crazy.*

Isn't it?

She could feel his note where she'd folded it carefully and put it in her pocket. *We'll talk tonight. —Beck.* It was short, but it gave her hope all the same. Hope that they could find a way through this. Together. She didn't want a man to sweep in and demand that she rely solely on him and bow to his will—not even Beckett. Samara trusted her instincts.

Right now, her instincts were hollering that this might be a huge mistake.

She forced a smile onto her face and opened the door to Lydia's office. The woman herself sat behind the large desk, her red-nailed hands steepled in front of her equally red lips. Journey occupied one of the two chairs opposite the desk, so

Samara strode in and took the other. "I got here as soon as I was able."

"Did you know?"

No preamble. No explanation.

Guilt flared, because Samara knew *exactly* what she was talking about. She lifted her chin. "I found out late last night."

Lydia narrowed her eyes as if she expected Samara to lie. "My darling nephew went around us to get that contract— a contract we *need*, I might add—and you didn't deign to...tell me? Call Journey here and let her know she didn't need to pull yet another all-nighter?"

Her guilt grew thorny spines that dug deep. Samara shot a look at Journey, taking in the circles under her eyes. Her friend gave the slightest shake of her head, but Samara ignored it. She faced Lydia. "It wouldn't have mattered if I told you last night. It's done. We lost the bid. I take full responsibility for not anticipating that Beckett would pull that move."

"Yes, well, you *should* have anticipated it." Lydia pushed slowly to her feet, sickly sweet menace rolling off her in waves. "You're sleeping with him, after all. You have been for months."

Samara went still. "Excuse me?"

"Did you or did you not have sex with Beckett King six months ago? You just *happened* to find your way up to his hotel room on that *work* trip in Norway and, how strange, you let him take you to bed."

There had been no *letting* him do anything. She'd been a full partner in the seriously questionable decision to have sex that initial time. "I don't see how it's any of your business one way or another who I sleep with."

"It is when you're spilling company secrets because you're so intoxicated with his cock."

She flinched, and hated herself for flinching. "I would never do that." Except she'd done *exactly* that by informing on Lydia's inconsistencies to Beckett. *Lydia, not Kingdom Corp.*

Lydia is *Kingdom Corp.*

"You would say that now."

More than anything, Journey's silence next to her hit Samara right in the chest. She pushed to her feet. "Correct me if I'm wrong, but did you not command me to get close to Beckett in order to distract him from whatever you're up to, Lydia?"

"Correct *me* if I'm wrong." Lydia mimicked. "But I never once told you to have sex with him and lose all sense of loyalty."

Another direct hit.

This time Samara didn't flinch. She raised her chin and straightened her shoulders. "Is that all?"

"Hardly." Lydia pointed an imperial finger at her. "You're fired. Sleeping with the enemy might be acceptable, but betraying the company *because* you're fucking Beckett King is not. I sincerely hope you weren't planning on continuing to work in the energy industry, because you're going to have a difficult time finding a job."

"That's enough, Mother." Journey pushed slowly to her feet, her mouth determined even as she seemed to shake. "You fired her. It's done."

"I'm nowhere near done."

Samara shifted, bringing Lydia's attention back to her. "Seeing as how I'm fired, fortunately, I don't have to sit here and listen to you rant." She stalked closer and leaned over the desk, getting in Lydia's face. "You are a vindictive bitch and you're positively soulless for what you've done to Beckett."

Nothing showed on her face. "I have no idea what you're talking about."

"Guess we'll see about that, won't we?" She turned and walked out of the office with her head held high even as a black hole opened up in her chest. After all her promises that she wouldn't make the same mistakes her mother had, she'd walked the exact blueprint.

Fall for a rich man from a prominent family.

Compromise everything she'd worked her entire life for.

Lose everything.

Not everything. I haven't lost Beckett.

She wasn't sure if that made it better or worse. She loved him. The hurt pounding through her, digging deeper with each heartbeat, didn't have any effect on what she felt for him. It was just everything else that had fallen apart.

He'd still offer you that job.

If I take it, I owe him everything and we'll never really be equals.

There was a way out of this—a way forward—but she couldn't see it right then.

"Samara."

She stopped in front of the elevators and waited for Journey to catch up. "I'm sorry."

Journey shook her head. "I'm pissed. It was shitty of him to do, but that's just business. I don't get you not telling me immediately, but . . ." She sighed. "I don't think you should be fired over it. I tried to convince my mother of that, but she's beyond reason. She'll cool down."

"No, she won't." Because the real reason Samara had been fired wasn't because of the bid. It was because of her relationship with Beckett—the appearance of putting Beckett over Lydia.

"She would if you'd dump him."

Samara jerked back. "You can't be seriously asking me to do that."

"Yes. No. Maybe." Journey shook her head. "He's just a guy, Samara. At the end of the day, he might be good in bed and not a total piece of shit outside it, but he's still someone you hated a week ago. Is he really worth it?"

The choice lay before her, clear as day. She could dump Beckett today and come crawling back to Lydia, promising to spill every single secret he'd shared with her as payment to securing her job once again. Lydia would punish her for a while, but she'd still have her job. She just had to throw Beckett under the bus to make it happen.

Samara let herself imagine it. Continuing to work in this office, going about her days as if she didn't have a gaping hole in her heart. She'd still have the job she'd worked her ass off for, but at what cost? Her mother never climbed over others to get ahead, even before she'd settled into the life she had now.

Her *father* had.

The realization slammed her thoughts to a halt. All this time, she was afraid of having her future cut off the way her mother's had been. It never occurred to her that she might be in danger of following in her *father's* footsteps.

She couldn't do it.

She *wouldn't* do it.

"I'm not..." She turned to face her friend. "I'm not making this call because of him, though it might look like that right now. The truth is that I can't work for someone like Lydia when I know what I know."

Journey huffed out a laugh. "I guess I can't blame you for that." She narrowed her eyes. "But if you think you're getting rid of *me* that easily, you're out of your damn mind."

"Drinks on Saturday?" she offered softly.

"Definitely." Journey pulled her in for a hug. "Now you better get out of here before she throws a hissy fit and calls security."

Samara pushed the button for the elevators. "I'll call you tomorrow."

"You better."

She stepped into the elevator and took it down to the main floor. No one jumped out to accost her, and she sighed at the colossal waste of time this had all been. Not the last decade of work, but this morning. Lydia didn't have to bring her in to personally berate her. It would have been just as easy either to wait until Monday or send a scathing email. She hadn't even kept Samara long enough to warrant the trip.

Unless...

Samara picked up her pace and dug her phone out of her purse. She dialed Beckett, but it clicked over to voice mail. *That doesn't mean anything. He's probably interrogating Walter Trissel and has his phone on silent. I'm being paranoid in thinking Lydia summoned me here to keep me out of that meeting.*

Wasn't she?

A man detached himself from the side of the building and fell into step next to her. She raised her eyebrows at Frank, not even remotely surprised. "I didn't realize you had time in your busy day to play babysitter."

"Wouldn't you do the same for Journey?"

There was no point in answering, because she *would*. If

Journey called her, she'd drop everything and go because they were best friends and both of them took that relationship seriously. Samara waved her phone at him. "I can't get ahold of Beckett."

"He should be at the hotel right now."

His calm demeanor made her feel a little like she was being paranoid, but Samara couldn't shake the growing suspicion that something was terribly wrong. She stopped. "You have a car around here?"

He gave her the look that question deserved. "Yes."

"I think Lydia orchestrated this meeting to make sure I didn't go to that hotel with Beckett." It sounded even crazier saying it aloud than it did in her head, but she pushed forward. "I think...I think she was protecting me." *And putting Beckett in danger.*

A stillness came over Frank that made the small hairs on the back of her neck stand up. "Let's go." He hit the corner and cut across the street, leaving her scrambling to keep up. Two blocks later he opened the passenger door to an Audi R8 coup painted a deep gray. "Get in."

Samara didn't hesitate to obey.

Seconds later Frank was in the driver's seat and they were shooting into traffic. He weaved between cars, heading for the 10. He didn't speak, and she kept trying to call Beckett.

Nothing.

Visions of smoke and fire and his bloody baby book flashed before her eyes. *He ignored the warnings. He went on the offense. She couldn't have possibly anticipated this, could she?* "He's okay. He has to be okay."

Frank said nothing, but the speedometer crept into triple digits as they flew out of town.

CHAPTER TWENTY-ONE

I want answers, Walter." Beckett leaned against the chair he occupied, watching the other man closely.

Walter scrubbed a hand over his eyes and then up over his head, making his thin hair stand on end. "Am I allowed to get dressed, or are you planning on having this conversation while I'm half naked?"

Beckett reached down and snagged a pair of pants and tossed them onto the bed. "That's good enough." He didn't think the man was a direct threat, but he'd been wrong about such things before. He wasn't about to take any unnecessary risks. This was Texas, after all. Walter no doubt owned a gun or three.

Maybe I should have brought mine.

But no. He wanted Walter to talk, not to piss his pants in fear. Beckett brushed his hand over his phone in his pocket. *Recording should be going.* He waited until the man had pulled on his pants to speak. "You drugged my father at Lydia's command so he'd will her Thistledown Villa."

Walter froze, his pale eyes going wide. "You can't know that."

That's almost an admission, right there. "And yet I do. How much did Lydia pay you? I want to know what your loyalty cost."

Walter's shoulders bowed half an inch before he seemed to make the effort to straighten them again. "Four. Million. Dollars."

Beckett didn't blink. The house and surrounding property was probably worth a cool ten million, but it wasn't money that had driven his aunt to such lengths. She would no more sell Thistledown than she'd sell Morningstar if she managed to see her plan through.

All we have in this world is family, even if we can never forgive them.

"Four million dollars just to drug my father." He caught the slight tightening around the man's mouth. "Ah. Four million to ensure she got Thistledown—and to make sure Nathaniel got behind the wheel the night he died." It was a shot in the dark, but Walter looked like he might throw up right then and there, which was all the confirmation Beckett needed.

Fuck.

"People drive drunk all the time." Walter looked out the window, seeming to shrink in on himself. "How was I supposed to know he'd drive himself right into a telephone pole?"

"That's not even close to a good excuse. You might not have put a gun in his hand and cocked it, but you directly set him on the path that resulted in his death. That's manslaughter at the bare minimum." Beckett leaned forward and lowered his voice. "She wouldn't let you off the hook after that, would she? What's a little fire after you killed a man?"

Walter pushed to his feet and weaved, almost floundering back onto the bed. "You don't know anything."

"I know that fire had to start right around the time you walked out of your office to accept an offer from Lydia. Strange coincidence, that. What do you think the fire investigator will find when he starts sifting through the evidence? You're no good at being a criminal, Walter. Look at you—you're still drunk from last night. Have you been sober since you killed my father?"

"*He deserved it.*" Walter swung around, his face a mottled purple. "That bastard was going to fire me. Did you know that? Ten years of being the sole attorney on retainer for Morningstar and he just up and decides that I'm no longer needed."

Beckett hadn't known that, but it didn't surprise him. Walter was crafty and conniving, which were positives in his business, but he was also lazy and drank too much for it to be completely casual. It was only a matter of time before he did something that forced Nathaniel's hand, and it must have happened while Beckett was out of the country, because his father hadn't had a chance to communicate the plan to him. "You had to know it was coming." He watched every move Walter made, ready to burst into motion if the man did something threatening. "Even if you didn't, why target me? I had nothing to do with it."

"You're Nathaniel's son." As if that was reason enough.

"How did you manage to break into my place without anyone seeing you—including the cameras?"

Walter gave a little smile. "Wouldn't you like to know? Maybe I'm just that good."

Not a chance. "Maybe you had outside help."

"You're just mad because you didn't see it coming."

If anything, Walter's smirk widened. "You never saw *me* coming."

Beckett replayed the whole conversation in his head. *Got everything I need. That's about enough of that.* He pushed to his feet. "Get a shirt on. You're coming with me."

"The hell I am."

He pointed at Walter. "Get your fucking shirt on or I will drag you out of here as you are now. Your choice. You have five seconds to decide."

Walter glared. "Fine. I'll get my damn shirt on."

"Thought you'd see things my way." He stepped back as the man went to round the bed, but Walter stumbled and fell against Beckett.

He caught the thinner man easily, but the second his hands closed around Walter's arm, a pinprick of pain hit him in the other shoulder. Beckett looked over to see a tiny syringe sticking out of him. "What the fuck?"

"She said you might come here. I was prepared." Walter leaned in, his breath reeking of stale alcohol. "Didn't see *that* coming, did you?"

He tried to respond, but his tongue felt too big in his mouth and his lips were numb. "What..."

"Just a little something to make you more agreeable." Walter caught him as he tipped sideways and shoved him onto the bed. "Hold still, Beckett. We're going for a drive."

Just like my father did.

Tingling spread through Beckett's body, followed by the damn numbness. He could move his arms and legs, but they wouldn't translate his brain's commands into anything but faint twitches. *Fuck, fuck, fuck.* He strained, but nothing happened. *It can't last forever. I can't drive like this and there's no alcohol in my system, so he can't fake it as another drunk driving accident. Lydia has something else planned, which means I have time.*

He forced himself to take as deep a breath as he was able. No telling how long the drug would last, but he'd conserve his energy and let Walter think he'd given up. If it meant the man kept talking, all the better.

Walter took what seemed to be a leisurely shower and came out of the bathroom dressed in a different pair of slacks and a dark gray button-down shirt that gave him the appearance of an undertaker with his cadaverous features. He chortled when he saw that Beckett hadn't moved. "Gave you the good stuff, didn't I? That tingling in your limbs can't be pleasant, but it'll keep you from being too much trouble in the meantime. We have a bit of a drive ahead of us."

Good. More time to let this shit work its way out of my system.

Walter guided him up and shoved himself under Beckett's arm. He had a good fifty pounds on the thinner man, and he had little control over his legs as Walter guided them to the door and out into the hall. It would look like he was helping a drunk friend, and when Beckett tried to talk, it came out as a jumbled mess.

"None of that, now." Walter huffed and they teetered dangerously as he shifted to push the button for the elevator. "Don't want to drag anyone else into this, do you?"

Considering Walter could barely handle maneuvering Beckett's uncooperative body around, he didn't know how much of a threat the other man was, but that was the problem—*he didn't know*. If someone else got hurt because he was trying to call for help, he'd never forgive himself.

Got to handle this one on my own.

Like I handle everything.

His phone buzzed in his pocket, and he groaned slightly to cover up the faint sound. If Walter took his phone out, he'd realize Beckett had been recording all of this—was *still* recording. He needed this evidence, and it was all too easy to delete if the man knew it was there. A short pause as the call went to voice mail and then it started buzzing again.

Samara. It had to be. Frank wouldn't call like that unless Lydia really *had* thrown Samara out a window, and Beckett didn't believe for a second that had happened.

They staggered into the elevator and Walter leaned them against the back wall as it descended. "Christ, you're a big fucker, aren't you? Thank God I parked close to the entrance."

Beckett expected him to head for the main entrance, but Walter turned them down the hall to the door leading out to a secondary parking lot. *He really did know I'd track him down eventually and planned for it—or, rather, Lydia did.*

Walter's car was a red Corvette—surprise, surprise—and he half collapsed Beckett against the side of it so he could wrestle open the door. He looked from Beckett's six-two frame to the cramped seat and cursed. "Should have rented a fucking van."

Seven minutes of cursing, banging Beckett's body parts against the door frame or dashboard, and more cursing, and Walter managed to get him inside. The calls to Beckett's phone had stopped, thankfully, but he still was under the full effects of whatever Walter had given him.

The man in question slid behind the wheel and gunned the engine. "Taking too much fucking time. Someone might have seen."

Even if he could have talked, Beckett wouldn't have

pointed out that no one who saw them was going to assume
that he was being kidnapped. This place catered to the rich
and, as such, they tended to look the other way whenever
something sketchy was going on. Normally, that was an asset, but not when a literal kidnapping was going down.

This is a fucking shit show.

His head lolled as Walter took the turn out of the parking
lot on two wheels. Beckett closed his eyes and took several
deep breaths. *Quite a drive could mean anything from fifteen
minutes to several hours. Focus on moving your body and
hope this asshole keeps talking.*

He concentrated all his will on his toes, hidden from view
by his shoes. *Move. Move, damn you!*

Nothing.

Samara pointed at the red Corvette that had just veered into
the road in front of them as they were slowing down to turn
into the hotel parking lot. "Did you just see—"

"That's Walter Trissel's car."

That wasn't what she'd been asking. She'd caught the
briefest glimpse of a man in the passenger seat, his body
slumped against the window as if sleeping or drunk. He'd
looked a whole hell of a lot like Beckett. "Follow him."

Frank nodded but didn't pick up speed. She saw why immediately. There wasn't much traffic on the road, so if they
followed too closely, he was bound to notice. She couldn't
imagine Walter Trissel expecting Frank Evans and her to
show up, but she wasn't willing to take any chances at this
point. "Beckett didn't look good. There's no way he'd get
into that car with Walter of his own free will." If they had to
drive somewhere, *Beckett* would be behind the wheel. Unless he couldn't drive for some reason...

Kind of like how Nathaniel shouldn't have been driving that night.

The thought took root, burrowing deeper and deeper with each mile they covered. Frank's tension only grew, choking the air in his vehicle, but she forced herself to keep breathing as if her heart wasn't in danger of beating out of her chest. She wanted to scream at him to go faster, to do something to force Walter to stop, to save Beckett.

But he kept a careful distance between them, following the Corvette south and then west along the edge of the Gulf. For a little bit, it seemed like he might drive back to Houston, but then he turned off the main road and into a group of trees.

Frank slowed and then slowed more. She thought he might turn into the same road, but he passed it and then pulled a U-turn about a mile later. He pulled out his phone and sent what looked like a flurry of texts.

"Why aren't we chasing him down right now?" Her hands itched to throw open the door and start running. It was *wrong* to sit here and wait while Beckett was most certainly in danger.

"Because we want him to live." Frank shoved his phone into his pocket. "Get out."

"Excuse me?"

"You're going to drive us over there and drop me off. Circle back around until I have Beckett, and then we'll make our escape."

She stared at him, waiting for the punch line—or at least something resembling an actual plan—but he gave her a flat look. Samara shook her head. "No way. I'm going down that road whether you give permission or not." When Frank didn't move, she glared. "You don't know how far he drove down there. What if it's half a mile and Beckett can't walk for some reason? Having me circle all the way out here isn't going to solve that problem. It's only going to make things more complicated."

"I promised him that I'd keep you safe." Every word sounded like it was dragged from him against his will.

She shook her head slowly. "That promise doesn't mean shit if something happens to him. I'm not a child, Frank. I'll follow orders, but you need me there. Trying to keep me out of this is just stupid."

For a second, it seemed like he might keep arguing, but he finally cursed softly. "You see it go sideways, you get the fuck out of there. You hear me?"

"I hear you." No way was she leaving with both him and Beckett, but if she said as much, he might tie her up and lock her in the trunk until this was all over.

Lydia, what did you do?

She could barely fathom that Lydia had orchestrated Beckett being kidnapped, let alone that she'd had *Walter Trissel* do it. There was nothing out in this area but marshes, and she couldn't think of anything good that would come from Walter parking in this nearly deserted area. *He's going to try to kill Beckett.* She pressed her lips together, waiting for Frank to give her the go-ahead.

He didn't make her wait long. "Let's go. I have reinforcements coming, but they won't be here in time to do anything but help with the cleanup."

Not for the first time, Samara wondered what the hell it was that Frank *did*. As far as the public was concerned, he was a real estate mogul who owned more than his fair share of Houston, and an eclectic mix of businesses at that. The Evans family had dabbled in politics before Frank's father was arrested for murder about fifteen years ago. Now there was only Frank and his solitary empire.

None of that matters. He's here. He obviously cares about Beckett. He's helping. That's enough.

She pulled off the shoulder and back onto the road, heading the way they'd originally come. The road the Corvette had disappeared down looked downright sinister now, but that was her imagination taking over. It wasn't any different from the first time they'd driven past it. Greenery encroached on the gravel drive as if waging a war to eliminate any evidence that men had ever settled in this place. The marshes had always been like that—a little too untamed for her tastes—but they had never left a cold spot in her chest before.

The marshes would be an excellent place to hide a body if someone was familiar enough with them to sink it correctly. The ecosystem would take care of any evidence, given enough time.

"He has to be okay."

"He is," Frank opened the glove box and pulled out a small handgun. "You know how to shoot."

It wasn't a question, but she answered all the same. "Yes, though I don't practice regularly."

He nodded and went through the motions of checking the cartridge and chamber as they bumped along the road. "You shouldn't have to use it, but I'm still leaving it with you."

In case things go all to hell.

She caught sight of a flash of red ahead of them and slowed until they barely crawled along. "Up ahead."

"I see it." He reached into the space behind the seats and pulled out a fucking shotgun.

Samara gripped the wheel harder to keep the shaking of

her hands under control. She wasn't trained for this. Her mother sent her to a gun safety course when she was in middle school because Samara was a woman and may have to protect herself at some point. She owned a handgun, but it was in a locked case at the top of her closet. She hadn't done more than clean it in years.

Beckett. This is for Beckett.

"Stop here."

She braked, grateful that she had a clear view of the Corvette. She could see the back of Walter's head, but not Beckett's. "Bring him back safely, Frank."

He passed over the handgun and waited until she nodded to shift his grip on the shotgun and climb out of the car. Samara watched him stalk toward the Corvette, keeping in what she suspected was the driver's blind spot. *I never want to be on his bad side.* She checked the mirror to ensure that no one had come in after them, blocking their getaway. There wasn't room to turn around, which meant she'd have to reverse a good portion of the way back to the main street. *Tricky. Trickier if we're being chased or in a hurry.*

"I can do it," she whispered, needing to say the words aloud to make them truth. She checked Frank's position. He'd reached the back fender of the Corvette.

Showtime.

CHAPTER TWENTY-TWO

Beckett had managed to regain control of all his toes. He suspected he had more than that, but he wasn't willing to risk testing with Walter so close. The man sat staring at the marshes in front of them as if psyching himself up for something.

Probably to put that gun in his hand to good use.

He'd stashed a .45 in the car and had brought it out as soon as they were parked. From what Beckett could see from his slumped position, they were somewhere within the many miles of coastal marshes that bracketed the area around Houston. *East of the city.* He wasn't sure *where*, though. Even if he'd managed to get a call out for help, he was too far for anyone to make it in time.

"It didn't have to be this way." Walter spoke softly, almost as if talking to himself. "If you'd just taken her offer, she would have let you walk away. I don't think she really wants you dead, Beckett. You're nothing to her. Just the son of the man she loathes." He chuckled. "The man we both loathe. Hell, the man we *all* loathe." His laugh took on a hysterical tinge.

Walter showed every evidence of being a man in over his head with no way of reaching the surface. Beckett knew better than to try to bargain. Lydia had the man by the balls and he'd see this through to the end because he couldn't imagine another way out. He'd killed Nathaniel and he'd try to kill Beckett, too.

And then she'd really own his soul.

Walter looked down at the gun cradled in his hands. "Can't do it in the Vette. Talk about evidence." He kept laughing as if hearing the funniest joke. "Then where would we be?"

If he let Walter get out of this car, his chances of survival dropped exponentially. Beckett could fight, but he wasn't at full capacity. Walter would hesitate to pull the trigger in here, which meant he'd hold back. It was Beckett's only chance.

He lunged, the move nowhere near as smooth as it had been in his head. Instead of snatching the gun from Walter's unsuspecting hands, he head-butted the man and half collapsed on his side of the car, pinning him in place. *Good enough.*

"Fuck! Jesus! Fuck!" Walter tried to scramble out from beneath him, but Beckett wedged his arm awkwardly in the way of the seat belt. He wasn't going anywhere.

Movement out the back window distracted him. He frowned, half sure the drug effects had evolved from paralysis into hallucinations, because there was no way in hell that Frank's R8 was sitting thirty feet behind the Corvette, *Samara* behind the wheel.

"Shuddup, Walter." He pressed down on the smaller man, concentrating on cutting off his ability to take deep breaths. Beckett had only one chance at this, which meant he had to get control of his fucking tongue. "You listening?"

"Fuck you, Beckett!"

"Good nuff." He shook his head, which only made the world spin. "Get out of Houston, Walter. Get out of Texas. Get the fuck off this continent. I ever see your face again, and I'll shoot you where you stand."

"You wouldn't dare!"

He leaned back to let the man meet his gaze, to let him see the truth there. Walter's curses sputtered out and he went silent. Beckett waited a few seconds longer. "Try me. You have six hours to get out of town."

Walter wet his lips. "Where will I go? I don't have my money yet."

"I doubt you're getting it." The thought brought him a vicious sense of satisfaction. While he could kill Walter right now, that would put him on the same level as this piece of scum, and he'd potentially have to deal with the fallout as well. Simpler—more justified—to exile him.

But if Walter did decide to test him, he would find out the hard way that Beckett didn't bluff.

"Six hours."

The driver's door opened, revealing Frank. The man looked from Walter to Beckett and back again. "You got it covered."

"Yeah." He nodded.

Frank leveled a shotgun at Walter's face. "If I were you, I'd pass that gun right over here nice and easy."

Walter shook and Beckett glared. "If he pisses himself while I'm stuck here, I'm going to kick your ass."

"Noted." Frank took the gun and tossed it into the water behind him. "I don't suppose we're killing him and leaving him to rot the same way he planned for you."

"Pesky thing about murder, Frank, is there's no statute of

limitations. Some part of him surfaces ten years down the road and we're fucked. Besides, I like the idea of this cockroach scuttling away from the light and spending the rest of his life looking over his shoulder and wondering when I'll change my mind about letting him live."

"*When?*" Walter squeaked. "You said you were letting me go."

"Yes, Walter. I did say that." He shook his arm out, the tingling slowly fading. "But you killed my father and tried to take my family home from me, in addition to a whole host of sins. That kind of thing pisses a man off. You understand."

"But—"

"May come a day where I change my mind and hunt you down. You'll never see me coming. There will be the hint of being watched, the feeling where you might not be quite alone, and then you'll take your last breath and know that I'm the reason why."

Without another word, he shoved off the man and climbed out his own door. He had to lean against the side of the Corvette. *Fuck.* This wasn't over—it was a long shot from over—and he needed to keep moving before Walter managed to make it back to a phone and call to warn Lydia.

She wouldn't flee. It was against her nature.

Which meant he had to make his move now as opposed to later, when she had time to plan and try to counter it. Catching her flat-footed was his only chance.

He yanked his phone out of his pocket and nearly fumbled it to the ground. *Slow down. Walter isn't going anywhere, but you toss that fucking phone in the water and this is all for nothing.* He thumbed off the recording, paused to make sure it was saved, and started for the Audi.

Which was right around the time he realized the damn car only had two seats.

Frank appeared at his elbow, the shotgun casually held against his hip as if he walked around with the damn thing during every waking moment. "Have Samara drive you back. My people will be here shortly and get me back to town."

His people.

Beckett paused. "I want him alive, Frank. There's enough blood to go around in this situation already. He was a pawn."

"Noted."

That wasn't a damn answer. Beckett opened his mouth to demand a promise to let Walter walk out of this situation alive, but Samara opened the driver's door and popped her head out. "Beckett, let's go."

Her window was down. She'd heard everything. He expected her to come down on his side of this, but there was a hard line to her lips he'd never seen before. He turned and frowned at Frank. "I mean it."

"I'm not going to murder him." Frank sighed and shook his head. "But I am going to drive that erectile dysfunction commercial on four wheels into the nearest compound and see it compressed into a tiny cube."

Beckett raised his eyebrows. "I didn't know you felt so strongly about Corvettes."

"It's not Corvettes, Beck. It's the type of people who drive them." Frank's expression stayed serious. "I'm glad you're good."

"Day's not over yet."

"Heading to Kingdom Corp?"

"Yep." He glanced back at the Corvette, but Walter hadn't moved. "Call me when you're back."

"Will do."

It took every ounce of willpower to keep his walk to the passenger side of the Audi relatively normal. He sank into the bucket seat and exhaled. "Hey."

"*Hey*. That's all you have to say to me?" Samara slammed the door and gunned the engine, backing up so fast Frank had to move quickly to avoid spraying gravel. "I thought you were going to be hurt, Beckett. I thought you could *die*." She kept her arm over the back of his seat, her narrowed eyes on the window as she expertly drove the Audi backward along the narrow road. "I realized Lydia called the meeting to ensure I wasn't with you when you met with Walter and it scared the shit out of me, and then we show up in time to see you slumped over and maybe unconscious and..."

He put his hand over her knee. "I'm okay, Samara. You're okay."

"Not through lack of trying," she snapped. They whipped around a curve and she used the minuscule shoulder on the road to turn around so they were driving the correct way. Only then did she exhale slowly. "Damn it, Beckett. I love you. I thought our last words might have been a fight and that I just found you only to lose you and..."

He waited for her to stop at the edge of the paved road and leaned over to kiss her. He kept it soft and sweet and re-assuring. "We're okay."

A sigh that he felt more than heard. "It's not over yet, is it?"

"No." He sat back. "Drop me at Kingdom Corp. My aunt and I are past due for a conversation."

Samara looked at him as if he'd grown two heads. "It's funny—the way you just said that made it sound like I'd drop you at the door and mosey my way on to safety while you battle that dragon alone." She gave a sharp shake of her head. "Not a chance, Beckett. You're barely standing on your own right now, though you get points for bravado. If you need to talk to her without witnesses, then I'll respect that, but I will be right outside that room and ready to ride to your rescue again."

"I just saved myself, woman."

"Was that what happened?" Her breathy laugh was more nerves than humor. "It sure as hell seemed like you let a man drive you out into the middle of nowhere with every intent of murdering you."

He touched his phone, the reassuring weight a steady reminder that at least it hadn't been for nothing. "He killed my father. Maybe not directly, but he was the tool Lydia used to ensure Nathaniel got behind the wheel that night. Walter's also behind everything from the will changing to destroying my apartment."

"Shit," she breathed. Samara took one hand off the wheel and reached over to lace her fingers with his. "What happens now?"

He'd spent enough time thinking about it while Walter drove. "I sent him away. If we went to court, he might go down, but ultimately my father was the one driving. Both the arson and the breaking and entering were admitted to verbally, but as yet there's no evidence to tie him to it. Going to the police isn't an option." When she didn't argue, he laid it all out there--the exile, the timeline. Everything.

Samara nodded when he finished. "He's going to spend the rest of his life looking over his shoulder as a paranoid mess."

"Good."

"Exactly what he deserves." She squeezed his hand. "I'm glad you're okay, Beckett."

He brought their clasped hands up and kissed her knuckles. "Thank you for riding to my rescue." He grinned, mostly to reassure her. "This will make for one hell of a story to tell the grandkids one day."

She arched her brows. "Getting a little ahead of ourselves, aren't we?"

He settled back in his seat. "You're right."

"I know."

"We'll talk after I deal with Lydia."

This time, her laugh was almost normal. "God, you're out of control."

She was right that it was too soon to talk about things like that, but he didn't want to think too hard about what came next until they were there. He wanted this quiet moment with Samara, separated from the rest of the world by the confines of the car. "Did you get my note?"

"The one about dinner tonight?"

"Yeah." A headache bloomed into being right between his eyes. *Probably the aftereffects of the drug.* He closed his eyes, but it didn't help in the least. "I'm sorry we fought this morning. I still think you made a choice out of pride, but I did, too."

"You were right. About Lydia. I didn't believe you until it was almost too late, and even then I almost made the wrong choice."

That roused him. Beckett opened his eyes. "What choice?"

"She fired me." Samara didn't take her attention away from the road. She sighed. "Sorry. You're trying to distract us both from what's coming next, and I'm just determined to throw us back into it, aren't I?"

They hit the city limits and their progress slowed along with traffic. He pinched the bridge of his nose, but it only made his headache worse. "It's almost over."

"We just have to survive it."

CHAPTER TWENTY-THREE

Samara purposefully parked the car several blocks from the Kingdom Corp building. She recognized the look in Beckett's dark eyes—if he had a chance, he'd try to keep her out of this the same way Frank had commanded her to sit in the car. She'd listened to Frank because that situation was clearly beyond her skill set. *This* wasn't.

She shut off the car and turned to him. "Ready?"

"Let's go."

She watched him closely as he climbed to his feet, but all evidence that he hadn't been at full health an hour ago was gone. He didn't shake or lean, and his pupils were normal. Beckett caught her looking and gave a grim smile. "Do I pass inspection?"

She wanted to say no. To tell him that he definitely needed a shower and a change of clothes and to take a vacation that would get him the hell out of Houston for a while. Samara didn't say any of it. Every distraction she could offer was just that—a distraction. A Band-Aid on a problem that wasn't going to go away without a direct confrontation. Even then, she didn't see how he could combat Lydia's entrenched position.

"Samara." Beckett crossed to her in two large steps and pulled her into his arms. "I have it under control. I promise."

He'd said something to that effect before and ended up drugged and almost murdered. She closed her eyes and leaned her forehead against his chest. This was it. Either she trusted him or she didn't. "Let's do this."

He took her hand, maintaining contact as they turned and started for Kingdom Corp. Samara thought she was ready to face down Lydia, to see justice. But her emotions tangled through her in an indecipherable mess. Rage and sorrow and something akin to hope. She trusted Beckett. She trusted his plan. There was no other option.

What happens if we fail?

She didn't know, and that scared her most of all.

Security met them at the door. Samara guided Beckett to a stop and lifted her chin. "Max. Jacob. Nice seeing you."

The guards exchanged a look. Max cleared his throat. "I'm sorry, Ms. Mallick, but we're under strict instructions to make sure you don't trespass on the property."

Damn you, Lydia. "I'm here to speak to Ms. King."

Another loaded look between them. "We're going to have to ask you to leave the premises. Immediately."

"For fuck's sake, Max, I know your kids' birthdays. And Jacob, who was it that made sure you were taken care of when you hurt your ankle falling down the stairs?"

Jacob wouldn't meet her gaze. "With all due respect, Ms. Mallick, you aren't with the company anymore."

And that was all that mattered to them. Years of learning details about the various employees to create a better working space in Kingdom Corp and it was all shit the second she stepped out of line. *So much waste.* Her throat threatened to close and she swallowed hard. "I would think ten years of employment would grant me a single meeting."

Max lowered his voice. "If you try to make a scene, we'll be forced to call the police."

Beckett finally spoke. "That's a great idea. Why don't you ring my aunt and let her know that Beckett and Samara are here and we'd be delighted to speak to the authorities about what she's spent the last week up to—specifically my father." He sounded charming and totally reasonable, and the two guards didn't seem to know how to deal with it. They'd prepared for a specific scenario—Samara trying to bully her way back into the building. They hadn't planned on Beckett being reasonable. *Smart man.*

He pointed at the deep purple chairs situated near the doors. "Why don't we wait there while you call up to her? I promise we won't try to bum rush you."

Max finally nodded. "Please don't move from the couch." He didn't have any weapons on him aside from a pair of handcuffs, but Samara had little doubt that he'd use them as he deemed necessary.

Since getting wrestled to the floor and cuffed in the middle of the lobby wasn't on her to-do list today, she let Beckett guide her to the couch. "What if she turns us away?"

"She won't."

She could do with some of his confidence right around then. Samara's knee got to bouncing and she couldn't force it still. So many things could go wrong. Why hadn't she thought of those things while they were driving in here and parking? Lydia could refuse to see them. She could have them arrested for trespassing. She could have had them followed while they chased Walter down. If

Samara and Frank could follow Walter and Beckett, there was no reason someone couldn't have been following *them*.

Round and round her thoughts went, circling until she had to fight to keep from jumping to her feet and yelling for Beckett to run, to get as far from this poisonous place as he could before it seeped into him, too.

"Breathe." He shifted closer, his thigh pressing the length of hers. His words were barely more than a whisper, designed not to carry beyond the two of them. Not even to the camera currently pointed at them. "Just breathe, Samara. You're safe."

She was no safer than he was.

Lydia was hardly the mob, but if she wanted to, she could have them smuggled out of here so she could follow through on her plan to remove Beckett—permanently.

"I have everything under control." He covered her bouncing knee with his hand. "Trust me."

"I do trust you. It's *her* I don't trust." How quickly things had turned around. A week ago, she'd been a confident businesswoman who knew her place in the world and embraced it without reservation. She knew there was an ugly underside to her job, but she'd never thought it was *this* ugly. Questionable—and maybe a little illegal—activities were a far cry from *murder*.

Jacob walked to them, looking like he'd eaten something sour. "I'll take you up."

Beckett squeezed her knee and rose. He gave her a reassuring look that did nothing to calm the fears inside her clamoring that something terrible was about to happen. She kept her back straight and her chin lifted and tried to keep her fear off her face. It was all she was capable of at that point. *Trust Beckett. Trust that he knows what he's doing.*

"Not too late for you to turn back," he murmured.

And leave him to face this alone? "No. I'm going up."

"Okay."

Then they stepped into the elevator and it was too late to change her mind.

Beckett could feel little shakes working their way through Samara's body, but she kept her eyes pinned on the back of the guard in front of them. He'd hedged his bets as best he could going into this confrontation, but despite his reassurances, he didn't know beyond a shadow of a doubt that things would play out like he'd planned.

The elevator doors opened and they followed the security guard into the hallway. It didn't look any different from the last time Beckett had been there, but it *felt* different. Menacing. Cold. Filled with the promise of violence.

The guard—Jacob—stepped aside and positioned himself with his back to the wall next to Lydia's office door. "Go ahead." He didn't have a weapon on him, but he had the feel of a solider protecting his commanding officer.

Beckett touched the small of Samara's back and they walked through the door together. Lydia sat behind her desk, looking every inch a queen in her white pantsuit, flanked on either side by Journey and Anderson. Journey looked like she hadn't slept in days, and he had a moment of regret that he might be the cause of it with all the government-contract bullshit. On the other side, Anderson was her polar opposite, from his blue eyes and dark hair right down to how well rested and alert he looked. His suit was perfectly unwrinkled, and if he'd been on a plane that day, there was no evidence of it.

He came.

No time for relief—not yet. He had to play this exactly right.

Beckett shut the door behind them. He had no intention of sitting or getting comfortable. The only advantage he had was driving this dialogue from the first moment. He strode to the desk and leaned on its surface with his fists, imposing himself into her space. "Next time you want someone dead, Lydia, you should send someone more capable than Walter Trissel. It may have worked for my father, but as you can see, I'm still among the living."

Anderson's eyes widened in recognition, the only outward reaction any of the three Kings had. Lydia sighed. "Wonderful, Beckett." She clapped mockingly. "Very dramatic. Now, if you're done wasting my time—"

"Let me tell you how this is going to go." He leaned down, lowering his voice and getting in her face a little. "I'm going to offer you the same deal I gave Walter. You leave Houston, Texas, the country, and you don't come back. You sign away Kingdom Corp to your children, release Thistledown Villa back to me, and take a small stipend to live off. And you never come back, Lydia."

No emotion showed on her face, not even a flicker. "I'm sure you're going to enlighten me on why I'm supposedly doing these things."

"Because if you don't, I'm taking this to the media." He took out his phone and pressed the button to start the recording. He never took his eyes from her face as Walter named her, as he admitted to putting Nathaniel behind the wheel that night…Beckett fast-forwarded to where Walter outlined his plan to kill *Beckett*. He hit the button to stop it, leaving strained silence in its wake.

She tapped a red nail on her polished desk. "Ravings of a madman. It will never hold up in court."

"It doesn't have to. I'm not taking you to court, Aunt." He spoke softly, almost gently. "I'm going to release it publicly and let things fall where they will. This might not be enough for a criminal conviction, but it's more than enough to turn the public against you and create a scandal the likes of which you've never seen. You know as well as I do that scandals make business partners nervous. How long before your shareholders start abandoning Kingdom Corp in waves? You'll lose key employees like rats from a sinking ship. Your contracts won't be renewed. You'll be left in this empty building, lamenting about the days when you were *almost* competition for Morningstar Enterprise."

Something akin to panic took root in her hazel eyes. "You're bluffing. You would never do that to your cousins."

Beckett leaned back and crossed his arms over his chest. "Anderson. Journey. You and your other two siblings are more than welcome to jobs at Morningstar. I can offer you comparable shares and salary matching what you've got now, in addition to the promise that any children you have will continue to hold positions within the company—as they should have before our family split."

Journey's jaw dropped, but Anderson just looked contemplative. Lydia shoved to her feet. "Don't you dare."

Beckett kept going. "If you'd come after my company legitimately, then we wouldn't be having this conversation. But you resorted to murder, and just kept digging yourself deeper from there. You want your legacy to live on in Kingdom Corp? Then sign it over to your children and leave. Or stay and watch everything you've sacrificed for come down brick by brick." He paused. "Like you wanted to do to me and Morningstar."

She went pale. "Why even offer me a choice at all?"

"I'm not you. I won't sink to your level." *And I know you'll live the rest of your life in misery because you've been cut off from the only things that matter to you—your legacy and your children.* Exile was crueler than death, crueler than grinding her company to dust. Lydia had proven herself more than capable of starting from scratch. If Kingdom Corp went under, she'd find a way forward. The only route to justice lay in the one he'd just spelled out for her. "Choose, Lydia. This is the only time I'm going to make this offer."

He saw the exact moment she realized she had no recourse. He'd already emailed a copy of the recording to himself and Frank, so destroying his phone wouldn't do anything. She could fight a criminal charge, but not a conviction of public opinion. She couldn't even play on his honorable streak, because he'd offered his cousins a convenient way out.

"You bastard."

"Not according to my mother."

She curled her top lip. "That bitch—"

"That's enough." This from Samara where she'd stood as silent witness. She moved forward with eyes only for Lydia. "You're outmaneuvered and you know it. Take his offer gracefully or don't do it at all. I won't stand here while you insult his dead mother. You're better than that, Lydia." She shook her head. "Or at least I thought you were. I thought you were better than a lot of things. Apparently I was wrong."

Anderson stepped forward, putting himself in front of his mother. "She'll take the offer."

"But, I—"

"Stop speaking, Mother. You've done enough damage." He turned those cold eyes on Beckett and then Samara. "I'll have the paperwork drawn up today and she'll be on a flight out Monday."

"She'll be on a flight out tomorrow," Beckett corrected. "This offer expires in twenty-four hours. If Lydia is still within Houston limits at that point of time, I'm releasing the tape."

"Consider it done."

He ignored Lydia's sputtering. Through all this, she'd become something larger than life, looming over his every move. Anticipating. Now, standing here in the pale light of her office, she was just a bitter and angry woman. Beckett took two steps back and gave her one last look. "You should have been happy with what you had."

"Morningstar was never supposed to be his, and it sure as hell was never supposed to be yours."

This is what thirty years of spite looks like.

He shook his head. "Have a nice life, Lydia. If you ever set foot in this city again, I'll personally see you and everything you've ever touched burned to ash." Beckett turned and, after letting Samara precede him, walked through the door.

Journey stared at the closed door, barely able to process the turn of events. Distantly, she was aware of her mother cursing, the legendary calm cracked beyond repair, but all she could focus on was how at peace Samara and Beckett had looked. There were no ghosts riding them, fear wasn't making this choice for them. He'd faced down one of the scariest people Journey knew without flinching, and he'd walked out with a solid win.

I could learn a thing or two from Beckett King.

"This is unforgivable."

She moved to the chair on the other side of the desk and sank into it, her legs not quite steady. Truth be told, they hadn't been steady since Anderson arrived a few hours ago bringing warnings that Beckett was up to something. Bringing warnings to *Journey*. Not to their mother.

He stood against Lydia's wrath, a solid pillar of stone, the one person who grounded their entire family no matter what the world tried to throw at them. Lydia moved as if to sweep everything off her desk, and Anderson caught her wrist. "That's enough, Mother."

Her expression went slack for the space of a breath, and then rearranged into rage. "You're just going to roll over and let him do this. You're going to sentence me to exile."

"*You* did this." He released her hand but didn't move back. "You went after him clumsily and now you're paying the price." Anderson shook his head. "Now it's up to me to clean up your mess. Again."

Lydia sneered. "You're not even attempting to pretend you're unhappy about this turn of events. You've wanted me out of the way for years."

Journey could almost see her mother working her way down the manipulation checklist. *Hurt, check. Guilt, check. Anger, check.* Journey would have cracked before now, but Anderson stood strong against the waves of emotion. "Sit down."

"I will *not*." Lydia turned on her heel and strode out of the office.

Anderson sighed and grabbed his phone. "Hey Jacob, I'm going to need you to guide my mother to the room on this floor... Yes, that one. Thank you."

As if on cue, a screech sounded from farther down the hall. Journey twisted to look at him. "You just ordered our mother restrained."

"If left to her own devices, she'd grab the first gun she came across and go hunt down Beckett to finish the job she ordered Walter Trissel to do." Anderson checked his phone and nodded to himself. "She's secure." He turned those blue eyes, so like their father's, on her. "How are you holding up?"

This was the brother she knew, not the cold bastard who'd stood there and dealt with Beckett. Journey gave him a wobbly smile. "About as well as can be expected."

He walked over and crouched down next to her chair. "I'll see us through this, Jo. I promise."

Just like he'd promised so many things in the past. For the first time since her father called and her mother fired her best friend, Journey managed something resembling a smile. "I know you will." She let the expression drop—it was too much effort to maintain. "You're really going to do what he wants."

"Yes." He gave her a tight smile. "We should probably send our cousin a gift basket this Christmas for doing us the favor of removing our mother."

Journey shook her head, because there was nothing to say to that. Dysfunctional parent-child relationships dominated the King family, and their branch was no exception. "What happens now?"

"Now, Jo . . . Now, we prepare for what comes next."

CHAPTER TWENTY-FOUR

You're more than welcome to have your position within Kingdom Corp back. Barring that, I'm happy to write you a letter of recommendation."

Samara studied Anderson King. She didn't know him as well as Lydia or Journey, but what she did know would make him a man who'd be a strong leader for the company.

He just wasn't the leader her heart wanted to follow.

"Thank you for the offer—to both—but I won't be staying on with Kingdom Corp. I'd be happy for the letter of recommendation."

Anderson sat back. "I don't suppose there's something I can offer you to stay? My sister values your relationship and it would mean a lot if you were still here. I'm prepared to offer a substantial raise."

She was tempted. Lord, she was tempted. But if she stayed only to make Journey happy, that would be taking the safe option. She'd never considered her career *safe* before, but looking back, that's exactly what it was. She'd thrown in her lot with Lydia and stubbornly clung to that path even when other options became available.

Samara wouldn't make the same mistake again. She smiled. "Journey isn't going to be rid of me that easily, but the next step for my career is in a different direction." She'd risen as far as she could within the ranks of Kingdom Corp. The top positions were all held by the King children, and they'd continue to be for as long as there were King family members. There was nothing wrong with that, but Samara wanted something more.

"If you're sure."

"I'm sure."

Anderson nodded. "In that case, I wish you the best." He opened a drawer and pulled out a set of keys. "I was going to send this over via courier, but something tells me you're headed for Morningstar Enterprise." He passed over the keys. "My mother followed Beckett's instructions and was on a plane Friday morning. It will take a little bit to untangle the paperwork fully, but Beckett should know we fully intend to ensure that Thistledown Villa stays his moving forward." He motioned to the keys. "A token in good faith."

Her heart swelled. "Thank you. That will mean the world to him."

"It's the least I can do to balance out the wrongs my mother committed."

She agreed, but she didn't say as much. Anderson wasn't behind Lydia's actions any more than Journey was. They were all pieces being moved around a board that was generations old, but hopefully that would change going forward. "See you around, Anderson." She stood and walked out of the office.

Samara paused in Journey's doorway and knocked on the frame. "Hey."

Journey looked up. "Hey." She looked like she hadn't slept all weekend, the circles beneath her eyes almost purple, but she smiled. "Guess you didn't take the job offer."

"Journey—"

"No, you're right not to. I'm sorry if I wasn't totally graceful about it when my mother fired you. I haven't exactly been living the highlight reel this week."

Samara hesitated. "Happy hour on Wednesday?"

"Definitely." Journey's smile warmed a little. "I really am happy for you, you know."

"I know."

She shooed her. "Now get out of here. Go hunt down that man of yours and celebrate a win." She raised her eyebrows. "You're going to have to work a lot harder for the next contract, though. I won't go easy on you just because we're best friends."

"Looking forward to it." Samara took her time leaving the building, silently saying her good-byes in a way she hadn't been able to last time. She might be back here at some point, but it would never be home again.

She walked the two blocks over to Morningstar Enterprise and made her way up to Beckett's office. He looked up when she walked through the door, and his smile had her grinning back. He rose and rounded the desk to take her in his arms. "You were gone too long."

"It was literally an hour." She ran her hands up his chest, part of her not quite believing that they'd gotten out in one piece. "Anderson offered me my job back with a large raise."

"Did he?" Beckett answered carefully, his dark gaze on her face. "What'd you say?" As if he was only distantly curious and not impatiently waiting for her response.

Samara let him wait a little longer. She finally rolled her

eyes. "I turned him down. You see, this really gorgeous and great guy offered me a job as COO of his company this weekend."

"Did he? I seem to remember you not giving him an answer."

She tilted her head to the side. "I didn't? Silly me. The answer is yes."

"In that case..." He released her and stepped back to a respectable distance, his tone going pure professional. "Welcome to Morningstar Enterprise, Ms. Mallick. I believe you'll be a welcome addition to the team."

"Looking forward to it." She managed to hold it together for all of five seconds. "Can you take a few hours? I have something to show you."

He shrugged. "It's going to be a late night no matter which way I swing it, but I can spare a few hours now."

"Perfect."

"Why did you bring me here?" Thistledown rose like a ghost from his past. Beckett had been able to keep it out of mind for the most part since he'd scattered his father's ashes, but seeing it now had that loss rearing up to slap him down.

He turned to find Samara leaning against her car, smiling. She moved to him and took his hand. "It turns out that your cousins aren't as monstrous as their mother, and Anderson is ensuring this ends up back with you."

Hope flared. He pulled her into his arms and held her close. "That's amazing news."

"I thought so, too." She nestled closer.

Beckett rested his chin on the top of her head and just let himself soak up the moment. The woman he loved in his arms, the future spreading out before them and filled to the brim with possibilities. His childhood home in the process of being restored. His business no longer under imminent threat. His enemy exiled.

He studied the house. "It's pretty fucking big."

"Mm-hmm."

A thought had been waiting at the edges of his mind since Thursday, when Anderson had stepped between Beckett and Lydia. "You know my cousins better than I do. Do you think they'd be amiable to the idea of getting to know their history?"

"What—you mean like here at Thistledown Villa?"

"It's part of their legacy, same as mine."

Samara twisted in his arms to face the house. She leaned back against him. "I don't know if you can fix the harm done by Nathaniel and Lydia. There's thirty years of bad blood between the branches of your family..." Samara took a deep breath. "But I don't think that bad blood extends to them the same way it didn't quite extend to you. They don't like you out of habit, not because of something you've done to them directly."

"I know there's no magic fix." He kissed her temple. "But it's a start, the first small step in the right direction."

"Yes, it is."

It felt right to start to mend those wounds. It might not be something fixed in the next year or two or five, but maybe they could build relationships close enough that the next generation wouldn't have to grow up separately.

Beckett rocked back on his heels as the image of Samara pregnant with his child formed in his mind. Their children would grow up here the same way he had, but they would have both parents and all the happiness that children deserved. All the happiness that he and Samara deserved.

Not yet. Not for a while yet.

But someday.

He released Samara and led her up to the house. Inside, it smelled slightly musty, as if the week since they'd been there last was closer to a month. Samara trailed behind, but he reached back and took her hand to pull her even with him. "I was thinking of redecorating."

"Oh?" She sounded amused.

"This was a happy place before my mother died. I think it could be a happy place again—*our* place. My father clung too tightly to the history before she died. I think it's time to move Thistledown into the future once and for all."

"I like that idea." She touched the drab burgundy drapes that hung in the entranceway. "We'll liven up the place."

He loved the way her laugh seemed to fill up the empty halls and breathe life into this old house. He could almost picture busy Christmases with children running down the halls playing chasing games, the smell of cooking permeating the space, the energy of love lifting the gloom that had been part of this house for so many years. "This was a happy place before all the loss."

"This *will* be a happy place again." She turned and went up on her toes to kiss him. "Give it time, Beckett. I think you're right. I think your cousins will come around and one day this place will be filled with family again."

He spoke against her lips. "Want to know a secret?"

"Always."

"When I picture the family that will fill this place, I picture *ours*." He kissed first one corner of her mouth and then the other, backing her slowly to the wall. "It's too soon to get into the specifics, but that's where this is headed, Samara."

She arched against him with a soft laugh. "Do I get a say in this theoretical family?"

"Of course." He nibbled her neck. "Would you prefer a spring wedding or a fall one? How do you feel about dogs? Should we have two kids or more?"

She burst out laughing. "Getting a little ahead of yourself, aren't you?"

"Never." Beckett pulled back enough to meet her gaze. "It's you for me. If that means waiting a year or waiting a decade, then that's what I'll do." He traced her bottom lip with his thumb. This part was more difficult to get out. "If you don't want kids...then we won't have any."

Her eyes went wide. "You just said you wanted kids."

"I do. With you. But that's not a decision I get to make without you." He leaned down and brushed his lips over the path his thumb had just traveled. "I'm head over heels in love with you, Samara."

She slipped her arms around his neck and kissed him. It wasn't an answer...but maybe it was. Beckett scooped her up and strode up the stairs, eliciting another infectious laugh from Samara. He went straight to his old room and laid her down across his bed. She looked around. "Tell the truth—you snuck girls in here all the time when you were a teenager."

"Never." He pushed her shirt up and kissed her stomach, working his way up to her breasts. "We had a full staff and they reported on my every move. Nothing kills a makeout session like having your dour housekeeper fling open the door." He pulled her shirt off and tossed it aside, quickly followed by her skirt. Beckett lowered his voice. "We're alone in the house right now."

"Thank God." She reached for his jeans and shoved them

down his hips. "I might throw something if we're interrupted."

He kissed her as he guided his cock into her. *This. This right here is fucking perfection.* Beckett thrust slow, savoring every touch, every sigh, every little gasp she made. "Happiness is you with me, Samara. Happiness is *this*." He picked up his pace and reached between them to stoke her clit the way she liked it.

She came with his name on her lips. Beckett couldn't hold out any longer. He didn't want to. He thrust into her again and again, chasing completion that he'd only ever found with this woman. "I love you."

Samara clung to him as their heartbeats slowed and their breathing returned to normal. She kissed his jaw, his neck, his shoulder. "Beckett?"

"Yeah?"

He felt her smile. "Want to know a secret?"

"As if you have to ask."

She shifted back and trailed her fingers down the side of his face. She wore a satisfied smile and there was no mistaking the love in her dark eyes. "Yes."

He went still. "'Yes' isn't a secret."

Her smile grew. "I think three kids is a nice number. I prefer cats to dogs, but I'm willing to be convinced. A fall wedding would be wonderful." She kissed him. "I love you, Beckett King. I think we should wait a few years before we start popping out babies, but let's fill these halls with a happy family. *Our* happy family."

LOOK FOR JOURNEY AND FRANK'S
STORY IN

The Kings #2

COMING IN EARLY 2019

Keep reading for look at the
first book in Katee Robert's
smoking hot series about the
O'Malley family—wealthy,
powerful, dangerous, and
seething with scandal.

*The Marriage
Contract*

Available now.

Brendan Halloran is dead."

Teague O'Malley didn't look up from the book he was reading. "And?" But he already knew where his brother was going with dropping that tidbit out of nowhere. And the death of an heir was a game changer, more so because the Sheridans had lost *their* heir less than six months ago. There was a potential power vacuum created as a result, and he had no doubt his father and brother would be racing to fill it.

Aiden dropped onto the coffee table and swatted the book from his hands. "And you know what that means."

"Shouldn't you be talking to our father about this?"

"I'm talking about it with you." His brother turned those guileless green eyes on him, a trick he'd learned from their oldest sister. It had gotten both Carrigan and Aiden out of a shit-ton of trouble while they were growing up—trouble then never failed to fall squarely into Teague's lap.

The prickling at his neck signaled that he was about to be on the receiving end of another round, and he wanted no part of it. "Go away."

"Not until you hear me out." Aiden and Teague both

looked up as Carrigan came into the library and closed the door behind her. Fuck. He really was about to get into deep shit if these two were settling down to plot. Aiden must have known he was about to bolt, because he slapped a hand down on Teague's shoulder, holding him in place. "Until you hear us both out."

He wasn't going to get out of this room until he did just that. "You have five minutes."

Carrigan crossed the room, her long dress swishing around her feet, and perched on the arm of the couch. "That's all we need." She looked particularly virginal today in the white dress with her dark hair falling loose around her face. It was a part she liked to play when it suited her—the devout Catholic good girl—and it had kept their father from pushing too hard for her to be married. Teague suspected their father thought a nun in the family would somehow magically balance the scales for all the evil shit he did, so he'd been driving her hard in that direction. After all, he had two more daughters he could use to secure a general's allegiance in marriage.

Only Teague knew she was anything but innocent when away from the watchful family protection, but he wasn't about to out her. Every one of them dealt with living in the O'Malley cage in their own ways. If her way of dealing helped her hold on to sanity, he wasn't going to judge the means. Not when he had just as many secrets.

His sister patted his foot. "With that despicable Halloran monster put out of his misery, we have an opportunity if we move fast."

Giving up the pretense of being relaxed, Teague straightened and swung his feet to the ground—and out of the reach of his sister. "The next words out of your mouth had better not be that we should take this chance to eliminate the Hallorans."

Aiden huffed. "Are you scared?"

"No, but I'm also not suicidal, either." He glared at his brother. "And that taunt stopped working on me when I was ten." It had taken months for his broken leg to heal from jumping off that bridge into the creek on their Connecticut property, and he still had the scar and fear of drowning from the result.

Carrigan laughed. "We're not suicidal."

That remained to be seen. "Then stop dicking around and tell me."

"The Sheridan daughter, the only one in the immediate family left, was set to marry Brendan Halloran. They were going to announce the engagement today." Carrigan twisted a lock of her dark hair around her finger.

That got Teague's attention. "I hadn't heard anything."

"No one did. That's the point. They brokered the deal in secret—or as secret as anything is these days. You already know the name of the game. They were consolidating power." Her tone told him her thoughts on *that*.

A deal between the Hallorans and the Sheridans would have sunk them. They held territory on either side of the O'Malleys, and he had no doubt that it wouldn't take long for them to start eating away at the edges, with the aim of crushing Teague's family and their business between them. The Boston underworld was a fat purse, but that kind of money only went so far when split three ways. Take out the largest competitor and...Yeah, he could see the reasoning behind Sheridan selling his daughter off to the Hallorans.

But, shit, everyone knew what a sadistic fuck Brendan was. His family didn't draw the same lines the other two did, and he had no problem exploiting the human trafficking they dabbled in and creating his own little harem. Word had it that when Brendan played with those girls, most of the time he broke them beyond repair.

What kind of man would knowingly sentence his daughter to that?

And why the hell were his two older siblings bringing this information to *him*? He glanced between them. "It sounds like the girl dodged a bullet."

"Most definitely." Now apparently it was Aiden's turn to talk. "She's the heir to the Sheridan fortune—and all their territory—which means she's going to be the most sought-after woman in Boston. The vultures will be circling by the end of the day."

"Which is bullshit."

Aiden glanced at Carrigan, his expression shuttered. "Which is bullshit, sure. But we'd be stupid to sit back and let someone else swoop in and snatch up this opportunity."

Teague's stomach twisted, and he couldn't shake the feeling that he was standing on the train tracks and feeling the rumble of an incoming engine. "I'm not seeing what this shit has to do with me."

"That's the thing." Aiden shifted. "If someone's going to secure an alliance with the Sheridan family, why not one of us?"

The twisting in his stomach developed teeth, but he fought to keep his voice light. "Then I suppose I should congratulate you on your impending nuptials."

"Actually, we're here to congratulate *you*." Aiden held up a hand. "Just hear me out. I can't marry her. Our father already has a couple candidates in mind for me, and any of them would expand our territory exponentially."

"Then what about Cillian? He's old enough to play husband to the Sheridan girl."

Carrigan shook her head. "That won't work and you know it. The Sheridans might forgive our passing over Aiden and offering you, but it would be insulting to go to any of our younger siblings."

Jesus Christ. Teague looked at the alcohol cabinet on the far wall. Surely it wasn't too early to start drinking? Even as the thought crossed his mind, he pushed to his feet. It might be too early, but this wasn't a conversation he was willing to have stone-cold sober. "No."

"Don't say no. You haven't even heard us out."

He didn't have to. He knew what they would say. *It's your duty to your family. Father has given you excessive freedom to mess around with your interests. It's time to repay all those favors you tallied up.* He poured himself a splash of whiskey and then kept pouring until the glass was full. "Didn't arranged marriages go the way of the dinosaurs a couple decades ago?"

"Maybe for other families. Not for ours."

He knew that. Fuck, he wished he *didn't* know it so well. The rules of polite society were different for his family than they were for your average Joe. He'd learned a long time ago that the money and connections came with more strings than a spider's web. And walking away wasn't an option, because that same money and those connections would be ruthlessly deployed to bring any prodigal sons or daughters back into the fold—whether they wanted to come or not.

Teague took a healthy swallow of the whiskey. "You can't seriously be asking me to marry some woman I've never met from a family we were raised to hate."

"I'm not." Aiden paused, and it was like the whole room held its breath. "Father is."

Just like that, the fight went out of him. He could argue his brother and sister to a standstill and even, occasionally, come out on top. Their father? His word was law, and he had no problem ruthlessly playing upon his children's weak spots to get what he wanted. Teague had learned that the hard way when he was still young enough to believe that there was another life—another option—out there for him. "I need some time to think."

"You don't have much."

Teague didn't turn at the sound of the library door opening and closing, because he knew both siblings hadn't left. "This is bullshit and you know it."

"I know." Carrigan plucked the glass out of his hand and took a sip. It was only then that he saw her hand was shaking. "You know Father made an offhand comment last night at the dinner you conveniently missed? He thinks it's time for me to shit or get off the pot." She laughed softly at the look on his face. "He didn't say it in so many words, but the meaning was the same. My goddamn biological clock is ticking away in his ear, and the man wants heirs to bargain with."

He watched her finish the whiskey. "What are you going to do?"

"I don't know." She set the glass down with the care of someone who wanted to throw it across the room. "I'm as much in a cage as you are—as we all are—but I can't talk to anyone about it."

He knew the feeling. It all came down to the bottom line—family. It didn't matter what was good for the individual as long as the family's interests as a whole were served. "You can talk to me."

Her smile was so sad, it would have broken his heart if he had anything left to break. "No, Teague, I really can't." With that, she turned and floated out of the room, leaving him alone in his misery.

He refilled his glass and went back to his seat on the couch. It was tempting to shoot the whole thing back and chase oblivion, but he needed his wits about him if he was going to get through this in the best position possible. The idea was absurd. The best position possible? He was a drowning man with no land in sight and the sharks were circling. There was nothing to do but pick the best way to die.

Each sip, carefully controlled, gave him some much needed distance. He mentally stepped to the side and forced himself to look at the situation without the tangled mess of emotions in his chest. There might be no way out, but he could make the best of it regardless. The Sheridans had been a thorn in the family's side for as long as there had been both Sheridans and O'Malleys in Boston. They might be looking to bolster their strength, but it wouldn't take much to weaken their position.

He took another drink. No, it wouldn't take much at all. And if he were with the Sheridans, he wouldn't be *here*, so there was something to be said for that as well. The further he got from his father's grasp, the easier it would be to slip free when the time came.

Slip free? The pipe dream of a child. He knew better by now...but that didn't stop the tiny flare of hope inside him. It was a mistake not to crush it--if he didn't now, then some-one else would, and it would hurt more that way. Reality had a nasty way of intruding on pipe dreams, and the reality was that marrying into the Sheridan family wasn't likely to give him an out. It would entangle him further in the type of life he wanted to escape. They may have a different last name and territory, but the type of beast was identical to the O'Malleys.

But if there was a chance to be free—truly free— wouldn't he be a fool not to take it?

He picked up the book his brother had knocked to the floor, and carefully marked his page before closing it. He couldn't leave Carrigan behind. Hell, he'd be a selfish prick to leave *any* of his sisters behind. And his youngest brother, Devlin, was the least suited of all of them for this life. The thought of hauling three women and Devlin into hiding with him...Teague shuddered. It was impossible. He couldn't run without them, and he couldn't run *with* them.

So what the fuck was he going to do?

He laughed, the sound harsh from his throat. He was going to do exactly what he was told, like a good little piece-of-shit son. He was going to marry the Sheridan woman.

ABOUT THE AUTHOR

KATEE ROBERT is a *New York Times* and *USA Today* best-selling author who learned to tell stories at her grandpa's knee. Her novel *The Marriage Contract* was a RITA finalist, and *RT Book Reviews* named it "a compulsively readable book with just the right amount of suspense and tension." When not writing sexy contemporary and romantic suspense, she spends her time playing imaginary games with her children, driving her husband batty with what-if questions, and planning for the inevitable zombie apocalypse.

Learn more:
www.kateerobert.com
Twitter @ katee_robert
Facebook.com/AuthorKateeRobert

FALL IN LOVE WITH FOREVER ROMANCE

USA TODAY BESTSELLING AUTHOR

HOPE RAMSAY

The Bride Next Door

"Every story by Hope Ramsay will touch a reader's heart."
—BRENDA NOVAK, *New York Times* bestselling author

THE BRIDE NEXT DOOR
By Hope Ramsay

Courtney Wallace has almost given up on finding her happily-ever-after. And she certainly doesn't expect to find it with Matthew Lyndon, the hotshot lawyer she overhears taking a bet to seduce her. Matt never intended to take the bet seriously. And moving next door wasn't part of his strategy to win, but the more he gets to know Courtney, the more intrigued he becomes. When fun and games turn into something real, will these two decide they're in it to win it?

FALL IN LOVE WITH FOREVER ROMANCE

TOTAL BRAVERY
By Piper J. Drake

Raul's lucky to have the best partner a man could ask for: a highly trained, fiercely loyal German Shepherd dog named Taz. But their first mission in Hawaii puts them to the test when a kidnapping ring sets its sights on the bravest woman Raul's ever met...Mali knows she's in trouble. Yet sharing close quarters with smoldering, muscle-for-hire Raul makes her feel safe. But when the kidnappers make their move, Raul's got to find a way to save the life of the woman he loves.

FALL IN LOVE WITH FOREVER ROMANCE

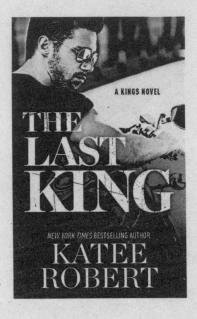

THE LAST KING
By Katee Robert

The King family has always been like royalty in Texas. And sitting right at the top is Beckett, who just inherited his father's fortune, his company—and all his enemies. But Beckett's always played by his own rules, so when he needs help, he goes to the last person anyone would ever expect: his biggest rival. Samara Mallick is reluctant to risk her career—despite her red-hot attraction—but it soon becomes clear there are King family secrets darker than she ever imagined and dangerous enough to get them killed.

FALL IN LOVE WITH FOREVER ROMANCE

THE AMISH TEACHER'S GIFT
By Rachel J. Good

Widower Josiah Yoder wants to be a good father. But it's not easy with a deaf young son who doesn't understand why his mamm isn't coming home. At a loss, Josiah enrolls Nathan in a special-needs school and is relieved to see his son comforted by Ada Rupp, the teacher whose sweet charm and gentle smile just might be the balm they *both* need.